STOLEN
by a sinner

USA Today Bestselling Author
MICHELLE HEARD

Cover Designer: Cormar Covers

TABLE OF CONTENTS

Dedication

To every book blogger who has taken a moment to share
my books.
Thank you.

Songlist

Available on *Spotify*

Prisoner – Raphael Lake, Aaron Levy, Daniel, Rayn Murphy

Lose Control – AG, Mindy Jones

Body To Body – X-Ray Dog

Another Day – Michele Morrone

The Hunter – The Rigs

Talking In Your Sleep – AG, Daniella Mason

Wicked Game – Daisy Gray

Obsession – Beds and Beats

Shallow – Tommee Profitt, Fleurie

Wake Me Up – Tommee Profitt, Fleurie

Synopsis

Cinderella said to be kind, have courage, and always believe in a little magic.

She's wrong.

To survive in my world, you have to be dead inside, be on guard at all times, and never dream of the impossible. You never dream of anything because you don't just get to stop working for the Polish mafia.

But you can be stolen from them.

Well, kind of.
When Gabriel Demir, head of the Turkish mafia, attacks my boss, I'm caught in the crossfire.
I'm taken captive, interrogated, and soon find myself in the position of maid again. Only this time, it's for the Turkish instead of Polish.

This time it's for a dangerously attractive man and not the insane one I've known all my life.

This time I find myself fantasizing about my boss instead of dreaming of ways to escape.

This time I'm not threatened with pain and death but with pleasure.

But can I step out of the maid's uniform and into a ballgown?

Do I dare cross that line just for a moment in the spotlight?

Stolen By A Sinner

Mafia / Organized Crime / Suspense Romance
STANDALONE in The Sinners Series
Book 3

Authors Note:
This book contains subject matter that may be sensitive for some readers.
There is triggering content related to extreme abuse, graphic violence, loss of a parent, and sexual slavery.
18+ only.
Please read responsibly.

Priesthood:

A gathering of Mafia dons that was in effect a convocation of the nation's priesthood of organized crime

---

"Be kind, have courage, and always believe in a little magic."

—— Cinderella

Family Tree

Gabriel Demir

↓

Family Business: Turkish Mafia

Father: Deniz Demir *(Deceased)*

Mother: Sinem Demir *(Deceased)*

Grandmother: Alya Demir

Cousin & Best Friend: Emre Demir

Aunt on mother's side: Ayesenur Altan

Cousin & in charge of Turkey: Eymen Altan

Cousin: Eslem Altan

Lara Nowak

↓

Father: *(Unknown)*

Mother: Agnieska Nowak *(Deceased)*

Employer: Tymon Mazur – Head of Polish mafia

Lara's Guard: Murat Eren

Chapter 1

Lara

Gabriel; 38. Lara; 22.

Cinderella said, 'Be kind, have courage, and always believe in a little magic.'

I suppress the bitter chuckle while walking down the corridor.

Cinderella's wrong.

A gunshot rings through the air, the sound rippling over my skin. I startle but catch myself in time so I don't drop the tray of black tea. With my heart lurching in my chest, I pause outside the door, and closing my eyes, I suck in a deep breath of air.

She's very wrong. To survive in my world, you have to be dead inside, on guard at all times, and never dream of the impossible.

Never dream of anything.

I open my eyes, raise my chin, and step into the sitting room. For a split second, I glance at the dead body. Blood stains the carpet. *Again.*

The guy didn't even work here for two weeks. Pity he didn't last longer. At this rate, Tymon will run out of people to kill.

Which means it's only a matter of time before I meet the bullet with my name carved into it.

I've seen it plenty of times whenever Tymon felt the need to threaten me. He keeps a wooden box full of bullets with all the staff's names engraved on them next to his favorite armchair.

Lord only knows how I've survived this long.

Tymon brought my mother over from Poland after I was born. She died when I was twelve, and ever since, I've been working for Tymon as a maid. Mom used to quote Cinderella to me, but after she passed away, I quickly realized life wasn't a fairytale.

Tymon Mazur is the head of the Polish mafia. He believes you can beat and threaten your staff into obedience. He's right. No one in this mansion will dare go against him.

You don't just wake up one day and decide you're no longer going to work for him. The only way out is death, and no matter how bad things get, I'm not ready to die.

"Get rid of the piece of shit," Tymon barks at the remaining three men.

They pick up the body and carry it out of the room as I set the tray down on a glass coffee table.

Tymon's black gaze rests on me, empty and cruel. "I want prawns and oysters for dinner."

I nod dutifully. "Yes, Sir." Not wanting to spend a second longer than I need to in his presence, I hurry out of the room.

"Did I say you can leave!" he shouts after me.

My feet come to a faltering stop, my shoulders slump, and even though every muscle in my body screams at me to not turn back, I obey.

I always obey.

It's either that or death.

Stepping back into the sitting room, I keep my eyes cast down, staring at the black fabric of the skirt that ends just under my knees.

When I hear the armchair creak beneath his weight, I peek up. Tymon's gaze is narrowed on me. He sets his gun down on the glass table, then closes the distance between us.

Power radiates from his bulky frame, the loss of half his hair doing nothing to lessen how dangerous and cruel he looks. He has round cheeks and a mustache that curls up at the ends.

Apprehension creeps through me, and I clench my teeth, fisting my hands at my sides.

His meaty palm connects with my left ear, the familiar pain exploding over my jaw and neck. The force has me falling to the right, my hip slamming into the golden corner of the coffee table, my hand crashing into the tray. The hot tea stings my skin before instantly cooling.

Staring at the carpet, I breathe through the sharp pain in my right hip.

That's going to leave another bruise.

I take a breath, my chest empty of emotions.

"You only leave when I give you permission," Tymon orders, his tone not leaving any room for arguments. Not that I'd dare argue with him. I'm not that stupid.

"Yes, sir," I murmur, still not moving from my spot on the carpet.

"The food better be here at six," he demands.

Shit. That only gives me two hours.

"Yes, sir."

"Leave!" he barks. It's followed by him grumbling, "Piece of ugly fucking shit."

Hearing the words is nothing new to me. I know I'm plain looking, and it doesn't bother me. Beauty will only get you raped in my world.

Wincing from the jarring ache in my hip, I quickly climb to my feet. I gather the overturned cup, and tugging a cloth from my apron, I wipe up the spilled tea before scurrying out of the sitting room.

I try not to limp, doing my best to ignore the pain in my hip. Stopping in the kitchen, I set the tray down, then glance at Agnes, one of the other maids. "Have tea taken to the sitting room. I'm going to get dinner for Mr. Mazur. He wants seafood."

"Okay," she murmurs, her tone the same as mine – void of emotion.

Everyone who works under this roof has been conditioned to just exist for one sole purpose – to serve Tymon Mazur, head of the Polish mafia.

We're his to do with as he pleases.

Leaving the kitchen that's fit for a five-star chef but hardly gets used to prepare meals for Tymon, I take the set of stairs at the back of the mansion down to the maid's quarters.

The basement holds two rows of beds and a single bathroom where the four maids, three gardeners, and two butlers sleep.

This has been my home since I can remember.

The dimly lit space is where Mom used to whisper fairytales to me and where I did my homework by flashlight after fulfilling my duties. That was only until I turned sixteen. I never got to finish school.

Crouching next to my bed, I pull the box from beneath it and take out a pair of worn sneakers. I slip the polished black pumps off, and after stepping into the sneakers, I tie the laces. Tucking the pumps into the box that holds my social security card, a photo of Mom, the worn Cinderella storybook, two sets of uniforms, two sweatpants, two shirts, and a sweater, I slide it back beneath the bed.

At twenty-two, it's all I have. A single box.

I hurry out of the maid's quarters and quickly make my way to the grand foyer where Mr. Kowalski, the head butler, is standing by the front door to receive any guests Tymon might have.

All the staff came over from Poland, and at first, I learned the language, but after Mom passed, I couldn't be bothered.

Mr. Kowalski is in his early seventies and dressed in a black suit, he looks like he's lived a hundred years too many.

"I have to go to Aqua," I murmur.

Mr. Kowalski lets out a heavy sigh as he pulls the credit card out of his jacket's inner pocket. We only use the card for Tymon's meals and anything needed for the mansion.

Handing the card to me, he grumbles, "Hurry."

"Yes, sir." I tuck the card safely into the breast pocket of my shirt, then remember to remove my apron. I quickly take it off and fold it into a bundle.

Mr. Kowalski rolls his eyes and holds out his hand to take it from me.

"Thank you," I murmur, my tone soft and respectful as always.

Opening the heavy wooden door, I step out of the mansion. Guards litter the property as I walk toward the SUV we're allowed to use whenever we have to run an errand for Tymon. Filip kills the cigarette he was smoking and slips behind the steering wheel while I climb into the passenger seat.

"Where to?" he mumbles as he starts the engine.

"Aqua."

I glance at the manicured lawn, and once we leave the property, it feels like boulders roll off my shoulders. Even though I have to hurry, I always cherish the time whenever I get to escape the mansion.

An automatic smile brushes over my lips as I take the bag from the server. I glance at the time on my wristwatch, and my heart kicks in my chest when I notice I only have twenty-six minutes to get back to the mansion.

Shit. I hope the traffic won't be too bad.

Hurrying out of the restaurant, I turn left and slam into a wall of muscle. Startled, a shriek escapes me, then I go down hard and fast. Unable to stop the motion, I fall onto my right side and the bag skids across the sidewalk.

In absolute horror, I watch as the containers open, and seafood scatters over the ground and a pair of brown leather shoes.

God. No.

Pins and needles erupt over my skin, and wincing from the ache in my hip, I move into a kneeling position, adjusting my skirt to cover my legs.

The food is ruined.

Tymon's going to kill me.

"Just what I fucking needed." The growl is dark, harboring a world of danger.

There's a whooshing in my ears, and as if in slow motion, I look up at the man standing among the scattered prawns and oysters.

Wearing a pristine, dark blue three-piece suit, testosterone and wealth exude from him, along with an ungodly dangerous vibe that makes the atmosphere around him seem darker than night.

He has styled black hair, and his light brown eyes are almost gold, reminding me of a lion. A strong jaw covered by a neat dusting of scruff rounds off his breathtaking features.

God, he's attractive.

I swallow hard as I keep staring at his ruggedly handsome face.

"Do you plan on sitting at my feet all night?" His voice is deep and velvety, sending a rush of goosebumps scattering over my skin.

When I notice he's looking at me as if I'm nothing more than a piece of dirt he stepped on, anger trickles into my chest.

Because of him, I'll be punished, and I'll have to pay for prawns and oysters with the money I don't have.

Blood. I'll pay with my blood.

Climbing to my feet, I scowl at him then glance at the ruined food. I'll have no choice but to use the credit card again.

God.

The impact of what just happened shudders through my body like a tsunami of horror.

Impatiently, the man snaps at me, "Jesus, get out of my way, woman."

Something cracks deep inside me, and totally out of character, I jab a finger at the rude man, letting him have a piece of my mind. "If you hadn't plowed into me, I wouldn't have dropped the bag. Now I'm late, and I have to order the meal again, and I don't have money and you being rude is not–"

"Does it look like I fucking care?" His annoyed expression clearly shows he doesn't give two shits about my problem, and my little tantrum is only irritating him more.

It's only then I notice the other two men. One is watching me as if I'm a bomb that can detonate at any moment, and the other actually looks like he pities me.

Taking in all three of the men, apprehension slithers down my spine.

They're cut from the same cloth as Tymon. I can feel the danger vibrating in the air around them.

Crap.

I take a step backward and anxiously glance into the restaurant.

The one looking at me with pity mutters, "Come, Gabriel. We have a lot to do."

The attractive one, who I assume is Gabriel, reaches into the breast pocket of his jacket. He pulls out a wad of cash, shoves it against my chest, and pushes past me, his shoulder bumping me out of his way.

Grabbing hold of the much-needed money, my eyebrow pops up, then I'm left to stare at his back as he stalks to one of the reserved tables with the other men.

Jerk.

Shaking my head, I enter the restaurant and make a beeline for the server who just helped me.

After placing another order, I have to wait outside the restaurant because all the tables are reserved. I wrap my arms around my waist and stare at the sidewalk, now clear of the ruined meal.

At least I didn't have to pay for food.

But I'm still late.

I glance at the time and close my eyes when I see it's already six o'clock.

I'm dead.

Chapter 2

Gabriel

After dinner, I sip on a tumbler of *raki*. That's why I like coming to Aqua. They're one of the few places that serve the traditional Turkish drink.

After taking the last sip of his drink, Emre, my cousin and second in command, murmurs, "The men are ready."

Emre's five years younger than me and has always been like a little brother. His parents died in a car accident just after his birth, so my parents took him in.

I nod, my thoughts turning to my parents. They came over from Turkey to make a better life for themselves and us in Seattle. After they were murdered, I only had my grandmother and Emre. The rest of my family on my mother's side remained in Turkey. Although they visit at least once a year, I'm not as close with them as I am with my Grandmother and Emre.

Tymon Mazur had my parents killed when they wouldn't sell their store to him. They owned a simple bakery, trying to make a modest living like everyone else.

It happened thirty years ago.

Time has done nothing to make the memory fade. It was an unseasonably hot summer's day. My t-shirt clung to my sweaty back as I packed flour bags onto shelves in the storeroom when Mazur's men came in. The threatening voices had me abandoning my work, and when I peeked around the partially open door, my father noticed and gestured for me to stay back.

Before I could obey, the first gunshot rang through the air. The bullet hit Dad in his stomach. Mom screamed. Someone cursed. Then more shots were fired.

I watched my parents fall.

I watched them bleed.

Dad's eyes locked with mine right before the light faded from them.

With the horrific scent of my parents' deaths hanging thickly in the air, I hid in the storeroom while Mazur's men trashed everything my family had worked so hard for.

At the age of eight, hatred filled every ounce of my being. I bit on my fist to keep myself from making a sound. My body shook with fear and sorrow.

Over the years, the hatred fed off my grief and need for revenge, becoming a living, breathing thing.

Over the past twenty years, I've built an empire and took over the Turkish mafia. All so I could avenge my parents' deaths.

Today's the day I step out of the shadows to show Mazur he didn't get away with killing my parents.

Finishing the last of my drink, I set the tumbler down and rise from my chair. Straightening my jacket, I mutter, "Let's go."

As I walk out of the restaurant with Emre by my side, Mirac takes the lead. He's my personal guard and one of my best men. His wife, Elif, is a damn good hacker who works at one of my clubs.

Emre gets into the back of the SUV with me while Mirac slides in behind the steering wheel.

"To the club?" Mirac asks.

"*Evet*," Emre replies, *yes*.

I use the club as a front for my headquarters. I had offices built beneath the building where we take care of anything mafia-related.

I made sure to never cross paths with Mazur, so the bastard has no idea what's coming for him.

I stare out the window at the lights from stores, restaurants, and bars brightening the sidewalks.

When we reach the club, Mirac parks the SUV behind the other vehicles in the alley. I shove the door open and climb out, on guard as I walk to the main entrance. One can never be cautious in my line of work.

Glancing at the line of people snaking down the side of the building, all waiting for their turn to enter the exclusive establishment, I only look for threats.

I have five clubs scattered around the city, all the names similar. Revenge, Retribution, Avenge, Reckoning, and Vengeance.

To most people, I'm just a successful club owner. The façade has served me well, lining my bank accounts with more money than I'll ever need.

Entering the club, I nod at the bouncers. Music pulses in the air, flashing lights giving an energized feel to the ambiance. There are two floors, the second holding the VIP section where many influential people like to hang out. We also have a bar and relaxing area set up on the roof.

I head toward the back, and as I approach a steel door, Scott opens it while Keith remains in place. "Sir," my men murmur with chin lifts as I walk by them and take the stairs to the lower level.

To the left is a hallway that leads to entertainment areas for illegal gambling. Many yachts, shares, and businesses have been lost and won at those tables. To the right is the office space we use for dealing in arms. The exit at the back leads to the loading docks where we receive any alcohol deliveries. It makes it easy to move the weapons hidden in beer barrels.

The area between the gambling section and the offices is where my men gather to let off some steam. Tables and leather armchairs fill the space, a bar counter lining the back wall. All the décor is black and gold, lending a dangerous but luxurious feel to everything. A smoke cloud hangs in the air. The music down here isn't as energetic as in the club upstairs.

My soldiers are already waiting, some caught up in deep conversations while others check their weapons.

I take a moment to look at every man. Some have been with me from the beginning, while others have joined over the years. They've all become my family.

"Ready?" I ask.

All eyes turn to me, then a jumbled chorus of affirmations sounds up.

Glancing at Emre, I gesture for him to proceed.

Emre takes a step forward, then lifts his chin as he sucks in a deep breath of air. "The mission is clear. Kill only those who are armed. Tymon Mazur is to be kept alive." Emre runs through the plan again, ensuring every soldier understands how the attack will be carried out.

When everyone's ready, we leave the club through the back entrance and pile into the line of SUVs filling the alley. This way, security footage shows me entering the club but not leaving.

It's always good to have a cover story, and if that doesn't work, there's the slush fund to pay off the police I have in my pocket to take care of any problems that might arise.

Driving to Mazur's mansion, my heart beats faster with every mile we put behind us.

Finally, the day has come.

Babam, Annem, bu gece sizin intikamınızı alacağım. Bu geceden sonra benimle gurur duyacaksınız.

Thinking about avenging my parents' deaths and how proud it will make them has adrenaline pulsing through my veins.

Chapter 3

Lara

When the cat-o-nine tail whip with metal spikes strikes, more pain explodes over my back as it tears through my shirt, ripping at my skin.

I bite harder on my bottom lip to keep the cry from escaping.

Whack.

Eighteen.

Don't cry.

Whack.

A wave of scorching heat engulfs my skin, sweat beading on my forehead. My back tingles as if tiny tongues of barbed wire are licking me, every strike intensifying the crippling pain.

Nineteen.

My arms threaten to buckle as I keep myself braced in a kneeling position, so I don't plow into the hardwood floor.

Whack.

Twenty.

Don't cry!

Unable to stop it, a tear spills over my cheek. I bite harder, my mind void of any thoughts.

There's only the pain.

"You have a call," Marcel, the head of the guards and Tymon's second in charge, mutters.

The whip hits my back so hard that I can't keep myself from falling forward and sprawling over the wooden floor. Air bursts from my lungs, my skin torn and on fire, my bones aching.

The whip drops next to me, the metal spikes coated with droplets of blood. I stare at it as I listen to Tymon taking the call and leaving the sitting room.

The moment I'm alone, my ears fill with a whooshing sound. My sight blurs, the intensity of the pain increasing tenfold.

You've survived worse. Don't cry.

You're stronger than this.

I push myself up into a sitting position. My skin feels stretched thin over my back, the drying blood pulling at the gashes.

I clench my teeth, suppressing groans while I climb to my feet.

The punishment is over. At least Tymon didn't kill me.

Using a hand to brace myself against the walls, I gingerly make my way down to the servant's quarters. Dizziness threatens to overwhelm me, but I shake my head.

Don't pass out.

A first aid kit lies on my bed. Like all the times before, I take it along with my sweatpants and sweater and walk into the bathroom.

I set everything down on the counter, then lift my eyes to the mirror.

I'm pale, my eyes too large, too dark.

You're okay.

My breathing starts to speed up, and once again, I shove the turbulent emotions deep down, not giving them the chance to surface.

You're okay.

Turning on a faucet, I cup my hands and splash water over my face before taking a couple of painkillers. Unbuttoning my shirt, I carefully pull the tattered fabric off, winching whenever it tugs at the fresh wounds.

You're okay.

Opening the first aid kit, I turn so I can see the right side of my back in the mirror. Old marks are now covered by fresh, red welts. Clenching my jaw, I begin the painstaking process of cleaning myself up.

It takes a while to tend to my wounds, my teeth aching from all the clenching. There are gashes I can't reach. The best I could do was draping a warm, wet cloth over them to get rid of some of the blood.

It's no use asking one of the other staff members to help. We never get personally involved because you don't know who will die next. It would be stupid to form bonds. It would only make things more challenging, so it's everyone for themselves.

I learned this lesson after Mom died, and I was left to fend for myself. She got bronchitis, and when she had breathing problems, she was taken away, and I was told she died.

There was no funeral.

When my time comes, I won't have a funeral either. Like all the ones before me, I'll just vanish.

Just wiped from existence while life in the mansion goes on as always.

You accept these things when you're given no other choice. It's better not to fight.

It's better not to hope.

It makes everything easier.

Knowing the other staff members need to clean up after a long day's work, I get dressed in my sweatpants and sweater. Gathering the bloody shirt, my skirt, and pumps, I leave the bathroom.

A new shirt lies on my bed.

I tuck the new shirt, my skirt, and pumps away in the box, then head up to the kitchen to throw the ruined shirt away.

The wounds keep tightening, and I know I won't get much sleep tonight. The next week will be brutal because I still have to see to all my chores.

I walk past the main part of the kitchen and into the section that's used for laundry and stocking the cleaning supplies. The smell of stew still hangs in the air, but having no appetite, I ignore the pot on the small gas stove.

Agnes prepares our meals, and it's always some kind of stew with egg bread. As long as our stomachs are full, we don't complain.

I toss the ruined shirt in the trash, then pour myself a glass of water. Standing by the sink, I only drink half and throw the rest down the drain.

A sudden popping of gunfire coming from outside has me quickly walking to the small window. Glancing into the night, lights illuminate the grounds at the side of the mansion. I can't see anything, but when more gunfire fills the air and I hear men shouting, I take a hesitant step away from the window.

Is the mansion under attack?

Suddenly the lights go out, plunging me into darkness. My heart kicks in my chest before continuing to beat frantically.

What's happening?

Something like this has never happened before, so I don't know what to do.

Hide!

I squint my eyes, and with my arms held out in front of me, I feel my way into the main part of the kitchen.

All hell descends on the mansion as gunfire pours through the hallways.

Dear God!

I duck behind the marble island, my arm pressing against it. I keep blinking, my eyes finally starting to adjust to the darkness. On all fours, I crawl to the side of the island and peek around it.

Where are the other staff? Do I try to make a run for it or hide?

The gunfire is sporadic, then I hear a man shout, "Clear all the rooms. I want Mazur found."

God, they'll probably kill me just for working here.

The gunfire comes closer, the shots sounding impossibly loud and making my heart beat faster in my chest.

Get to safety! You've survived too much to die tonight.

I glance to the other section of the kitchen, and as I stand up to make a run for the backdoor, it bursts open, and men pour inside.

Crap!

Panicking, I run in the opposite direction, and darting into the hallway, bullets fly past me. My mouth instantly grows bone dry, and before I can take another step, a bullet slams into my side, tearing through my flesh and insides with excruciating pain.

Another bullet hits me in the stomach, and as pain engulfs me for a second time, my body drops into a pit of darkness.

Chapter 4

Gabriel

It happens fast. One second, I'm firing at Mazur's soldiers, and the next, someone darts right into my line of fire.

Reaching the body, I notice the person isn't wearing any combat gear, and there's no weapon. I crouch down, on guard for any threat, while my men sweep through the mansion.

"Dead?" Emre asks as he crouches on the other side of the body.

"Looks dead," I mutter, not able to see the person clearly.

Then Emre shines a light over the body, and I stare at the familiar face of the woman I bumped into outside Aqua.

She belongs to Mazur?

Just like earlier, her light brown hair is tied back in a tight bun that does nothing to flatter her average features. By the worn sweatpants and sweater, it's safe to guess she's probably a maid or some kind of employee. I've heard Mazur doesn't give a fuck about his staff.

My eyebrows draw together when I hear the gunshots tampering out.

As I climb to my feet to continue my search for Mazur, Emre asks, "Is it the same woman from earlier?"

"*Evet*." I lift an eyebrow at one of my soldiers. "Any sign of Mazur?"

"Not yet, boss," he answers before disappearing down the hallway.

Emre searches the woman's neck for a pulse, then glances at me. "She's still alive."

I doubt it's a coincidence that she bumped into me on the same day I planned to attack. I swear, if Mazur got away and she had something to do with it, I'll make her wish she was never born.

An edgy feeling ghosts over my skin, increasing the restlessness already tightening my muscles.

I want to know why she was at Aqua and any other information she has on Mazur. "Take her."

Emre signals for two of my men to come closer. "Where are they taking her?"

"Home. One of the cottages at the back of the property. Get the doctor to take care of her."

"Home?" Emre questions me.

"I want every piece of information she can give me."

"If she survives," my cousin mutters.

While my men take care of the woman, I continue to walk through the house, and when every soldier shakes their head, intense disappointment starts to fill my chest.

"No sign of Mazur or Dydek," Daniel, one of my lieutenants, informs me as he comes into the sitting room. His words hit a nail in the coffin containing my hope that tonight would be the night Mazur pays for what he did to my parents.

I wanted that fucker to die tonight. I wanted his blood coating my hands, his screams filling my ears.

I bite out the instruction, "Find out if any of our men were wounded, and get the lights turned on."

"Yes, boss."

To another soldier, I say, "Gather the maids and every other staff member that's still breathing for questioning."

He nods and quickly darts out of the sitting room.

Minutes later, when the lights come on, I glance around me. "Tear the mansion apart."

Getting to destroy the place Mazur calls home doesn't do anything to lessen the frustration swirling inside me.

Fucking, bastard! You can run, but I swear I will find you – if it's the last thing I do.

While my men get to work destroying every piece of furniture, a wooden box grabs my attention. Thinking it's a cigar holder, I flip the lid up, then stare at the rows of bullets. Taking one out, I see a name inscribed on the side.

Agnes.

I check another one.

Nikodem.

So the rumor is true. Mazur keeps a bullet for each of his employees.

Where he uses fear to inspire loyalty, I chose a different method. There's only one thing that overrules fear. Money. People will do a lot of dumb shit for the right amount.

"The staff are gathered in the basement," Kerem, one of my soldiers, informs me.

Nodding, my lip curls in distaste, and with one last hateful glance around the sitting room, I follow Kerem to where the staff are waiting to be questioned.

The basement is dimly lit, eight beds lined against the walls. I only count seven people and assume the girl I shot is number eight.

"Where's Mazur?" I ask, my sharp gaze checking each of their faces for any sign of emotion.

They remain silent, their eyes trained on the concrete floor.

"The sooner you talk, the quicker you can get back to your lives," Emre adds.

The oldest, a man who looks like a butler, says, "We don't know. There's a tunnel beneath the house. Mr. Mazur probably left via it."

"Where's the entrance to the tunnel?" I ask, glad they're not making this hard for themselves. I get no pleasure from torturing innocent people.

"It's in the garage," the elderly man answers.

"You have no idea where Mazur will go to hide?" Emre asks.

The man shakes his head. "We know nothing about his business. We only work here."

Glancing at Daniel, who joined us during the questioning, I say, "Find the tunnel, and check where it goes."

"Yes, boss."

I gesture for Emre to take care of the staff, then head toward the stairs.

"Pack up and leave," Emre instructs Mazur's staff. He also gives orders to some of our soldiers, and when he catches up to me, he asks, "What now?"

"Now we fucking start over and find out where the bastard is," I growl, unhappy as fuck that tonight didn't go as planned.

"Mazur will probably hear that you're out for his blood. We've lost the advantage of a surprise attack."

Leaving the mansion, we get into the back of the SUV. Mirac slides behind the steering wheel. "Home?"

"Evet."

That woman better survive. She might have information that will make the hunt for Mazur easier. It can't be a coincidence that she bumped into me today.

I start to check my clothes for any kind of tracking device she might've planted on me, but not finding any, I relax back against the seat.

Sucking in a deep breath of air, I exhale slowly, then mutter, "It's fine if Mazur knows I'm coming for him. Let him fucking scurry around like a rat trying to figure out why I attacked."

I fucking hope he's consumed by fear and confusion.

When I get home, I shrug out of my jacket and hand it to Nisa, my housekeeper. "*Selam*," I greet her.

Nisa makes sure the entire household runs smoothly, and she provides company for my grandmother.

"*Selam*, Gabriel *Bey*." Her words are accompanied by a relieved smile.

I head up the grand staircase, making my way to the east wing of the mansion. The moment I step into my grandmother's private sitting room, her eyes scan every inch of my body, relief washing over her wrinkled features.

"I'm fine," I murmur to set her at ease.

"Good. And Emre?" She asks, her eyebrows drawing together again.

"He's in good health," I assure her.

"*Tanrıya şükür*." She murmurs her *thanks to God*.

Reaching the armchair she's sitting on, I drop down to one knee and take hold of her hand. With my head lowered, I swallow hard on the bitterness as I admit, "Mazur got away. I failed."

She lifts her other hand to my head, her touch loving and forgiving. "You'll find out where he ran to."

I nod, and lifting my eyes, I look at the woman who raised me. She's only worn black since my father died. Over the past thirty years, not a day has passed where she didn't mourn her son.

"I will." Steel laces my words.

Climbing to my feet, I bend over her and press a kiss to the top of her head. "*Söz veriyorum*." (I promise.)

Chapter 5

Gabriel

There's no fucking sign of Mazur. It makes my blood boil, knowing I was so close, but he managed to slip away.

Walking down the cobbled path, the landscaped garden bathing the grounds with green ferns and rose bushes forms an oasis around me. My grandmother has always loved gardening. Whenever she's pruning a bush or strolling through the greenery, she's truly at peace.

I open the door to the cottage, and stepping inside, I look at Murat, the soldier I have guarding the woman I stole from Mazur.

"Has she woken up?" I ask.

He shakes his head, glancing toward the bedroom. "But Dr. Bayram said she's out of the woods. You just missed him. He'll be back in a couple of hours to check on her."

"She's healing?" I ask. It's not out of concern. I just hope she'll have information I can use against Mazur.

Mazur nods. "Everything went well with the surgery. Dr. Bayram has her on an IV for medication."

Letting out a sigh, I walk to the bedroom, then stare down at the unconscious woman. She's pale as fuck.

She's probably in her early twenties, her light brown hair now loose and forming a halo around her face. Even though she's plain-looking, a small button nose and wide mouth give her an innocent look.

"Why were you at Aqua?" I murmur, the need to find out everything she knows making me want to shake her awake.

A soft gasp escapes her, and as her features tighten with pain, her lashes slowly lift, revealing the striking blue eyes that annoyed the ever-loving shit out of me when she bumped into me outside the restaurant.

Jesus, they're the clearest blue I've ever seen.

A frown deepens on her forehead, and the moment I take a step closer to the bed, her gaze snaps to me. Instantly confusion flutters over her face, then she weakly whispers, "You?"

Tilting my head, my eyes sharpen on her, but before I can demand any answers to my questions, her eyes drift shut, and she slips back into unconsciousness.

"Fuck," I mutter. "You couldn't stay awake for one minute?" Not having more time to waste, I stalk out of the room and instruct Murat, "Call me when she's awake."

Leaving the mansion, Mirac drives me to the club, where Emre's already hard at work, receiving a shipment of Glocks fitted with tactical flashlights and suppressors from Luca Cotroni that are destined for Nikolas Stathoulis in Vancouver.

Being a part of the Priesthood, a group formed by the five heads of the respective mafias that rule the world, we help each other out.

Years ago, we formed an alliance. I wouldn't call any of the men friends, but having fought alongside them has tightened the bond between us.

I make sure Luca's shipments reach Nikolas, and in return, Luca transports weapons to Turkey for me. Once they reach Eymen, my cousin on my mother's side, he sells them on the black market.

Over the years, we've streamlined the entire operation, rarely getting any trouble from rival criminal organizations. They've actually become regular customers.

"Everything in order?" I ask Emre as I glance over a beer barrel. The weapons are all in airtight sealed bags with actual beer filling the barrels to cover them. Whenever there's an inspection, which doesn't happen often, the guards at the border only find beer.

"*Evet*. It's all here," Emre answers. "We're loading the truck. As soon as it's on the road, I'll call Nikolas with the estimated time of arrival."

"Good."

For the most part, we speak English, having practically grown up in Seattle, but some Turkish words have stuck with us, always slipping through in conversation.

I watch as my men load the barrels into our eighteen-wheeler. To make transport across the borders easier, Nikolas opened a club as well. That way, it doesn't look suspicious that a shipment of alcohol is en route for him.

As soon as the truck leaves the docking yard, Emre and I head back inside and walk to the gambling section. We check that the cleaning staff did a good job and the tables are ready for tonight.

Finding Justin, the manager in charge of the floor, in his office that overlooks the tables, I say, "Give me an update."

"Everything is running smoothly. I've hired a new dealer. He used to work in Las Vegas and has a good eye to catch any card counters."

"Good," I murmur.

"Profits are up by five percent," Emre adds. "Business has been great."

I smile at my cousin. "I'll see you at home."

"Don't eat all the food," he calls after me.

Leaving the office, I go upstairs to check with the other floor managers before heading back home.

Just in time for dinner, I take a seat and offer a smile to my grandmother. "*Selam, babaanne.*"

"*Selam,*" She returns my greeting. Her eyes, the same light brown as mine, rest warmly on me.

The table is already loaded with food, and we don't wait long for Emre to arrive and Nisa to join us.

After Emre greets our grandmother, I pick up a spoon and enjoy the Turkish soup. It's only because of our grandmother and Nisa that we've continued our Turkish traditions in America.

For a couple of minutes, we eat in silence, then my grandmother says, "Nisa tells me there's a woman in the cottage."

I wipe the corners of my mouth with a napkin, then explain. "She's one of Mazur's employees who got hurt in the attack. Once I've questioned her, she'll leave."

Changing the subject, my grandmother asks, "Are you busy at work?"

Emre nods, then gives me a playful grin. "I'm overworked and underpaid."

"Like hell, you are," I mutter while I help myself to some vegetables and shredded beef. Before I take a bite, I glance at my grandmother and ask, "How are the plans for your birthday coming along?"

She scrunches her nose. "I regret it every year. Why do I still have parties at my age?"

"Cancel it if you don't want a party," Emre mentions.

"Then Gabriel will never see his family on his mother's side," she mutters. Letting out a sigh, she adds, "I've never gotten along with Ayesenur and Eslem."

"*Allah Allah*," Nisa mutters. "I can't stand them."

I can't say I get along with my aunt and cousin, but because we're family, I can't just turn my back on them.

Also, working so closely with Eymen, who's the opposite of his sister and mother, makes it impossible to cut ties with them.

"It's only for a week," I say, giving the women an encouraging smile. "Thank you for putting up with them for my sake."

My grandmother reaches across the table and gives my hand a squeeze. "*Gözümün nuru*," she calls me the light of her eye, one of her favorite terms of endearments.

Chapter 6

Lara

Waking up, I blink against the bright light streaming into the room.

Weird.

It takes a moment before I realize nothing is familiar.

No dimly lit basement.

No sounds of snoring from the other staff.

It's quiet.

Once my vision focuses, I glance around the room, taking in the cream bedding with an embroidered flower pattern. Cream curtains. A high-back chair in the corner.

Everything looks soft, warm, and luxurious.

Again I glance at the bed as I try to pull myself into a sitting position, then, all at once, everything floods back.

The pain from the whipping.

The attack on the mansion.

Panic rockets through me, my skin turning ice cold. My breathing speeds up, my eyes wildly darting around me.

My body protests when I try to sit up again, a deep ache in my stomach stopping me. Noticing the IV inserted into the back of my hand, my eyes widen even more.

God. Where am I?

Just as I remember I was shot, a man appears in the doorway. His black cargo pants and shirt are the same as the ones Tymon's guards wear. With no expression on his face, he mutters, "You're up."

Nervously, my tongue darts out to wet my dry lips. "Where am I?"

"You'll find out soon enough." He disappears again.

Oh, God.

This time I clench my teeth against the pain, and I manage to sit up. Sliding my legs from the bed, I sag against the side of the mattress when I try to stand. I'm wearing only a white nightgown that reaches to my feet.

Come on, Lara. You have to move faster.

With my heart pounding in my chest and zero strength in my legs, I don't even make it halfway to the door before dropping to the carpet, the IV stand toppling beside me.

No. Get up!

The pain becomes so intense it feels like something is trying to claw its way out of my stomach.

You're okay.

You can do this.

You're okay.

You've survived worse.

My head snaps up when I hear murmuring voices, then another man appears in the doorway. Unlike the guard, who's dressed all in black, this man is wearing an expensive charcoal-colored, three-piece suit.

It takes a couple of seconds before I recognize him.

The rude man from the restaurant.

I can't remember his name.

"Finally," he mutters, already looking annoyed with me. "Unless you plan on crawling out of here, I suggest you get back in the bed."

Apprehension tightens my muscles, increasing the pain. "Will you even let me crawl out of here?"

His eyes narrow on me, then slowly, he tilts his head. "No."

Dear God.

"Why?" I wet my lips again, frustration swirling in my chest because I'm not even strong enough to crawl out of here. "Why am I here?" I shake my head as my fear darkens into a powerless feeling. "How did I get here?"

The man glances down the hallway, then talks to someone I can't see, authority lacing his words. "Get the woman back in the bed. Secure her."

"Yes, boss."

Boss?

Crap.

Oh. Crap!

The guard comes back into the room, then I'm hauled up into the air and placed back on the bed, nauseating waves of pain rippling through me.

Sweat beads on my skin, an exhausted tremor shuddering through my body. I have no strength to stop the guard from clamping a shackle around my ankle. The chain rattles as it settles, hanging down the side of the bed. I didn't even notice it was lying beneath the bed.

What is going on?

Panic steals the last warmth from my body, leaving me a shivering mess.

"Why are you doing this?" I ask weakly, my fear drenching my words.

The boss stares at me, and just as it starts to feel like he's trying to cut me in half with his piercing gaze, he says, "You work for Mazur."

A slight frown forms on my forehead. "Yes?"

He waves a hand over the length of me. "You got shot during the attack. I saved you, and in return, you'll answer all my questions."

My frown deepens, and hesitantly I ask, "Did you attack the mansion?"

He nods before taking a seat on the high-back chair, making the thing look like a throne. The guard leaves the room, pulling the door shut behind him.

One less man to deal with.

My eyes settle back on the boss, the fact that *he* is responsible for the attack on the mansion making me absolutely terrified of him.

"I got shot because of you," I breathe, quickly realizing this man is Tymon's enemy, and by default, it means he'll view me as his enemy as well.

My heart thumps rapidly in my chest, my mouth growing dryer than the desert.

Panicking, I ramble, "I'm just a maid. I know nothing about Mr. Mazur's business dealings. I–"

He cuts me off, his tone brutally harsh, "It's quite the coincidence that you bumped into me at Aqua the same day I was planning to attack."

What?

My lips part, my frown deepening.

Aqua?

Then I remember, and my eyes widen. Quickly, I exclaim, "I don't know who you are."

His lion-like eyes lock with mine, and instantly I feel like prey that's a second away from being torn apart.

God. Help me.

The corner of his mouth twitches, making my heartbeat hammer crazily against my ribs. More sweat coats my skin, prickles of fear rippling through me.

"I'm Gabriel Demir." *I've never heard the name before.* "Head of the Turkish mafia."

Pins and needles turn me into a block of ice. My lips part, then my heart sinks to the deepest pits of hell.

I won't get out of this alive.

Slowly, I inhale a shocked breath, the gasp clearly audible.

His eyes narrow again as he takes in my shocked reaction. "Why were you at Aqua? Were you sent to spy on me?"

My head starts to shake, my hair tossing wildly over my shoulders. "I wasn't there… to spy on you. I was at Aqua to get dinner… for Mr. Mazur. You saw the food… it splattered all over the sidewalk." My fear tightens my voice.

Again, Gabriel stares at me until shallow breaths rush over my lips with terror.

He doesn't believe me.

"I swear," I exclaim, "I was only there to get an order of seafood for Mr. Mazur."

I even got whipped. The proof is on my back.

Something stops me from showing the marks on my skin to this man.

He wouldn't care.

The predatory look in his eyes and the dangerous aura around him tell me as much.

As soon as this man is sure there's no information to gain from me, he'll kill me.

My silence might be all that can keep me alive. Not that I have any information to share.

I just need to buy myself time until I'm stronger.

Slowly, Gabriel shakes his head, and as if he can read my thoughts, he warns, "Don't try to lie to me. I know many creative ways to make someone talk."

Torture.

God.

Again, pins and needles spread over me, reminding me I'm still shaking like a leaf in a hurricane-force wind.

My eyes flick to the shackle around my ankle.

I've survived so much, but how will I escape this nightmare?

Slowly, my gaze lifts to meet Gabriel's, then he asks, "What's your name?"

I swallow hard on my fear before answering, "Lara... Lara Nowak."

"How long have you worked for Mazur?"

"Since I was twelve."

His head tilts slightly, and I'm not sure if he believes me because I can't get a read on him. All I can say for sure is he's dangerous, and I'm in a world of trouble.

With Tymon, I knew what to expect. I grew used to the punishments.

But with Gabriel, I have no idea what he's capable of doing. Beatings I can handle. Wounds and broken bones heal.

What if...

Oh, God.

My cheeks go numb, a lump forming in my throat.

I'm a virgin. Tymon never allowed relationships between staff, not that it mattered because I'm too plain looking. It was my one saving grace. No one showed any interest in me.

Instinctively I scoot as far back on the bed as I can go. "Please don't hurt me," the feeble plea falls over my lips. "I'm just a maid."

Still, Gabriel only stares at me, putting the fear of God in me.

"Where would Mazur go to hide?"

A wave of dizziness hits, making dots dance before my vision. I'm not used to all the emotions spiraling through me.

With Tymon, everything was a routine. One I grew accustomed to since birth.

Being in the hands of the enemy, not able to anticipate his next move, is nerve-wracking as hell.

"He has homes all over the world." I swallow hard, wishing I could have some water. "I have no idea which one he'd run to," I admit, still unsure whether remaining silent would be the best option.

Gabriel's eyebrow lifts. "Where are these houses? Give me addresses."

The fact that he thinks a mere maid would know the actual addresses almost makes a cynical burst of laughter leave me. "I'm just a maid," I tell him again. "I didn't have access to that kind of information."

Again he's eyes narrow on me. "Yet, you know he has many properties? You're contradicting yourself."

Crap.

Gabriel stands up, the movement sending a fresh wave of debilitating fear through me. Unable to stop myself, my chin starts to tremble, tears threatening to fall.

Don't cry.

Lifting a hand to his chin, he swipes the pad of his thumb over his bottom lip, his gaze still resting intensely on me. "You have three days to decide whether you'll tell me everything you know or face the consequences."

What kind of consequences?

Gabriel inhales deeply as if he's savoring the scent of my fear. "A word of advice." He starts to walk out of the room. "I'd talk if I were you."

The words sound ominous, causing my stomach to burn from all the fear and tension.

The bedroom door is drawn shut behind him, then I'm left alone.

What am I going to do?

How in God's name am I going to get out of this alive?

Chapter 7

Lara

I've spent the last forty-eight hours panicking and trying to free myself from the shackle and drifting fitfully in and out of sleep.

The only human interaction I've had was when the guard brought me food and gave me toilet breaks, and the doctor came to check on my wounds.

I'm exhausted, in pain, and scared out of my mind.

When the bedroom door opens, I quickly sit up, ignoring the ache in my stomach. Dr. Bayram comes in, followed by a woman who seems to be in her early fifties.

Yesterday I begged the doctor to help me escape, but he just checked my wounds, stuck fresh bandages on, then left without a word.

Maybe the woman will help me?

I watch as she sets a stack of clothes down on the chair. When she comes to stand next to the doctor, I try to make eye contact, but she won't look at me.

As if I'm not here, Dr. Bayram shows her how to change my bandages and what to look out for in case of infection.

Either these people fear Gabriel, or he pays them well.

Crap. How am I going to escape?

"Has your appetite returned?" the doctor asks without bothering to look at me.

"I'm being held captive. Do you really think I can eat under the circumstances?" I snap at him.

It's weird. I wouldn't dare speak to Tymon in that tone, but since I woke up in this foreign bed, it's as if I can't stop.

Maybe it's because my sixth sense tells me I won't get out of here alive, so I might as well fight with everything I have.

"Eat, or you won't regain your strength," the doctor mutters, then he leaves the room with the woman following right behind him.

He showed her what to do. Maybe that means she'll check in on me from tomorrow. If I can talk to her alone, I might be able to gain her sympathy.

Just as my muscles start to relax, the door opens again. This time Gabriel comes in, and it has me moving to the side of the bed. I'm ready to jump off the mattress should he try anything.

Not that I'll get far with the chain that's bolted to the bed.

My eyes are glued to him, every movement from him making me feel more on edge. He walks to the window and stares out of it until the silence grates against my nerves.

God, he's intense.

Suddenly his deep voice breaks the silence. "How old are you?"

I swallow hard on my frayed nerves. "Twenty-two."

"And you've worked for Mazur since you were twelve?"

"Yes." The single word is nothing more than a whisper, my eyes burning from not blinking as I cautiously watch him. Every muscle in my body is wound tight.

He's tall, firm, and strong. I won't stand a chance against him in a fight. He'd kill me in seconds.

The hopelessness of the situation is starting to sink in, making me feel like a caged animal.

"How did you end up working for the Polish mafia?"

I hesitate, not wanting to share my personal life with this man.

Gabriel turns around, and locking eyes with me, he raises an eyebrow. "Are you related to Mazur?"

God no. Not wanting him to think something so awful, I give in and answer, "My mother worked for him. Mr. Mazur brought us over from Poland after I was born."

"You don't sound Polish." Gabriel tilts his head, a flicker of interest in his eyes. "Your mother works for him too?"

"No." My tongue darts out to wet my dry lips. I lower my eyes to the bedding. "She's dead."

"How did she die?"

Shaking my head, I frown at him. "Why are you asking me personal questions? It won't help you find Mr. Mazur."

"Just answer me," he orders, his tone clearly stating I better comply if I know what's good for me.

Letting out a sigh, I mutter, "She died of bronchitis when I was twelve."

Gabriel nods, then gives me one of his unnerving stares that has a tendency to rattle me. "What did your work entail?"

My fingers fist the covers, and I wrap my other arm around my waist, hoping to lessen the pain.

"I cleaned the mansion, prepared beverages, and got Mr. Mazur's meals for him." I really don't understand Gabriel's line of questioning.

"Were you the only one who took care of his meals and beverages?"

The frown deepens again on my forehead. "No. Agnes, another maid, would sometimes help."

"So just the two of you touched his food and drinks?"

The apprehension thickens in my chest. "Yes."

Gabriel nods, his piercing gaze cutting right through me. "Mazur trusts you."

Shit.

Now I understand the line of questioning, and I've stepped right into the damn trap he set up for me.

Desperately wanting to get myself out of the hole I'm stuck in, I say, "Mr. Mazur doesn't trust anyone. I just did my job so he wouldn't kill me."

His eyes narrow. "How much did he pay you?"

"Nothing." I swallow hard on the fear this man makes me feel. "We got food to eat and a bed to sleep in."

"Are you legally in America?"

I nod quickly. "But my personal documents are at the mansion." Along with the only belongings I owned.

Gabriel walks to the chair, and when he takes a seat, my heart sinks. If he's getting comfortable, it means the interrogation is far from over.

After he unbuttons his jacket, he settles his arms on the armrests. His fingers lightly tap against the upholstery.

Everything about this man feels calculated.

Our eyes lock, his light brown irises filled with intelligence.

He inhales deeply, then asks, "Have you traveled with Mazur?"

"Rarely," I whisper.

Giving in to my thirst, I reach for the glass next to the bed and take a couple of sips, savoring how the cool liquid soothes my mouth and throat.

"Where have you traveled with him?"

I set the glass down. For the millionth time since I woke up, I glance around the room, unconsciously looking for anything I can use as a weapon.

"Only to Poland."

"Where in Poland?"

I shake my head. "I don't know. We traveled by private jet, and I always stayed in the house."

Gabriel lifts a hand to his face, his fingers brushing over his jaw. "Who are Mazur's allies?"

How am I supposed to know something like that?

"Ahh… Marcel? He's the head of the guards. If Mr. Mazur trusts anyone, it's Marcel." I'd gladly throw Marcel under the bus if it got me out of the hot seat.

A frown line forms between Gabriel's eyes, making him look more threatening. "Dudek. How long has he worked for Mazur?"

I don't know. "He has always been there."

"Why were you at Aqua?"

The question is random, but the moment the words register, ice pours through my veins.

"To get dinner for Mr. Mazur," I answer the same as before.

Gabriel leans forward, and resting his forearms on his thighs, he links his hands. His intense gaze bores into mine. "Did you try to plant a tracking device on me?"

What?

"No!" I shake my head vehemently.

"Were you supposed to kill me?"

God.

My chin starts to tremble. "No."

"Why were you at Aqua?"

I gasp for air, fear gripping my throat in a strangling hold. It's hard to squeeze the words out. "To get dinner for Mr. Mazur."

Gabriel stands up, and as he buttons his jacket, he slowly walks closer to me.

I struggle up from the bed, the chain rattling. My legs feel weak, and sweat beads on my forehead.

He stops in front of me and stares me down until I feel more vulnerable than I've ever felt in my life. I keep my head lowered and my eyes trained on the carpet, every muscle in my body on high alert.

"I really hope for your sake, the next time we talk, you will have something of importance to tell me."

Or else?

When I glance up, Gabriel's eyes slice through mine, his expression cold, merciless, and filled with promises of pain.

He turns around and leaves the bedroom, then air whooshes from my lungs, and I slump down on the side of the bed.

Dear God.

Chapter 8

Gabriel

It's been an entire week, and Lara keeps giving me the same answers. It's clear as fucking day she's scared shitless, and my gut tells me she hasn't lied to me.

Yet.

Still, I'm no closer to finding Mazur. The fucker vanished into thin air.

Walking into the cottage, I ask, "Still the same?"

"*Evet*," Murat answers. "She eats, showers, and tries to get out of the shackle. She hasn't asked Nisa *Hanim* to help her escape again. Nothing new."

Nodding, I walk to the bedroom and let myself in. Just like every other day, Lara moves to the side of the bed, her body tensing with fear. Since yesterday she's been wearing the dresses I had Nisa bring to the room. The colorful patterns make her look even younger.

Some color is returning to her face, and she seems to be gaining weight. She doesn't look as gaunt anymore, her striking eyes sparkling brighter.

Lara never keeps eye contact because she's always on guard and scared shitless.

That doesn't mean she's not brave.

Not once has she cried, and not a day has passed where she hasn't tried to break the fucking shackle.

Yesterday, Dr. Bayram removed the IV and said Lara was recovering well.

Trying a different strategy today, I shut the door behind me and take a seat on the chair. Removing my gun from behind my back, I release the clip.

As I lift my eyes to Lara's, I say, "For every right answer, I'll remove a bullet. By the time I'm done questioning you, I'll use the remaining bullets on you."

I watch as fear darkens her eyes until they almost look like the night sky, light blue flecks shining like stars.

The woman's eyes are something else. She can keep her facial expression neutral, but her eyes give away her emotions.

"Why were you at Aqua?" I ask for the hundredth time.

Lara takes a deep breath and lets it out slowly. "To get dinner for Mr. Mazur."

Again, my thoughts turn back to the scene outside the restaurant. Lara's shocked expression. Her outburst. Her fear. How she ordered another meal and left without looking at our table.

Unfortunately, I'm really starting to believe her.

My thumb moves, ejecting a bullet. I set the round down on the armrest.

Lara's eyes widen, and I watch as relief trickles into them.

"Does Mazur have any romantic relationships?"

Her brow creases, and for a split second, she looks repulsed. "Not that I know of."

I focus on the emotion she let slip by her defenses. "Why are you repulsed by the question?"

She shrugs. Her gaze darts to the clip in my hand before meeting my eyes again. "It's hard to imagine Mr. Mazur being intimate in any way."

"No girlfriends? No wives?"

She shakes her head. "None that I've seen."

I remove another bullet. When I set it down next to the other one, Lara relaxes more.

Questioning the woman, I've learned a couple of things. She has zero loyalty to Mazur. I have no idea what her life was like, but I can imagine it wasn't good. I've heard

Mazur has a habit of killing his staff for the slightest offense.

Lara might have expressive eyes, but I've never seen a flicker of hope in them. This woman has been conditioned to survive at all costs, which means if she had information on Mazur, she would've given it to save herself.

My only hope is that she knows something she's unaware of. Working in the mansion, she could've overheard something of value that meant nothing to her.

"How have you managed to survive twenty-two years?"

There's a flash of a frown before her features become expressionless again. This time the light in her eyes dim.

When she doesn't answer me immediately, I slowly repeat. "Working for Mazur, how did you survive twenty-two years?" To get a reaction out of her, I add, "I can only assume you're of value to him. He must care about you."

Lara's features tense with a flash of hatred. Again it's only for the slightest moment.

"I mean nothing to him. I survived by doing my job and not causing any trouble."

To encourage her, I take another bullet from the clip and set it down on the armrest. "How did you explain the ruined meal to him?"

I watch as all emotion leaves her eyes until they almost seem lifeless. "I didn't tell him."

I stare at her for a moment, but this time there's no increasing fear on her part. "But something happened," I murmur.

"I was late."

For the first time since I took her prisoner, Lara seems to shut down completely. Having done it myself many times before, I recognize the emptiness in her eyes.

Out of curiosity, I ask, "And?"

"I was punished."

Which reminds me. "Does Mazur keep a bullet with your name on it?"

She immediately nods. "Yes."

"Do you know of someone close to Mazur who doesn't have a bullet with their name carved on it?"

Slowly, she shakes her head, and only then do I realize she has her hair up in a bun.

"I've never looked inside the box," she answers.

I slip another bullet out of the clip. "Still, I find it interesting that you've lasted this long."

There's a spark of life in her eyes again. "Mr. Kowalski worked for Mr. Mazur since I was five. I'm not the only one who's managed to stay alive."

"Who is Kowalski?"

"The head butler."

I remember the elderly man who spoke on behalf of the group in the basement and assume he's Kowalski. I have men stationed at the house in case Mazur is stupid enough to return. I'll get them to question the butler.

Wanting to test Lara some more, I ask, "If I were to let you go, would you run back to Mazur?"

Lara's fair complexion turns pale, her eyes looking twice their size. Her breathing picks up until they're short bursts of air over her lips.

Her reaction tells me everything I need to know. She can't go back because he'd probably kill her.

Fuck, this woman is of no value to me. She knows nothing.

I gather the bullets from the armrest and slowly push each one back into the clip. When the clip clicks into place in the gun, Lara closes her eyes. A visible tremble shudders through her, her fear palpable in the air.

"You have no documents, no belongings, and nowhere to go."

Slowly, her eyes open. They're dull and empty again.

She thinks I'm going to kill her and is already mentally checking out.

Rising to my feet, I move closer. I lift the gun, training the barrel on her. "Give me a reason to not kill you."

She lifts her chin, and her gaze locks with mine. "I'm a good maid."

"I already have a housekeeper."

Downright terrified, she whispers, "I won't tell anyone about you."

"That's not a chance I'm prepared to take."

Her shoulders hunch as if she's trying to make herself a smaller target, then the woman surprises me when she drops down on her knees.

I've never had anyone kneel before me. No one has lived long enough to beg for their lives.

"Please." The word is strained with unshed tears, yet her cheeks remain dry. "I'll work my fingers to the bone."

Nisa could use the help, and should Mazur find out I have Lara, it might piss him off enough to make contact with me. I know I'd hate it if he had one of my employees.

Tucking the gun behind my back, I turn around and walk to the door as I say. "You start tomorrow. You'll do exactly as Nisa instructs. Break any of the rules, and you won't get a second chance."

I open the door and glance back at Lara, who's gaping at me in utter shock.

"Under no circumstances are you allowed to enter the east wing of the house. The punishment will be death."

Still kneeling, she respectfully murmurs, "Yes, sir."

Stalking out of the bedroom, I stop to talk with Murat. "From tomorrow, Lara will start helping Nisa *Hanim*. You're to keep an eye on her at all times. Move her to the room next to Nisa *Hanim*'s. She's not allowed near the east wing. I don't want any contact between my grandmother and the woman."

"*Tamam*." (Okay.)

Only time will tell whether I did the right thing by sparing Lara's life.

Chapter 9

Lara

Still reeling from one hundred percent believing Gabriel was going to kill me, I slump onto my butt.

What just happened?

I wrap an arm around my tender waist, my breaths coming too fast, my heart hammering against my ribs.

God, that was close.

Gasping, I try to grasp the fact that I'll be working for Gabriel.

It's a way out. At least I'm alive.

I'll work hard, so he doesn't regret sparing me.

So far, everything is different here. They give me three meals a day, where we only got dinner at Tymon's.

Gabriel is scary as hell. With Tymon, I at least knew when to expect a slap, a whipping, a broken arm or ribs.

I'm confused, struggling to keep control of my emotions while still healing from the gunshot wounds and whipping to my back.

Everything is different. I've been dropped into a world where I don't know the rules.

Murat, the man who's been guarding me, comes into the room. Quickly, I climb to my feet, the long dress swooshing around my legs. I've never worn anything so colorful.

When Murat comes right at me, I move backward until I bump into the bedside table.

"Relax, I'm taking off the shackle," he mutters.

On guard for any sudden movements from him, I watch as he crouches in front of me and unlocks the shackle. The metal falls away from my ankle.

Before the thought can cross my mind, he says, "If you try to run, I'll shoot you. Just do as you're told, and you'll be fine."

I nod quickly while he straightens up again.

Murat locks eyes with me. "I'll watch your every move, so don't try anything."

I nod again.

"You're not allowed near the east wing of the house."

Good. Rules. I need to know them so I won't get in trouble.

"You are not allowed to talk or look at Mrs. Demir."

Gabriel's married? Not that it matters. I'll stay away from her if that's what they want.

"Just do a good job. Okay?"

I nod, still unable to process what's happening.

"Gather the clothes and follow me," Murat instructs.

I do as I'm told, and with my arms filled with the nightgowns, dresses, and underwear I was given, I follow Murat out of the place I've been held the past week, which seems to be at the back of a large property.

I glance around, taking in all the beauty. The garden is nothing short of a paradise.

Gosh, it's breathtaking.

My eyes devour the colorful roses, the greenery, the huge pool, and the rocks where water happily splashes down into the pool.

With sweat beading on my forehead from moving so much, only a week after I've been shot, I step into the mansion.

It looks nothing like Tymon's home.

I find myself being led through a living room. There is a gorgeous red tapestry against the main wall. Dark blue couches and an inviting fireplace make the space feel warm.

There are potted plants everywhere. All the walls are a sandstone color.

When we enter a grand foyer where a stunning chandelier sparkles in the sunlight shining in from the floor to ceiling windows, I notice a staircase. We turn right toward the west wing before I can take in anything else.

Down a hallway, Murat opens a door, then gestures for me to walk inside.

I glance at the large bed with peach bedding and curtains. There are closets lining the one wall and another door that leads to an en suite bathroom which I can see through the open doorway.

"This will be your bedroom. Stay here until I come to get you."

My lips part and my eyes widen with shock.

Before I can ask Murat if he's sure this is my room, he shuts the door behind him.

This isn't the maids' quarters.

Crap.

I don't want to get in trouble before I've even had the chance to show Gabriel I'm a good worker.

I stand dead still with the clothes in my arms, my heart pounding a mile a minute, my midsection aching.

What do I do?

I look around again, this time taking in the plush white carpet that looks soft enough to sleep on. There are nightstands on either side of the bed, two rectangular mirrors against the walls, with two lights hanging from the ceiling. It looks warm but modern. There's also a small round table with two armchairs by the window and a TV mounted on the wall.

It's unlike any room I've ever lived in.

The door opens again, and I let out a breath of relief when Murat steps back inside. A frown forms on his forehead. "Why are you still standing there?"

Nervously, I glance around the room, then say, "I think you brought me to the wrong room. I don't want to get in trouble."

Murat stares at me for a while. "This will be your room for as long as you work here."

Again my lips part with shock. "Really? Are you sure?"

Murat nods his head, and I don't miss how the corner of his mouth lifts as if he's struggling not to laugh at me. "Put down the clothes so I can take you to Nisa *Hanim*."

I quickly set them down on the bed and nervously wipe my hands on my dress as I follow Murat out of the room. I'm taken to a five-star kitchen where Nisa is busy wiping down the marble countertops.

As soon as I can start working, I'll probably feel better. I might still be weak, but I'll just have to push through, so Gabriel won't want to get rid of me.

Nisa crosses her arms and stares me up and down until I feel the need to wrap my arms around myself.

Pointing a finger at me, she says, "You'll do everything I say."

"Yes, ma'am."

She shakes her head. "You'll call me Nisa *Hanim*."

"*Hanim* is your last name?" I ask.

This time she scowls at me. "No. *Hanim* means Ms. You'll call me Ms. Nisa the Turkish way."

"Oh. Okay." I glance around the clean kitchen, wondering if I should just get to work or whether I have to wait for her to tell me what to do.

It's hard being in a new house. Working for Tymon, I at least had a routine. I knew where everything was and what was expected of me.

This is all strange and confusing. It feels like I've been dumped into the twilight zone.

Nisa's features soften, then a tentative smile graces her lips. "Let me show you where everything is."

Relief washes through me. "That would be great. Thank you."

I follow Nisa from cupboard to cupboard, learning where everything goes. The laundry is done in a room that's separate from the kitchen, and I can still smell the dryer sheets. Lilies and linen. The familiar scent helps ease my nerves.

I stay close to Nisa as she shows me the whole west wing of the mansion. There's a formal sitting room, TV room, entertainment area, four bedrooms with en suite bathrooms, and a study.

All the bedrooms are decorated in light colors, except for Gabriel's room. The dark gray tones fit his demeanor. It definitely looked like a man's room, and honestly, I felt uncomfortable setting foot inside it.

When we head back to the kitchen, I ask, "Is there anything I can do now?"

Nisa shakes her head. "You can go to your room and settle in until it's time for dinner."

I stop dead in my tracks. "But… won't I get in trouble?"

I'd love to get some rest to soothe the ache in my midsection, but I can't see how that can even be an option. I have to work to prove my worth.

She turns to face me, a slight frown forming on her forehead. Her thick black hair is braided down her back, and even though she's in her fifties, it hasn't dimmed her beauty.

"Why do you ask that?"

Having forgotten Gabriel's last name, I try to remember it. Unable to, I murmur respectfully, "The boss said I have to work, and I don't want to give him any reason to punish me."

I'm in enough pain as it is.

Nisa's frown darkens. "Just do as I say, and you'll be fine. You're still recovering from your wounds. Go to your room, settle in, and get some rest. I'll call you when it's time for dinner."

Not wanting to argue and feeling a little relieved, I nod. When I turn around, Murat's waiting to escort me back to the bedroom.

"Oh, I'll bring you fresh towels and toiletries after I've taken the afternoon tea to Alya *Hanim*."

I nod again, assuming Alya *Hanim* is Gabriel's wife.

Crap, this is all too confusing.

Chapter 10

Lara

I'm up at the crack of dawn after a restless night of tossing and turning.

When I'm done showering, I check the lashes on my back, glad to see they're healing and not infected. Still, they'll leave horrible marks.

Yesterday Nisa brought me the softest towels, the same peach color as the bedding. She also brought me shampoo, conditioner, a brush, and hair ties. There are products I've never used or had access to before.

It feels wrong, though. Like I shouldn't have these luxuries.

While I wonder if it's too early to get to work, I also think about everything that happened during the past eight days.

It's surreal.

Not once have we had stew here, and the food is delicious. It's like there's an explosion of tastes in my mouth during every meal.

Last night we sat at a table in a quaint little room filled with potted plants. I didn't have to shove the food down as fast as possible while standing by the sink.

Also, Nisa and Murat have actually been nice to me. No one barks orders at me. The atmosphere in the house is pleasant and not filled with tension.

But all of this makes the apprehension grow in my chest.

It's not what I'm used to, and it's making me feel emotions I've never felt before.

Just do your best.

Keep your guard up and your head down.

Bey for mister. Hanin for miss. Evet for yes.

I go over the Turkish words I learned yesterday so I won't forget them.

I take five minutes to squash all the new emotions down and to gather the strength for the day ahead.

Today I'm wearing a pale yellow dress with a light brown pattern. The flat shoes are comfortable, unlike the pumps I used to wear.

I noticed Nisa doesn't wear a maid's uniform, and I wonder if that means I won't be wearing one as well.

There's a lot I wonder about, but not wanting to overstep any boundaries, I keep the questions to myself.

Walking to the window, I glance outside and notice the sun's rays are just starting to break through the darkness.

It must be past five o'clock already.

Not wanting to be late, I make sure every strand of my hair is neatly tucked into the bun before walking to the door.

Now that I have hair ties, I can maybe braid my hair like Nisa's. Tomorrow, though. There's no time for that now.

It's still hard to believe I don't have to share my sleeping space with anyone. Or a bathroom.

It's too good to be true, which means this could be a trap of some kind. Maybe Gabriel is hoping I'll let my guard down, and I'll give him information on Tymon.

If only he knew I don't know anything of worth. Not once have I lied to him.

Feeling tense and unsure in the foreign house, I cautiously open the door and peek up and down the hallway. There's no sign of Murat.

Can I leave the room without Murat?

Crap.

I don't know what to do, and I really don't want to be late for my first day of work.

With my hand clutching the doorknob, I worry about what to do.

Do I wait?

Do I go to the kitchen and get to work?

This is so hard.

A door opens to my left, and when Nisa steps into the hallway, I almost let out an audible sigh of relief.

She notices me and says, "You're up early. Let's have some tea."

Still hesitant, I ask, "Is it okay if I leave the room without Murat *Bey*?"

"Tsk." She gestures for me to come. "As long as you're with me, it's okay. Just don't wander around alone."

That's good to know.

I follow Nisa to the kitchen. While she opens the backdoor, I fill the teapot with water so it can boil. I peek into all the cupboards again to refresh my memory of where everything goes.

There's even a dishwasher.

Last night it was weird loading all the dirty dishes into it and not washing them by hand.

Moving closer to the dishwasher, I ask, "Do I just open the machine to unload the dishes?"

"*Evet*," Nisa murmurs.

I watch as she takes various ingredients from the pantry and fridge. Opening the dishwasher, I get to work.

Honestly, I'm surprised everything is clean.

As I pack the dishes and utensils away, I have to admit it's more convenient than washing and drying it all by hand.

I notice Nisa takes out curved glasses in which she serves the tea. Beneath each glass is a small plate with a light blue and gold pattern.

I try to memorize everything as quick as possible as Nisa shows me how to pour the tea. She uses a double teapot contraption, the bottom half holding the boiled water and the smaller teapot containing brewed tea.

"I like my tea strong, so I never add boiling water," Nisa explains. She glances up at me. "How do you like your tea?"

Ahh…

We only had water at Tymon's mansion.

"I'm not sure? Normal?"

Nisa lets out an amused chuckle and pours an equal blend of water and tea, the red color much lighter than hers. She also adds sugar to mine.

The whole process took thirty minutes.

Gone are the days of making a quick cup of tea.

"Thank you, Nisa *Hamin*," I murmur as I take my glass of tea from her. I sip tentatively on the hot liquid and have to admit it's much better than water.

A small smile tugs at my mouth as I drink some more, then I catch Nisa grinning at me.

"It's delicious," I compliment her.

"You won't get any work out of me before I've had my tea," she says, her tone light and friendly. Her eyes flick over me, then she says, "Tell me about yourself."

I set the glass down on the small plate. Not knowing what to say, I shrug. "I'm a hard worker."

Nisa shakes her head. "Tsk. No, tell me where you're from, about your family, how you ended up working for someone like Tymon Mazur."

My eyebrows lift slightly. Is this a Turkish thing? I never had conversations with the other staff.

"Ah... I'm Polish." Then I think to quickly add, "But I have citizenship in America." I fidget nervously with the fabric of the dress. "My mom died when I was twelve, and

I have no other family." I shrug again. "I took over her position as a maid after she passed."

Nisa blinks at me. "You've been working as a maid since you were twelve?"

I nod.

"*Allah Allah*," she exclaims dramatically, making me stare wide-eyed at her. "That's no childhood." She pins me with an intense look. "Did you go to school?"

"Yes. Until I was sixteen."

"*Allah Allah*."

It's not that bad.

Just then, Gabriel walks into the kitchen. I quickly straighten my posture, fold my hands in front of me, and respectfully look down.

"Gabriel *Bey*," Nisa says, her tone still pitching. "The girl didn't even get to finish school."

Gabriel says nothing as he takes a bottle of water from the fridge.

Today he's dressed in a pair of jeans, a white t-shirt, and an olive green jacket. Gone are the brown leather shoes, and in their place are black boots.

He almost looks like a normal human being and not a mafia boss.

A very attractive human being.

91

Isn't he going to work? What day is it?

"Will we be having breakfast soon?" he asks.

Nisa waves a hand at him, and again my eyes widen as she shoos him out of the kitchen. "Have I ever let you starve?"

"There's always a first time." The teasing tone in his voice has me peeking at them.

When we're alone again, Nisa says, "Let's get to work. You can continue telling me about yourself while we prepare breakfast."

While I help Nisa prepare *pide* which is a Turkish flatbread, I tell her how we weren't allowed to have any kind of relationships. Friendships of any kind were strictly forbidden.

When she's gaping at me like a fish out of water, I murmur, "It's not something I'm used to." I give her a sheepish grin. "But I'll do my best to learn."

She lifts her eyes to the ceiling as if she's praying, then mutters, "*Allah Allah*." Patting my shoulder, she gives me a comforting look. "I'll teach you everything, Lara *Hanim*."

Emotions shoot through me like a rocket, and I have to swallow hard to keep them down. Clearing my throat, I get back to work.

You'll be okay.

Chapter 11

Gabriel

After breakfast, where I was glad not to see Lara serve us, I settle in a chair to enjoy some tea with my grandmother.

"I hear you gave the woman a job," my grandmother casually says before sipping on her beverage.

"It's temporary," I mutter.

Emre comes in and helps himself to tea. "What are we talking about?"

"About the woman," *Babaanne (grandma)* informs him. "I'm curious as to why Gabriel gave her a job."

Letting out a sigh, I ask, "Would you rather I kill her?"

"*Allah Allah*." She gives me a scowl. "Don't make the food sour in my stomach."

"It was the only other option," I state.

"I suppose you couldn't let her return to Mazur," *Babaanne* agrees.

Letting out a sigh, I explain, "It's just for the time being until I figure out what to do with her."

"It might be a good thing. Nisa isn't as young as she used to be and could use the help," *Babaanne* agrees.

"I've instructed the woman to stay away from your side of the house so you won't be bothered by her," I inform my grandmother.

"Pfft." She waves a hand. "I'll have to meet her at some point."

Not if I can help it.

"What's her name?" she asks.

"Lara Nowak," I answer. "She's Polish."

My grandmother nods, then murmurs, "Lara. Such a beautiful name."

With the tea finished, I get up and excuse myself, so I can catch up with the news. It's my Saturday routine before I head over to one of the clubs.

I walk to my private living room on the west side of the house, and when I pass by the sitting room, I hear Nisa say, "Slow down, Lara *Hanim*! You don't have to clean the entire house in an hour."

"Sorry, Nisa *Hanim*," Lara murmurs respectfully.

Stopping, I turn back to glance inside the sitting room. Lara's polishing the ever-loving shit out of the coffee table.

Nisa places her hand over Lara's, then gives her a compassionate look. "Slow down. There's plenty of time, and you're still healing. We don't want your wounds opening up."

Emotion washes over Lara's face, and for a moment, it looks like she might actually cry, but then Nisa says, "It's okay. You'll learn everything soon enough, but you don't have to work yourself to death. Okay?"

"Okay." The single word sounds small and vulnerable, and it does something weird to my heart.

Jesus, the woman must've worked her ass off in fear that Mazur would kill her for the slightest thing.

Shaking my head, I walk to the living room and settle into my comfortable recliner. I switch on the TV and select CNN, then pick up my tablet so I can read my newspapers.

I get to relax for an hour before Nisa and Lara walk into the living room. "Do you want us to come back later, Gabriel *Bey*?"

I shake my head. "No, go ahead."

They start to clean the room, and when I hear Lara whisper 'sorry' for the third time, I glance up. I stare at her, which probably isn't helping her nerves. She peeks in my direction, and catching me looking at her, she lowers her eyes and starts to dust the ornaments on the mantlepiece as if her life depends on it.

"Slow down," Nisa whispers.

"Sorry."

Before I can stop myself, I mutter, "Are you going to apologize for breathing?"

Lara's eyes snap to mine, and a visible tremor hits her. "If that's what you want, sir."

Jesus.

My temper flares instantly. I get up, dropping the tablet on the side table. "If I hear you say sorry one more time, there will be hell to pay. Understand?"

Confusion and fear flutter over her features. "Yes, sir."

Stalking out of the living room, I figure I'll get more rest at the club and make my way out of the house.

Since she bumped into me, Lara has an uncanny way of annoying the shit out of me.

———————

It's already past nine pm. Sitting at a table, where I have a clear view of the floor, I watch men and women illegally gamble their riches away.

It's all about the money. They could gamble ten million and only win a hundred thousand back, and still, they'll leave here feeling like they actually won something.

As long as it lines my pockets, I don't care.

I watch as a senator bets two million, and a businessman matches it.

Idiots.

One of the waitresses bumps into a patron. "Sorry."

It's funny how that word doesn't bother me now, whereas earlier, it pissed me off.

Lara is only twenty-two, and growing up in Mazur's house must've been hell.

I might be known for being quiet, demanding, and never giving second chances, but I'm not heartless. I just don't like the fact that I'm stuck with her. The moment I let her go, she could run right back to Mazur. The last thing I want is that man knowing anything about me.

Although, he'd probably kill her.

Or not.

Fuck if I know.

Hopefully, Lara turns out to be an asset.

I pull a disgruntled face when I realize I'll have to discuss her wages with her. I'm definitely not looking forward to that.

My gaze lands on Emre. Lifting an arm, I signal to him to come over to my table.

"The place is packed," he says as he takes a seat.

"It's always packed." Taking hold of the tumbler of whiskey, I watch the liquid slosh as I pick it up. "I'm heading home. I need to discuss Lara's wages with her."

Emre turns his attention away from the floor to look at me. "How much are you going to pay her?"

"Fuck knows. Can you remember what wage *Babaanne* started Nisa *Hanim* on?"

The corner of his mouth lifts in a smirk. "How do you expect me to remember? I was in diapers when Nisa *Hanim* started working for us."

Locking eyes with my cousin, I tilt my head. "True."

"I have a question." When I nod, he asks, "Why did you employ Lara if she clearly annoys you?"

"It's the whole vulnerable-innocent vibe she's giving off," I mutter. "I'm starting to think it's why Mazur couldn't kill her. I sure as fuck couldn't when she was down on her knees in front of me."

Emre's smile grows, a mischievous gleam entering his eyes. "Look at you getting all soft because of a woman."

"Fuck off," I growl. Having had enough of this conversation, I finish my drink and get up from the chair. "Take care of things here."

"Always."

While Mirac drives me home, I deliberate about Lara's wages. She's not a permanent employee yet, so I'm not going to pay her what I pay my other staff.

When Mirac stops the car in front of the house, I get out and take the steps up to the front door.

While she's on probation, I'll pay her two thousand dollars a month. If she proves to be of any worth, I'll increase it.

Walking through the west wing, I cross paths with Nisa and ask, "Is Lara in her room?"

"*Evet.*" Before I can walk away, she adds, "Even though she's still healing, she worked hard today."

I nod, then head in the direction of Lara's bedroom. I only knock once before opening the door.

Lara's sitting at the table in front of the window, her hair half braided. She startles, darts up, and winches with pain from the sudden movement.

Like earlier, she folds her hands in front of her and lowers her head.

"I've decided your wages will be two thousand for the next three months. Give me your banking details."

Shocked, she lifts her eyes to meet mine. "Banking details, sir?"

I've only been five minutes in her presence, and already annoyance is creeping up my spine. "Your bank account number. What is it?"

Looking confused and scared, she shakes her head. "I don't have a bank account."

Unexpectedly compassion slithers into my heart like a fucking thief in the night, only making me feel more irritated.

My mind races to ignore the unwelcome emotion and to come up with a quick solution that won't inconvenience me, but then I remember she said her personal documents are still at Mazur's house. "I'll have one of my men bring your belongings. Murat will take you to open an account."

"Yes, sir." She hesitates, her tongue darting out to wet her lips, then she looks at me as if I just promised her the fucking world and whispers, "Thank you, sir."

I've been thanked millions of times but never have the words hit as hard as they do now. My heart constricts, and as I stare at the woman that's become my problem, I feel another wave of intense compassion.

Jesus, this is the last thing I need.

I stalk out of the room, yanking the door shut behind me, thinking things must've been seriously fucked up at

Mazur's place if the woman is so damn thankful even though I practically kidnapped her.

She's just another employee.

Chapter 12

Lara

Since Murat placed the box on the table in my bedroom, I've been swallowing hard on my emotions.

My belongings.

It might not be much, but it's mine.

How long have I been here? Almost eleven or twelve days? Not once have I been shouted at, slapped, or whipped. So far, these people have been kind to me.

Even though I'm still scared of Gabriel, the fear has lessened some. He's going to pay me to work here. Two thousand dollars. It's hard to wrap my mind around the large sum of money, and I have no idea what I'll do with it.

Just save it.

And now he's had my personal belongings brought over from Tymon's mansion.

It's surreal.

My hand trembles slightly as I lift the lid. Carefully, I remove the sets of clothes and my sneakers. My eyes threaten to tear up at the sight of the worn Cinderella book Mom used to read to me.

Taking hold of the storybook, I swallow hard. I turn to the first page, and seeing the only photo I have of my mom, my chin starts to quiver.

Don't cry.

My eyes drink in her light brown hair and blue eyes.

I can't remember what she smelled like, and over the years, her smile and the sound of her voice have faded. Without the photo, I'm scared I might forget what she looked like.

Pressing the photo to my heart, I close my eyes and breathe through the pang of emotion welling in my chest. It's a mixture of longing and loss that has only increased over the years.

Since I started working for Gabriel, I've been finding it hard to bury my feelings. It's all too overwhelming.

In Gabriel's house, people are allowed to have relationships and friendships. Nisa is motherly to everyone. Murat is always smiling, his presence becoming comforting instead of threatening.

It's too much to process.

What if I let all these emotions in, and I have to go back to Tymon? Then working for him will be so much harder.

Just focus on doing a good job, and you might not have to go back.

Taking my social security card from inside the pages of the book, I tuck it into my bra. If something happens where I'm unconscious again, at least the document will go wherever I go.

I place the photo back in the book before tucking it all beneath the clothes. Putting the lid back on the box, I glance around the room.

Where am I going to keep it?

There's no space beneath the bed. Opening the closets, I decide to slide the box onto the top shelf. I have to stretch, and when there's a sharp pain in my stomach, I almost drop it.

By the time I shut the closet door, sweat is beading on my forehead. I press my hand to the healing wound over my stomach and suck in shallow breaths.

You're okay.

There's a knock before the bedroom door opens, and Nisa comes in. She takes one look at me then her eyes widen. "What's wrong?"

I shake my head and force a smile to my lips. "Nothing."

Not taking my word for it, she comes closer, shoves my hand out of the way, and starts to unbutton the dress.

Like an idiot, I stand rooted to the spot, not even trying to stop her.

When Nisa has access to the bandage, she gently peels it away. "Tsk! I told you to be careful. You'll have all the stitches tearing open. Sit on the bed."

Even though she's scolding me, the fact that she's once again taking care of me becomes too much. With a trembling bottom lip and a lump in my throat, I sit down and lower my head.

I never knew how much I missed and needed a caring touch until Nisa. I got so used to just existing.

Nisa quickly retrieves the first aid kit she keeps in my bathroom, and while she gently cleans both my wounds, I keep swallowing on the tears threatening to spill from my eyes.

The last time anyone cared about my wounds was when Mom tended to my scraped knee.

Once Nisa's happy and the bandages are back in place, she sits down beside me. Without a word, she grips my hand and holds it in both of hers.

I close my eyes, focusing on my breaths.

Need for acceptance, to belong to something bigger than just surviving, shoots through me with an incredible force.

Nisa wraps an arm around my shoulders, and when I flinch from the tenderness still left over after the whipping, I can feel her eyes burning on my face. "Is it okay if I hold you?"

Not wanting her to stop, I nod quickly. My voice is thick with unshed tears as I whisper, "It's just the lashings. They're still tender."

"Lashings?" Her voice is sharp as she darts to her feet. For a second time, she unbuttons the dress, and when she pulls the fabric over my shoulders to expose my back, she inhales sharply.

"*Allah Allah!*" she exclaims.

My eyes dart to her face and seeing the horror etched into her features, a wave of shame hits hard. Slowly, she shakes her head, then her face contorts as if she can actually feel my pain.

Opening the first aid kit again, she begins to clean the scabbed-over lashes. It doesn't even sting but just having Nisa show me such kindness has me losing the fight for a fragile moment. A tear rolls down my cheek, and I duck my head lower.

"You poor thing," she murmurs, her words filled with a world of compassion. She clears her throat, the gentle pats over the lashes on my back, both soothing and tormenting.

Soothing because no one has shown me such care since I lost my mother, and tormenting because it's making it so much harder not to cry.

The single teardrop reaches my jaw, then falls and splats onto my hand. I quickly wipe it away, trying harder to not crumble beneath the weight of the kindness being given to me.

"I will not have you working today," Nisa informs me.

Instantly all the foreign but good emotions evaporate, and ice pours through my veins. My head snaps up, my eyes widening on Nisa. "But I'll get in trouble. I don't think I'm strong enough to handle another beating. Please let me work."

Nisa shakes her head before I'm yanked into a motherly hug. She brushes a hand over the braid I struggled to make. "*Allah Allah*. This is breaking my heart." Pulling slightly away, she locks eyes with me. "You won't be beaten or whipped here. This is a safe place, Lara *Hanim*."

Not understanding, my eyebrows draw together. Needing to know so I can mentally prepare myself, I cautiously ask, "What kind of punishments do we get?"

Again she shakes her head. "There are no punishments here. Gabriel *Bey* isn't a monster like that despicable man you worked for."

That can't be possible, can it? How does Gabriel control his employees, then?

"What if I break something, or I'm late?" I ask.

Nisa pats my arm. "We're all human, Lara *Hanim*. We're bound to break a plate or glass."

Absolutely dumbfounded, I try to process everything. My world has totally done a one-eighty turn on me.

Nisa seems to understand my predicament because she says, "You'll get used to our way of life, which is actually quite normal. It's Mazur who's the abnormal one." She gives me a comforting smile. "Life is not meant to be lived in pain and misery, Lara *Hanim*. I'll show you everything. Okay? Never worry about asking me anything. If you don't understand, I'll explain it until you do."

Again my eyes begin to well with tears, and I swallow hard. "Thank you, Nisa *Hanim*."

Gabriel might be responsible for my being shot, but because of it, I've been given this chance to work in a house where people care.

It might all be a farce to get me to let down my guard, but my gut instinct tells me that's not the case.

My heart beats a little faster as excitement trickles into my chest.

Do I dare hope that a life without punishments exists? That there's more to life than being on guard all the time and living in a bubble of loneliness?

Chapter 13

Gabriel

When I walk into the kitchen to grab a bottle of water and find Nisa working alone, I ask, "Where's Lara?"

The woman that's like a second mother to me makes a disgruntled sound through her nose, then pins me with a scowl. "She's resting. You do remember she was shot less than two weeks ago, right?"

How can I forget? I was the one who shot her.

Not answering, I open the fridge and take a bottle from it.

"Lara's been through hell. Tymon Mazur is the scum of the Earth," Nisa begins to rail, visibly upset.

Leaning back against a counter, I take a sip of the water, my eyes resting on Nisa. Once something's upset her, all you can do is listen while she offloads whatever's on her mind.

"I've never wished ill on anyone, but I hope you find that monster and make him pay."

My eyebrow lifts. "You must like Lara a lot that you're out for blood on her behalf."

Nisa drops the rag she was using to wipe the counter, plants her fists on her sides, and locks eyes with me. "My heart bleeds for the poor young woman, Gabriel *Bey*. Watching her struggle isn't easy. She keeps asking if she'll get in trouble, and she's terrified out of her mind that you'll punish her."

It probably didn't help that I threatened her life.

"She'll grow accustomed to how we do things here," I murmur, already annoyed again even though Lara's not in the kitchen. Just the mere mention of the woman is enough to make me feel frustrated. It's really starting to bother me.

"Do you know," Nisa moves closer, the expression on her face secretive as she glances around to make sure we're alone, "Lara won't even cry. She fights it so hard that it makes me want to cry on her behalf."

Letting out a sigh, I set down the bottle on the counter and cross my arms over my chest. "Why does it feel like you want me to fix the problem?"

Nisa jabs a finger at me. "Because she's terrified of you, Gabriel *Bey*. Just give Lara a kind word and set her mind at ease that you won't beat her if she accidentally breaks a plate. It's not right for someone to live in so much fear."

The woman is becoming a bigger problem than I anticipated. She's already wrapping Nisa around her little finger.

"I've given her a job, a bed to sleep in, and food to eat." *And I fucking spared her life.* "I've done more than she deserves."

Nisa starts blinking, her head snapping back as if I physically struck her. "*Allah Allah!* You almost had Lara *Hanim* killed. You practically kidnapped her and brought her here. Of course, it's your responsibility to take care of her. Alya *Hanim* and I raised you better than this!"

I let out another sigh knowing this is one argument I'm not going to win. "Fine, I'll tell her I won't beat her. Happy?"

Nisa gives me a look filled with warning. "*Evet.* Now hurry and leave so I can prepare breakfast before you complain about starving."

God help me.

Letting out a chuckle, I press a kiss to Nisa's forehead, then mutter, "You drive me insane."

As I walk out of the kitchen, Nisa calls after me, "I'll add extra pastrami to your eggs."

To keep the peace in my house, I walk to Lara's room and knock once before opening the door. Just like before, Lara's sitting at the table. With wide eyes and visible fear tightening her features, she darts up, folding her hands in front of her.

I step inside and glance around the room that's neat, not a single thing lying around to say the woman now lives here.

My eyes rest on Lara, who's wearing another dress. It doesn't suit her. She's only twenty-two, and wearing something a fifty-year-old woman would wear is unflattering on her slender frame.

I let out another sigh, then notice her hands are trembling. Moving forward, I take a seat at the table and murmur, "Sit down, Lara."

She instantly listens, dropping down in the other chair. Cautiously, her eyes flit to mine before lowering back to her lap.

I stare for a moment, wondering if I shouldn't just send her back to Mazur, but something tells me not to. My gaze sharpens on her as I try to figure out why it would bother me to send her back.

She gives me another cautious glance, worry knotting her eyebrows together.

"Nisa tells me you're living in fear that I'd beat you for the slightest mishap."

This time her eyes fly to mine, and with a look of alarm, her lips part, but she doesn't say anything.

She just looks fucking terrified.

I glance out the window as I inhale deeply. "I don't find joy in beating people, Lara. That's not how I punish my employees."

She nods, and even though I can see the questions forming in her eyes, she doesn't say a word.

Those goddamn eyes. They're so expressive... and wounded.

"I'll never hit you. You can relax. I'm not Mazur."

Her eyebrows knot tighter together, and she looks extremely vulnerable. The sight makes my heart melt.

Now I understand why this woman has Nisa wrapped around her little finger. Hurting Lara would equate to kicking a puppy.

Suddenly I have the urge to set her at ease, not because it's what Nisa wants, but because I don't want this innocent creature living in terror.

Tilting my head, I settle my hands on the chair's armrests. "Is there anything you want to ask me?"

114

She hesitates but then lifts her chin and asks, "How do you punish your employees?" Her fingers start to fidget with the fabric of her dress. "If I'm allowed to know, sir."

I either dismiss or kill them. It all depends on how much they know about me and what the transgression is. "Unless you betray me, there is no punishment."

"Betray, sir?" The fear in her eyes lessens, and slowly the blue becomes lighter, filled with an eagerness to please me.

The punch to my gut is instant and forceful.

Jesus.

"Don't speak to people about what happens in my house. Don't disclose any information about me."

She nods quickly. "I won't." Her teeth tugs nervously at her bottom lip, then she says, "So I'm not to talk to anyone about you, and I must stay away from the east wing."

"That sums it up." For a moment, we stare at each other, then I ask, "Do you have any other questions?"

Again she hesitates, and it's clear she was never allowed to question anything. It makes her uncomfortable, but still, she pushes through and asks, "Are relationships allowed?"

She has a love interest?

Instantly I frown, totally caught by surprise. "Why do you ask?" She better not start parading men through my house.

"Ah… it's just, Nisa *Hanim* is really kind, and it's becoming hard to keep my distance from her."

I end up blinking like Nisa did earlier, then anger unfurls in my chest. "Are you asking me whether I'll allow a friendship between you and Nisa?"

"Yes, sir."

With a pissed-off frown, I stare at the woman, wondering just what kind of life she's had until I shot her.

Lara squirms in her chair, then she quickly murmurs, "I'm sorry. I didn't mean to upset you."

"You didn't upset me." Mazur fucking did. "Of course, you're allowed to be friends with Nisa. In fact, I encourage it." Just to save myself from a future headache, I add, "But no boyfriends. If you're going to have a romantic relationship, it better happen outside and nowhere near my house. Don't bring men here."

I watch as absolute confusion washes over her face but then understanding sets in, and the woman blushes something fierce. The color in her cheeks actually makes her look pretty. "I… I'll never do that."

Hold on a minute.

I find myself leaning closer, my eyes inspecting her strong reaction of discomfort. "You've had a boyfriend before, right?"

Lara quickly shakes her head. "It wasn't allowed."

Jesus.

A wave of protectiveness rears inside my chest, and before I can think about the consequences, I say, "In that case, you're not to get romantically involved unless I approve of the man. You're living under my roof now, which means you're my responsibility."

Instead of arguing because I'm placing a restriction on her personal life, Lara looks relieved by my request. "Yes, sir."

It's probably because she doesn't have a fucking clue how to navigate through life. Mazur seriously did a number on this woman.

The fucker.

"If there's anything you're unsure about, just ask. You'll never get in trouble for asking a question." I might be a criminal and murderer, but I'm not a dick.

More relief washes over her features. "Thank you, sir."

The fact that she's thanking me for allowing her to ask questions fills me with more compassion.

Now that Lara seems to be more at ease, I decide to add, "If you remember anything about Mazur you think might be of worth to me, please tell me."

She tilts her head. "Like what, sir?"

"Any relationships he had. Phone calls you overheard. People you saw coming and going."

Lara nods. "I'll think hard, and the moment I remember something, I'll let you know."

"Good." Climbing to my feet, I glance around the room again. "Did they bring your belongings from Mazur's house?"

"Yes, sir." Lara stands up and walks by me to open the closet. "I placed it in here because it wouldn't fit beneath the bed. I hope that's okay?"

My eyes land on the plastic box. Without thinking, I remove it from the closet, drop it on the bed, and take off the lid. I stare down at the meager clothes, pair of shoes, and children's storybook.

Unable to believe this is all Lara owns, I grab the maid's uniform and toss it on the bed. Disgust fills my chest as I turn to look at Lara. "This is everything you own?"

Her gaze touches on the worn items with a fierce possessiveness that lends more color to her cheeks. "Yes,

118

sir." Moving around me, she gathers the clothes and starts to fold them neatly.

Jesus Christ.

Pulling cash from my pocket, I take a couple of thousand dollars and drop it on the bed. "Have Murat take you shopping when you go to open the bank account. Take Nisa with you and get yourself decent clothes."

Lara stares at me with the same expression as yesterday when I told her how much her wages would be – as if I just gave her the fucking world.

"It's so much, sir," she breathes, the emotion on her face making her look vulnerable and downright beautiful.

Again there's a tug at my heart.

Needing to get away from Lara and the unwanted emotions she's making me feel, I mutter, "Take a couple of days to heal properly while you get settled."

"Yes, sir." Her words are soft as I stalk out of the bedroom. "Thank you, sir."

After the emotionally loaded moment in Lara's room, I need to fucking kill someone to restore my equilibrium.

Chapter 14

Lara

Sitting on the chair, I stare at the bed that's covered with shopping bags.

I got to go out without having to check the time.

I opened a bank account and have one hundred dollars in it. It's the first time I have any kind of money that I'm allowed to use for myself.

Nisa helped me shop for clothes until my legs were trembling and my arms were numb. Poor Murat must be exhausted from all the bags he had to carry.

Nisa also had me go to a hairdresser where, for the first time since my mom passed, someone else cut my hair.

Today feels like a dream. An incredibly good dream.

I lift my arm and tentatively pull my fingers through the long bob style. The strands feel so soft and healthy.

Is all of this really happening to me?

Yesterday, Gabriel was so kind. Not once did he threaten me, and he even allowed me to ask questions.

I'm allowed to form attachments with other people without fearing they'll be killed the next day. It's scary how quickly I'm growing attached to Nisa. It feels like she's becoming my fairy godmother. It's silly, I know, but it's as if, by some sort of magic, I've been thrown into a storybook where happiness does indeed exist.

Once I have some strength in my legs, I get up and start to pack the clothes away. I smile at every piece, admiring it all over again.

I got jeans, leggings, t-shirts, beautiful silk blouses, soft sweaters, jackets, the prettiest underwear, and a bunch of shoes. Everything from sneakers to boots to high heels. I'm not sure if I'll be able to walk in the heels, though.

I find myself smiling, and the moment I realize it, emotions wash through me like a tsunami. I haven't smiled in years. Not a genuine smile anyway.

A wave of excitement rolls through me, and I quickly strip out of the dress. As I put on a pair of soft jeans and a pale purple blouse, my chin quivers, but I suppress the urge to cry. I decide to match a pair of silver ballet flats with the outfit.

When I'm dressed, I quickly walk to the bathroom and look at my reflection in the mirror.

Gosh.

Instantly my eyes tear up, and I blink furiously to keep from crying.

I look like a woman.

Not a maid or someone's belonging, but a feminine woman.

I look young and free and not like a caged animal that's kicked around every other second of the day.

A knock at the door tears my eyes away from the mirror. When I step out of the bathroom, Nisa comes into the bedroom.

She stops, her eyes slowly drifting over me, then a wide smile spreads over her face. "Beautiful." She comes to stand in front of me and touches my hair. "Let's celebrate your new look with some tea."

Following Nisa out of the bedroom, I struggle to school my face into an obedient expression. A smile keeps tugging at the corner of my mouth until we enter the kitchen. Gabriel has taken steaks from the fridge and is busy placing them on a plate. His eyes snap to us, then he freezes and stares at me.

My mouth drops open from seeing Gabriel working with food.

Are we in trouble?

Just as panic and fear flood my chest, Nisa asks, "Doesn't she look beautiful, Gabriel *Bey*?"

Gabriel takes his time to look at me until my cheeks flush, and I lower my eyes to the floor.

There's a weird sensation in my chest.

"*Evet*, now she looks like a twenty-two-year-old woman."

The heat in my cheeks increases, and so does the sensation in my chest.

"I love the hairstyle," he adds.

My eyes dart to his, and when I see a smile tug at the corner of his mouth, there's a rush of warmth through my body.

He's too attractive for me to handle right now.

"I'm going to put the steaks on the grill," he says, his tone not harsh at all.

Again my lips part as I watch Gabriel leave the kitchen with the plate of meat.

"He likes to grill on Sunday evenings. Sit at the table while I prepare the rest of the food," Nisa instructs me.

Gabriel helps make food? Nisa wants me to sit and watch while she works?

He likes my hair?

Amazement fills me, and I swallow hard as I take a seat, my hands trembling from how wonderful it feels to be in this house filled with good people.

To not just exist, but to get to experience new things. Amazing things.

"It's so nice here," the admission slips from me.

Nisa smiles while she starts to make a bean salad. "It's nothing like the hell hole you came from, Lara *Hanim*."

That's for sure.

I soak in all the positive feelings until Gabriel walks back into the kitchen. The grilled meat's aroma quickly fills the air and makes my mouth water.

He sets the plate down, and without a word, leaves.

"Set our table while I serve Gabriel *Bey*," Nisa says.

I nod and slip off the chair to get to work. When I have everything ready, I pour two glasses of water, then wait for Nisa.

I wonder what the east wing of the mansion looks like and whether Gabriel's wife is also a kind person. She must be if she's surrounded by these amazing people every day.

The fear I feel for Gabriel is slowly fading, but I'm still cautious, not wanting to upset him. I really don't want to go back to Tymon, who'd probably kill me on sight.

"Let's eat," Nisa says when she returns.

Once we're seated, she places a massive chunk of meat on my plate.

My boss prepared it, and I get to eat it?

Never in my life did I imagine something like this would happen.

I give Nisa a tentative smile, then cut off a piece and pop it into my mouth. The tender meat practically melts on my tongue, my eyes drift shut, and I almost moan.

So good.

The meal is easily the best I've ever had, and I eat everything on my plate even though my stomach is threatening to burst.

When we're done eating, Nisa sips on a cup of tea, her eyes resting warmly on my new haircut. "You have some color on your face. How do you feel after all the exercise?"

I'm exhausted but don't care.

"I feel okay." My teeth tug at my bottom lip. "Thank you for everything. Today is the happiest day of my life."

Emotion washes over Nisa's face, she reaches across the table, and taking hold of my hand, she gives me a squeeze. "You're welcome, Lara *Hanim*. I enjoy watching you experience new things. It's like watching a flower blossom."

We sit in silence, my thoughts filled with how much and how quick my life has changed.

Getting shot was the best thing that ever happened to me.

The stitches will come out tomorrow, and this time I don't mind the marks that will be left behind. They're a reminder of the day I left hell and found heaven.

Chapter 15

Gabriel

It's been a month since I attacked Mazur, and there's no sign of the bastard. It pisses me off to no end.

I had my men pull away from his house and only left two to keep watch, one at the front of the property and the other at the end of the tunnel Mazur used to escape. It led to a storm drain outlet.

The employees at his house keep working as if they expect him to return any moment. None of them asked about Lara, though. It's like they don't even care that she disappeared.

Over the past four weeks, she's settled into a routine, following Nisa like a shadow. Yesterday I heard her laugh out loud, and I found myself smiling.

She seems to fit right in with the way we do things and have not once argued. She's a damn good worker as well.

Now that I've become used to seeing her around the house, she doesn't annoy me as much as she did at first.

However, it does bother me that she doesn't smile often. I caught her smiling once, and it made that twisting sensation return in my chest.

When I walk into the security room at the club, it's to find Mirac keeping his wife, Elif, company.

"You're keeping her from work again," I joke as I take a seat behind the monitors. Elif once tried to explain how everything works, but hacking will never be one of my strong points.

"She's distracting me from working," Mirac mutters.

"Right." I nod toward the monitors. "Anything on Mazur?"

Elif shakes her head. "It's dead quiet out there. He'll come to the surface at some point. They always do."

Just then, my phone starts to vibrate in my pocket. Pulling the device out, I see Emre's name flashing on the screen.

"*Evet?*" I answer as I rise from the chair and walk toward the doorway.

"Where are you? One of Mazur's men just showed up, demanding to talk to you."

My right eyebrow lifts as I leave the office.

"He just showed up? Armed?" I ask Emre.

"Unarmed."

That's not fucking weird at all.

"I'm close to my office. Take the man to the freezer where we keep the beverages."

Turning around, I head toward the section holding all the freezers and meet Emre, where he's talking with Daniel, the head of the guards.

"So, this guy knocked on the door and demanded to speak with me?" I ask again, unable to believe someone would be that stupid or desperate to die.

"*Evet*," Emre nods. He gestures to the freezer's door, and opening it, I'm on guard as I step inside.

I come face to face with a middle-aged man who looks more like a sickly accountant than a soldier.

Frowning at him, I demand, "What's your name and what are you doing at my club?"

"Filip," he answers, his arms wrapped around himself for some warmth. "My name is Filip. Mr. Mazur sent me to check if the girl you shot is dead."

What?

Surprise slithers down my spine, then every muscle in my body tightens. "What girl?"

"Lara Nowak. One of the maids. The CCTV showed you shot her during the attack and took her away."

Frowning, I give the man a look of warning. "You're fucking brave walking into my club, demanding to talk to me, and then demanding I give you information." I take a step closer, narrowing my eyes on him.

He's scared shitless, but he had to know he was undertaking a suicide mission when he came here.

"Did Mazur guarantee to pay your family for your death?" I ask.

He doesn't even bother to withhold the information. "I only have months left. At least this way, my family will be well off."

I lock eyes with the dead-man-walking. "You're carrying a listening device," I state the obvious, to which the man nods. Knowing Mazur is listening to this conversation, I say, "You can't hide forever, Mazur. I will find you."

The man clears his throat, his features drawn tight with the fear of his impending death. "Mr. Mazur also wants to know why you attacked him."

I let out a dark chuckle, slowly shaking my head. "If Mazur wants that information, he'll have to ask me in person."

The man's eyebrows draw together, nervously licking his lips. "And the girl? Is she dead?"

If Mazur sent a man to check if she's alive, Lara is worth something. Or she's been fucking lying to me and doing a damn good job of it.

"Why do you want to know if the woman is dead?" I counter his question.

"Mr. Mazur just cares about his employees."

Right, and I'm fucking Santa Claus.

"She's dead," I lie. Taking my gun from behind my back, I keep eye contact with the man. "May you find the rest you so desperately came to seek." Sparing him the time to agonize any further about what lies in the beyond, I train the barrel between his eyes and pull the trigger. I hope, for his sake, Mazur will pay his family for his sacrifice.

"Bury him," I order before stalking out of the freezer.

"Where are you going?" Emre asks, following after me.

"I'm going to find out what Lara's been hiding from me," I snap, anger already pulsing through my veins.

Chapter 16

Lara

Life is wonderful. I can't stop smiling.

Every day my heart fills with more warmth, and I've grown so attached to Nisa I can't imagine life without her.

Murat has also grown on me. He's always quiet in the shadows, but his presence is comforting, offering me a sense of safety I didn't even know I needed.

I'm making *pide* the way Nisa taught me and have learned I enjoy cooking and baking.

Placing the dough mixture into the oven, I quickly rinse my hands and dry them. Nisa's busy making jam from fresh raspberries. It's incredible, and I love watching her.

"I'll get started with the *manti*," I say.

I'm busy placing a small amount of shredded beef on a square of dough when Gabriel stalks into the kitchen, his features drawn tight with anger. Without a word, he grabs hold of my forearm and yanks me out of the kitchen.

I almost stumble over my feet as I try to keep up with him, my heart instantly setting off at a wild pace.

Over the past month, my fear has lessened, and I've started to let my guard down. The sudden aggressive anger from Gabriel has my mouth going bone dry and a tremble shuddering through my body.

I'm pulled into his study, then the door slams shut behind us.

My eyes flit over his face, and having his anger directed at me almost makes my legs go numb. Instantly, my survival instincts from the past flood back. I lower my gaze to the carpet and fold my hands in front of me, waiting for the punishment for whatever I've done wrong.

"Have you lied to me?" Gabriel's tone sounds downright dangerous and merciless.

It makes my fear multiply until it feels like it's strangling my heart.

"No, Gabriel *Bey*," I whisper, my voice respectful.

I scramble to shut down, to shove all my emotions back into a box so the punishment will hurt less, but I can't. After weeks of getting to feel, it's impossible to become a closed-off robot again.

I should've kept my guard up.

Gabriel takes a threatening step closer to me, putting him so close to me that I can smell his woodsy aftershave. I can hear his angry breaths.

I cower into a smaller target, bracing myself for the slap that's bound to come.

"Why the fuck is Mazur looking for you?"

My eyes flick up, but seeing his rage, I quickly lower them again. "I don't know." My mind races so I can give him an answer. "Probably to kill or punish me for leaving?"

I really can't think of another reason.

Suddenly Gabriel's fingers wrap around my throat, and I'm shoved back against the wall. With his hand around my neck, I'm forced to look at him. My eyes are wide, my breaths nothing but shallow gasps.

With his fierce gaze locked on mine, he growls, "You're lying. Mazur would only want you if you were worth something to him. What the fuck are you keeping from me?"

Even though he can easily strangle me, or worse, break my neck, his hold isn't too tight. It doesn't hurt.

Yet.

Turbulent emotions wreak havoc in my chest, forcing tears to my eyes. I swallow hard, refusing to cry. "I'm not hiding anything."

Gabriel stares at me long and hard, the intense moment stretching between us until I'm highly aware of every inch of his solid body so close to mine. His cool fingers around my throat. His breaths skimming over my skin. The gold around his irises shining brighter than ever.

After experiencing all the good life has to offer, there's so much more to fear. I have a lot to lose. It's not just my life that's on the line anymore.

I can't bear the thought of returning to Tymon. I won't survive a day.

When it all becomes too much, my face contorts into a pleading expression. With fear drenching my words, I whisper, "I really don't know why. I promise." I swallow hard again, my voice trembling as I beg, "Please don't send me back."

Gabriel lets go of me and takes a step back, his eyes still burning with anger.

Panic flares through me, robbing me of my ability to think. I just react, grabbing hold of his arm and dropping to my knees. Clinging to his jacket, the pleas fall over my lips, "I beg you, don't send me back to Mr. Mazur. I'll do anything you want. He'll kill me. I can't go back."

Gabriel yanks his arm free from my hold and takes another step back. "Get up."

Instead of obeying the order, my palms meet the carpet, my shoulders shuddering from the effort it's taking to not wail at his feet. "Please," I whimper, my voice hoarse from all the fear and panic.

I won't survive. Don't send me back.

"Get up, Lara," he snaps.

I scramble to my feet, a trembling mess of chaos and confusion.

"You're not going back." My eyes flit to his, searching for the truth in his words, then he adds, "The only way you'll leave my house is in a coffin."

God help me.

The sudden anger from Gabriel and all the past trauma it's brought to the surface makes me feel faint. I rock on my feet, my back colliding with the wall. My hands slap against the plaster, so I don't lose my balance. The breaths rushing frantically over my lips only make me feel dizzier, my lungs starving for air.

It feels like something has a tight hold on my chest, pressing and pressing until my heart flutters like a wild bird.

"Lara?"

It sounds like Gabriel's talking through the other end of a long tunnel, then black dots dance in front of my eyes.

Gabriel takes hold of my shoulders, and through the dots, I see his face, now filled with worry instead of rage. "Breathe."

I inhale, and as the air fills my lungs, I feel an overwhelming urge to cower against his chest and beg him to never send me away. My throat strains from not being able to cry, my eyes stinging as if tiny flames are licking at them.

"Take another breath," he instructs while lifting his right hand to my cheek. The touch is comforting.

Instead of beating me or sending me away, Gabriel keeps telling me to breathe until the dots fade and my heartbeat slows down.

He pulls back, his eyes settling on me with something intense burning in them, then shaking his head, he yanks the door open and stalks out of the study.

Nisa rushes in, and the moment her arms wrap around me, my breath catches in my throat.

"*Allah Allah*, the man will give me a heart attack." She keeps hugging me, making it much harder for me not to cry.

Needing the comfort she offers more than ever, I lift my arms and hug her back. My fingers dig into her clothes, and

I bury my face in her shoulder, taking deep breaths of her flowery scent.

"I don't want to leave," I whimper.

"You're not going anywhere." Nisa pulls back, her dark brown eyes filled with concern. "Why was Gabriel *Bey* so angry?"

I shake my head, the strands of my hair flying wildly around my shoulders. "I don't know. He asked why Mr. Mazur wants me back. I don't want to leave here."

Nisa brushes a hand over the side of my head, her determined gaze promising me she won't let me go anywhere. "You're a part of the family now, Lara. Gabriel *Bey* will never send you back. Okay?"

All I want is to be enveloped in Nisa's motherly hug again, but instead, she takes hold of my arm and pulls me out of the study. "Let's have some tea. It will make you feel better."

Now that the peaceful boat I found myself on has been rocked, I feel rattled to my core.

I know Nisa said Gabriel would never send me back, but that doesn't mean he won't kill me. Like he said, the only way I'd leave is in a coffin.

All the warmth gathered over the past month is gone after the altercation, and I feel chilled to the bone. I've never wanted to cry more in my life.

I should've kept my guard up.

Chapter 17

Lara

The past two days, everything feels weird again, as if I just started working here.

I haven't slept much, too worried to find any rest. Gabriel has not spoken a word to me since the altercation, and it feels as if the air keeps tensing with my impending doom.

I stare at the teapot as the water boils, wondering how much time I have left before Tymon finds me or Gabriel ends me. It's either one or the other.

No matter how Nisa tries to comfort me, I can feel my time running out.

A sob threatens to build in my chest. It takes a lot of effort to fight the urge to cry.

"Staring at the pot won't make it boil any faster," Nisa says.

Nodding, I turn away from the stove to find any kind of work to keep me busy. The kitchen is already spotless, but I pick up a cloth to wipe down the counters again.

Nisa sighs, shaking her head at me, then a smile splits over her face as she looks at something behind me. I glance over my shoulder and find an elderly woman standing in the doorway.

"Alya *Hanim*, the tea is almost ready," Nisa says.

Alya Hanim.

Oh, God.

Ice pours through my veins. There are only three rules. Stay out of the east wing and away from Alya Demir. Don't talk to anyone about Gabriel.

My lips part as fear bleeds into my soul.

"I thought it's time I meet Lara *Hanim*," the woman says. "I'm Alya Demir, Gabriel's grandmother."

No. No. No.

I stand frozen on the spot.

Mrs. Demir walks closer, the same golden eyes as Gabriel slowly drifting over me. "Nisa can't stop talking about you."

My lips are dry, refusing to part.

Then the ground might as well open up beneath me and swallow me whole when Gabriel walks into the kitchen.

141

Everything spins around me, fear and panic forming dark clouds. It feels like I've been sucked into a tornado.

"*Babaanne*?" Gabriel's eyes snap between his grandmother and me. "What are you doing down here?"

"I came to meet Lara *Hanim*. You can stop hiding her from me," she answers, her gaze still resting on me with curiosity. "Nisa tells me you're Polish?"

My eyes lock on Gabriel, and I watch as his gaze sharpens as if he's ready to kill me should I make the slightest movement.

"Gabriel *Bey*, you're going to give Lara a nervous breakdown. Leave, so we can enjoy our tea," Nisa scolds him.

I swear I can almost feel my soul up and leave my body. I grab hold of the counter so it can help me remain standing under the severe tension swirling around me.

Instead of lashing out at Nisa, Gabriel looks at me again before he leaves the kitchen.

A breath whooshes from me, sweat beading on my forehead.

He'll probably corner me once his grandmother isn't around.

Dear God, I'm in so much trouble. As if things weren't bad enough.

A headache starts to throb behind my eyes, and I feel uneasy in my skin as I turn my attention back to Mrs. Demir.

"You look like you're about to faint," she mutters, sounding upset.

My tongue darts out to nervously wet my lips. "I'm fine."

"Sit while I pour us tea," Nisa says, taking hold of my arm and forcing me down on a chair.

Mrs. Demir sits down, then she shakes her head. "You have to forgive my grandson. After his parents died, he's overly protective of me."

Activity returns to my brain as I take in what she just said, then she continues, "I raised Gabriel and Emre since they were little boys. If only they would settle down so I can see my great-grandchildren before I die."

I know Emre is Gabriel's cousin. He's rarely home, so I haven't interacted much with him.

A smile forms on Mrs. Demir's face. "Do you enjoy working here?"

My head starts to bob up and down. "Yes. Very much." At least, I did until my world was turned upside down again.

"That's good," she murmurs. "Nisa tells me you're twenty-two and hardly got to experience life while working for that madman."

I nod again, feeling awkward. I'm also worried out of my mind about Gabriel and what he'll do because I interacted with his grandmother.

It's only then her words start to sink in, and I realize *she's* Mrs. Demir. There's no wife. Not that it matters, because I still broke the rule even though it wasn't my fault.

Nisa places the glasses of tea down and takes a seat. "I've taught Lara how to bake. She's a quick learner," she says with pride in her voice.

Mrs. Demir lifts an eyebrow. "That's good to hear." She turns her gaze to me. "Do you have any hobbies?"

I shake my head. "But I love baking."

"You should spend tomorrow afternoon with me, and I'll teach you how to knit. It's a wonderful way to pass the time."

Gabriel will definitely wring my neck right off if I did that.

Instead of answering, I keep quiet and sip on the tea, hoping it will help ease the headache still throbbing behind my eyes.

Nisa and Mrs. Demir talk about a pattern Mrs. Demir is currently knitting, and by the time they're done with their tea and we get to return to work, I feel sick from all the worry.

My throat aches from the strain, and my chest is starting to burn.

My mind is filled with worry, not knowing when Gabriel will drag me to the study to lay into me because I talked to his grandmother.

Every time Murat peeks into the kitchen, my heart lurches to my throat.

After dinner, which was tasteless for the first time since I started working here, I retire to my bedroom.

I shower quickly and change into a pair of leggings and a t-shirt. Eyeing the bed, I just want to crawl beneath the covers and hide from all the worry, but instead, I take a seat at the table and stare out the window.

Every couple of seconds, I clear my scratchy throat, and by the time it's time for bed, the headache is so bad I know I won't close an eye.

I glance at the door, wondering if Nisa has any painkillers. Getting up from the chair, the world spins a little as I walk to the door and open it. I glance up and down the hallway, then step out of my bedroom.

I quickly walk to Nisa's room and knock on the door. When there's no answer, I knock again.

"She's probably sleeping," Gabriel suddenly says.

My head snaps in his direction, where he's walking toward me. My heart plummets to my feet, the pounding in my head instantly increasing tenfold.

I hunch my shoulders and press close to the wall as I quickly dart back to my door, but before I can open it, Gabriel reaches me.

"About my grandmother…"

I keep my head down, pinching my eyes shut.

I can feel his gaze on my face, and it makes my anxiety spike to unhealthy levels. My head spins again, and I rock on my feet.

Gabriel raises his arm, and I instinctively flinch, bracing myself for the hit. Instead of punching me, his cool hand settles over my forehead. I flinch again, an icy tremble shuddering through me.

"Jesus," he mutters, sounding upset. He throws my door open, then his arm wraps around my lower back, and I'm ushered into my bedroom. "Get in bed," he orders, and not wanting to upset him more, I quickly obey.

Before I have the covers pulled over me, Gabriel rushes out of the room, leaving the door wide open. I sit awkwardly, wishing I could rest my throbbing head on the pillow.

I close my eyes again and startle when I hear Gabriel come back into the room. He's carrying a tray with a glass of water and other things on it. Only when he sets it down on the bedside table, do I see there's medicine.

"Take the pills for your fever and get some sleep." His tone is still harsh.

I pick up the medicine and quickly swallow it down.

"We'll talk in the morning," he instructs.

Feeling more confused than ever, I cautiously lie down.

Without another word, Gabriel leaves the bedroom, drawing the door shut behind him.

He gave me medicine?

Does that mean he's not as angry with me as I thought?

I don't get to worry about things for too long before exhaustion drags me into a restless sleep and feverish dreams.

Chapter 18

Gabriel

Guilt creeps into my chest as I walk away from Lara's bedroom. She probably got sick because I scared the living shit out of her.

I've never second-guessed my actions until two days ago when I lost my temper with Lara. I regret how I handled the situation, and since then, it's clear Lara's frightened of her own shadow again.

I hate how she flinches and cowers away from me. It makes me feel like shit.

Ignoring the guilt, I head to the east wing. When I enter my grandmother's private sitting room, she tells me, "I'm going to teach Lara how to knit."

I drop down in one of the plush armchairs and meet her eyes. "I think it's too early for you to interact with her."

"*Allah Allah*," she huffs. "She's been here a month, Gabriel! I'm tired of staying in the east wing, and Nisa loves her. You and Emre are in and out all day, busy with work. You know I get lonely, right? I need fresh company. Lara doesn't look like she could hurt a fly. Don't make the poor young woman pay for Mazur's sins. Nisa tells me Lara has suffered a great deal."

Christ, give me strength.

"I don't trust her," I voice my opinion.

At least, not entirely. I'm not as guarded after having her in my house for a month, and my gut still tells me she's being truthful about everything. The woman is too scared to lie to me. She'd offer Mazur up on a fucking platter to save herself.

Letting out a sigh, I mutter, "But if it pleases you, I'll allow her to have access to the east wing."

I'll never win when it comes to the women in this house. They have me wrapped around their little fingers.

After giving my approval, my grandmother leans forward, an eager expression lighting up her face. "Now that Lara's no longer banned from the east wing, there's so much I can teach her, seeing as you and Emre refuse to get married and give me great-grandchildren. I wonder if she loves gardening?"

"I wouldn't know," I say as I get up from the chair. I don't want to spend the rest of my evening talking about

Lara. "I'm heading to bed. Don't stay up too late." Walking to my grandmother's chair, I press a kiss on her temple.

"*Iyi geceler*," she wishes me a good night. "*Gözümün nuru*." Hearing her call me *the light of her eye*, the corner of my mouth lifts as I leave the sitting room.

On my way to my own bedroom, my thoughts turn to Lara and how quickly Nisa accepted her and how eager my grandmother is to get to know the woman.

Stopping by Murat's bedroom, I knock on the door.

"*Evet*?" he calls out.

I let myself in. Murat turns down the volume on his TV. "Something wrong?"

I shake my head. "You've been guarding Lara since she got here. What do you think of her?"

His eyebrows draw together. "Boss?"

"Do you get along with her?"

He shrugs. "She's a good person. Hard-working, as well." One of his eyebrows darts into his hairline, then he rambles, "I just think she's a nice person. There are no feelings. Nothing like *that*."

I let out a sigh. "Relax. I just want to know if you get along with her, seeing as she has Nisa and my grandmother in love with her."

"Lara is always respectful. I have no reason to dislike her."

Nodding, I open the door again. "I'll let you rest."

When I leave the room, I start to think the problem lies with me. If everyone in my household gets along with Lara and practically embraces her as part of the family, maybe I should ease down on the suspicion and give the woman a chance.

She's given me no reason not to trust her since she started working for me.

Then why did Mazur want to know whether she's alive?

While thoughts of Lara and Mazur fill my mind, I shower and prepare for bed. When I'm dressed in a pair of sweatpants, I stand in front of the window and stare out over the yard, the outdoor lights illuminating the garden my grandmother loves so much.

My thoughts turn to the fever Lara had when I made her get in bed.

Is she sick because of the worry I'm causing her?

Again the guilt creeps to the surface.

I let out a disgruntled sigh, then decide to check on her before I turn in for the night. Walking into my closet, I grab a white t-shirt and pull it over my head.

Barefoot, I take the stairs down to the ground floor, and not wanting to wake Lara, I slowly push her bedroom door open. The bedside lamp is still on, giving me a clear view of her sweat-drenched face and hair. Her lashes lift, and with feverish eyes, she stares at me, looking like a lost puppy.

Fuck.

I step inside and shut the door behind me. I don't even make it halfway to the bed before Lara tries to get out from under the covers. "I'm sorry," she starts pleading as if I'm holding a gun to her head, then she drops to the carpet, hacking up half a lung from a tight cough that sounds painful as fuck.

I dart forward, and slip my arms beneath her. Picking her up, I place her back on the bed. "You're fucking sick," I state the obvious, sounding like I'm about to rain hell-fire down on her.

"I can work," she protests weakly. "I can still work."

The beating organ in my chest that's been threatening to soften with compassion and guilt gives up the fight and aches for this woman. Even feverish and clearly sick, she'll probably clean the whole fucking house if I give her half a chance.

'It's not right for someone to live in so much fear,' I remember Nisa's words.

"I can work," she mumbles half deliriously.

I pull the covers over her trembling body, and sitting down on the side of the bed, I place my hand over her forehead.

She's burning up something fierce.

"I can..." her breath hitches in her throat, then she's overwhelmed by another painful coughing fit that shakes her entire body.

I quickly pull her up until she's convulsing against my chest and pat her back, hoping it will help loosen the tightness in her lungs.

When the coughing fit passes, Lara slumps against me, wheezing as she sucks in deep breaths.

I'm tempted to wake Nisa so she can watch over Lara but decide against it. If Lara doesn't get better before morning, Nisa will need to take care of her.

I help Lara lie back down, saying, "I'm going to get more medicine. Don't you dare get out of this bed while I'm gone."

"I'm sorry," she whimpers, her face contorting as if she might cry, but no tears fall.

Picking up the tray I used earlier, I hurry out of the room. I get a bowl of boiling water from the kitchen, putting in a couple of eucalyptus oil drops. Nisa makes us inhale it whenever we're sick, and it always helps.

I also grab cold medicine and a bottle of water from the fridge, not wanting Lara to dehydrate from the fever.

When I walk back into the room, the woman looks sick as fuck, and I wonder if it won't be better to take her to the emergency room.

It's probably just the flu. Don't fucking overreact.

I pull the table closer to the bed and set everything down. Reaching for Lara's shoulders, I help her sit up and pull her closer. "Position your face over the bowl and take a couple of deep breaths."

The moment she does as she's told, she starts coughing again. I wince at how painful it sounds and begin to rub a hand over her back. With each cough, Lara leans closer to me until I'm all that's keeping her upright. I wrap an arm around her and reach for the bottle of water. "Take a couple of sips."

She tries to nod, strands of hair plastered to her clammy skin. When she's done taking a couple of gulps, I set the bottle down and pour cough syrup onto a tablespoon. Lara takes the medicine, some strength returning to her body.

Once I've helped her lie down again, I walk to the bathroom and wet a facecloth under the cold water. The moment I enter the bedroom again, her eyes lock on me.

I sit down on the side of the bed and gently wipe the cool cloth over her heated face. "Since when have you been feeling sick?"

She clears her throat before she whispers, "This morning." She takes a breath, then quickly adds, "I'm sorry."

"Stop apologizing," I mutter. "You can't help that you got sick."

The stress I put you under probably didn't help as well.

I pick up the electronic thermometer to check her temperature. The gadget reads one hundred and three.

"Fuck," I mutter. I grab two Tylenol and help Lara sit up again so she can take them. "Maybe I should take you to the hospital."

She starts to shake her head, panic flashing over her face. "I'm fine. I can still work. I promise."

What the ever-loving fuck?

"Stop saying you can work. You're sick."

Her features crumble into a pleading expression, intense panic making her look even more feverish. It has me

155

reaching for the thermometer just to make sure her fever hasn't gone up more.

"Please," she begs, her eyes shining with unshed tears, "I'll get better."

I stare at Lara, taking in her fear and panic, then realizing she's fucking terrified I'll no longer have a use for her.

"Did Mazur kill employees when they couldn't work any longer?"

Lara nods, the pleading look still etched into her features. "That's how my mom died. She kept coughing until she couldn't breathe, and once she left for the hospital, she never returned."

Her words hit me unexpectedly hard, and for a moment, I can only stare at Lara.

"Jesus," I mutter. Shaking my head, I say, "You're not going to die. It's just the flu. But you need to rest so you can get better."

"I can rest?" she asks, her eyes burning on me.

My heart constricts as I nod. "I want you to rest, Lara." I pull the bowl of steaming water closer. "Take another couple of breaths to loosen your chest."

She seems to relax a little.

After she inhales the steam, I do my best to help her through the coughing fit. When she slumps against me, I can't stop myself from wrapping my arms around her.

"Shh," I try to pacify her the way Nisa comforted us whenever we didn't feel well. "You'll be better soon."

"You're not angry?" Lara asks, her voice filled with a world of vulnerability.

"No, I'm not angry."

I rub a hand up and down her back, keeping my other arm wrapped around her shoulders. Lara sits dead still, and minutes later, when I think she's fallen asleep, I start to lay her down on the pillows, only to see she's wide awake.

"You can sleep," I murmur as I get up so I can fetch more boiling water.

"Gabriel *Bey*," she whispers, once again looking at me like I gave her the world, "thank you."

"Rest, Lara," I say before I leave her bedroom. It's only when I reach the kitchen, and I have the pot boiling on the stove, that I pay attention to the weird sensation in my chest.

Compassion. That's what it must be.

When I return to the bedroom, Lara's finally asleep. I rinse the facecloth beneath the cold water, and taking a seat on the side of the bed again, I gently wipe the strands of hair away from her skin.

I stare down at the woman everyone seems to love so much, and as the minutes tick over, I let the compassion I feel for her surface.

I take in her parted lips, her breaths shallow with a slight wheezing sound on every exhale. It has me standing up and heading back to the kitchen to look for one of the humidifiers my grandmother likes to use when the air is dry.

Rummaging through the cupboards, I finally find one and spend ten minutes trying to figure out how the thing works. When steam eventually spirals from it, I grin and head back to Lara's bedroom. I plug the device in next to her bed and position it, so the steam wafts in her direction.

Hopefully, it will help.

I check her temperature again, and seeing it's come down to a hundred, I take a seat on the armchair and rest my feet on the side of the bed.

Crossing my arms over my chest, my eyes settle on her sleeping face. She manages to rest for an hour before a coughing fit wakes her. I quickly get up and help her to sit so she can breathe easier.

Lara seems dazed, and as she leans against me, she makes a whimpering sound that tears right through the middle of my heart. Instinctively, I wrap my arms around her and hold her while she struggles through the painful coughs.

Long after she's fallen asleep again, I lay her back onto the pillows and move to the armchair to try and get some sleep myself.

I only manage to get thirty minutes, here and there, woken by Lara coughing up a lung throughout the night. By the time Nisa comes into the room, I'm dead on my feet.

"What happened?" Nisa asks, her eyes wide between a sleeping Lara and me.

"She's sick. I think it's the flu. It's your turn to watch over her." I walk to the door then add, "She had Tylenol and the cough mixture two hours ago. The eucalyptus oil in boiling water helps to open her chest."

As I walk out of the room, I hear Nisa exclaiming, "*Allah Allah*, my poor baby."

An eyebrow lifts as I head down the hallway because it's clear Nisa's practically adopted Lara as her own.

Chapter 19

Lara

Waking up, it's to find Gabriel asleep in one of the armchairs for the third morning in a row. He has his feet propped up on the side of the bed, his arms crossed over his chest.

I stare at my boss as the last sleep clears from my head.

During the days, Nisa and Murat kept checking in on me, and at night Gabriel's been taking over.

As if they were all worried I'd die if they left me alone.

Even Alya *Hanim* visited me, telling me about the flowers she wants to plant and what TV show she's currently watching.

My chest fills with warmth, and I'm overcome with emotion. Especially because Gabriel has been so kind to me. Not once did he snap at me, and he even held me whenever I coughed so severely I had no strength left in my body.

It felt good being able to lean against him.

It felt good having his arms around me.

My eyes drift over his mussed hair and the dark scruff on his jaw. His arms look strong, the lines of muscles visible now that he's not wearing a suit but a t-shirt. The fabric stretched tightly over his chest.

Curiosity trickles into my heart, along with the gratefulness I feel toward this man who cared for me instead of letting me die.

I've never felt any kind of interest toward a man until now.

But Gabriel's my boss, and I'm just a maid in his house.

I shove the curiosity deep down, and it's just in time because Gabriel's eyes open, and he catches me staring at him.

I quickly sit up and self-consciously pat a hand over my wild bed hair.

"How do you feel?" he asks, his voice deep and hoarse with sleep.

There's a burst of heat in my stomach, and I quickly press a hand to my midsection to stop the sensation. "Much better. I can work today."

I'm not going to lie, I will miss all the attention. There were moments it felt like I was dying, but it felt amazing having everyone caring for me.

It felt like I was a part of a family.

"You'll return to work when I say so," he mutters as he stands up. Picking up the thermometer, he checks my temperature. When he reads the result, a smile forms around his full lips that has me gaping at him like a fish out of water.

"No fever," he praises me, making my own mouth lift into a smile, then he gives me a look of warning. "You'll only return to work on Monday."

That's another four days!

Not wanting to upset Gabriel in any way, especially now that things are so good, I nod. "Okay."

What am I going to do in bed for four days?

I watch as Gabriel walks to the door, still not used to seeing him in sweatpants and a t-shirt. He looks different from when he's dressed in a suit. He's more approachable and not cold like when he's the head of the Turkish mafia.

Right before he pulls the door shut behind him, he glances at me again, and my stomach does a weird flip-flop.

It's just gratitude.

Not long after Gabriel has left, the door opens again, and Nisa comes in. "Gabriel *Bey* says you're much better today," she beams as if it's the happiest news she's ever heard.

"*Evet*," I answer, trying to use more Turkish words.

"Good. I hope it means your appetite has returned. You're losing all the weight you gained."

My stomach grumbles, and I slap my hand over it.

Nisa lets out a chuckle while she fluffs out a pillow. "I'll prepare breakfast and bring a tray up to you."

My eyebrows draw together. "Do I really have to stay in bed? It's all I've done the past three days. Can't I keep you company in the kitchen?"

She shakes her head. "You'll stay in bed. Tomorrow we'll see about you moving around."

Reluctantly, I slump back against the pillows, my eyes following Nisa out of the room.

With plenty of time to think, my thoughts are filled with everything that's happened. What it was like growing up in Tymon's house. How much I miss my mother, now that Nisa has reminded me of how it feels to be cared for.

The ups and downs since I started working for Gabriel. Whenever he got angry with me, he never hurt me. He's taken care of me while I was sick and didn't discard me like trash.

I turn onto my side and bury my face in a pillow, emotions whirling inside me until they spill from my eyes.

Silently, I shed a few tears because there's one thing I've realized the past three days – Gabriel is not Tymon. He won't kill me if I'm sick, beat me if I make a mistake, or threaten me with death just for the sadistic pleasure it gives him.

Gabriel really cares about his employees, and I'm one of them.

Thank you, God.

Having been deprived of any kind of affection for so many years, I don't know how to process all the appreciation pouring into my heart. These people have become very important to me, and I'll do anything to stay with them.

I find myself crying for the cold years I had to endure and the blessings that have come into my life.

All because of Gabriel Demir, I no longer have to just exist. Instead, I get to live and experience all the goodness life has to offer.

I owe him everything.

The most intense feeling I've ever felt fills my chest. I press a hand to my heart and manage to stop crying. My gaze rests on the armchair he spent the night in, and I remember all the times he got up to help me, how gentle he was, his voice soothing and patient.

Slowly the corners of my mouth curve up.

He might not be my prince, but he's definitely my savior. I'll spend the rest of my life thanking him. I'll never disobey him.

Not out of fear but because of loyalty.

Chapter 20

Gabriel

I arrive at the club just in time for the conference call with the rest of the Priesthood.

It's been a while since I heard from any of them, and I assume it means business is going well for them.

Opening my encrypted laptop, I go to the application Viktor, the head of the Bratva, created. His ally and best friend Luca, the head of the Italian mafia, had to go to Italy for business, so we couldn't meet in LA like we usually do.

One by one, each of the men signs into the chat. Viktor is first, followed by Nikolas, who's in charge of a Greek syndicate, then Liam, the head of the Irish mafia, and lastly, Luca.

"Gentlemen," Luca says as he gets comfortable in a chair.

I've only joined the Priesthood for the peace treaty it ensures. The last thing I want is to go up against one of these men, and forming an alliance with them was the better option. It also brings in more money, so I can't complain.

"How's business?" Luca asks.

"It's quiet now that the Sicilians have been dealt with," Liam answers.

Nikolas nods. "Yeah, no problems on my side."

"How's married life?" Viktor asks with a chuckle.

Liam fucking grins from ear to ear. "Good."

"My wife hasn't tried to kill me, so I'm taking it as a win," Nikolas jokes.

I'm not one to chat about idle things, so I just listen.

Suddenly Viktor says, "I hear you attacked Tymon Mazur?"

My eyes flick to his face on the screen. "I did."

Interest flickers in all the men's eyes. It's Luca who asks, "Why?"

"I have a debt to settle with him," I answer vaguely, feeling I don't have to explain my actions. "Does anyone have a problem with it?"

They all shake their heads, then Viktor says, "Just say if there's anything we can help with. We know you like to work alone, but we're here for backup."

"Thank you," I murmur.

Luca steers the conversation toward the shipments of arms we currently have on the road, and once we're discussing everything, the meeting comes to a close.

As I shut my laptop, Emre comes into the office. "I hear Lara's better today?"

"Yes, she didn't wake up so much last night." I glance at my wristwatch, checking the time. It's only two in the afternoon.

"Do you have somewhere to be?" my cousin asks.

I shake my head. "Just finished the meeting with the Priesthood."

"I have a new buyer arriving in a couple of minutes. Want to sit in on the meeting?"

"*Evet.*" I get up from the chair and follow Emre to the boardroom. I usually let him handle any new business so I can focus on the bigger clients, but with Lara being sick, my routine went to hell. I figure a business meeting will get my head back in the game.

As I sit down at the head of the table, my phone vibrates. While Emre goes to welcome the client, I check the message that came in from Elif.

Mazur was seen in Poland. I've asked for proof. Will let you know when I receive it.

"That's good news," I murmur to myself.

Emre comes back to the boardroom, this time with Daniel by his side and two men following after them. I remain seated as they all gather around the table.

"This is Cairo Mohammed and Darius Ibrahim," Emre introduces them.

I nod and gesture for them to take a seat.

Emre sits down to my right while Daniel remains standing. He's an Israeli soldier I found living on the streets while I was in Israel for business.

I almost let out a chuckle when I realize it seems I have a soft spot for broken things. First Daniel, now Lara.

Emre starts the meeting, and we listen to the order of weapons the Egyptians want.

It takes close to seven hours to negotiate a price both parties are content with. By the time the Egyptians head up to the club for a complimentary night of drinking, I'm itching to go home.

As if he can read my mind, Emre asks, "Are you heading home?"

"*Evet.*" I walk down the hallway toward the stairs.

"At least you can sleep in your own bed tonight." The teasing tone in my cousin's voice doesn't escape my attention.

Glancing at him, I ask, "Is it a crime to make sure one of my employees doesn't die?"

He holds up his hands, a mischievous look in his eyes. "I didn't say anything."

"Right," I chuckle. As I take the stairs to the upper floor, I admit, "Besides, I like sleeping in the armchair."

Emre's laughter follows me right through the doorway before it's drowned out by the pulsing beat filling the club.

As I walk through the groups of early partiers, I stop to greet VIP clients, and I finally make it out the door well after ten pm.

Lara's probably asleep already.

Mirac holds the backdoor open, so I can slide into the SUV, and as he drives us home, I think back to the past three days.

Taking care of Lara, it felt like I was doing something worthwhile.

Yeah, just like that, the woman has grown on you.

I let out a chuckle that has Mirac glancing at me in the rearview mirror.

When I finally get to walk into my house, I unbutton my jacket and stop in my bedroom to shower quickly. It's too late for dinner, so I change into my sweatpants and a t-shirt before heading down to Lara's room.

Not knocking, in case she's asleep, I open the door. I'm met with a startled shriek as Lara quickly yanks a shirt over her head.

I pull the door shut, then stand rooted to the spot, my hand still on the doorknob.

Shit. I should've knocked.

A couple of seconds later, the knob turns beneath my hand, and Lara opens the door. "Sorry," she apologizes for my mistake.

I step inside the room, and narrowing my eyes on her, I say, "You need to stop doing that."

Her wide gaze darts to mine. "What?"

"Stop apologizing for everything. It was my mistake. I'm sorry for not knocking before I let myself in."

Her eyebrows draw together, and when it looks like she really wants to say something, I mutter, "Out with it. Speak your mind."

She shakes her head. "I'm really grateful, Gabriel *Bey*." Genuine appreciation shines from her eyes. "For everything you've done for me."

The corner of my mouth lifts slightly. "You're welcome, Lara." I gesture to the table. "I think it's time we have a serious talk." Instantly, her features tighten with nerves, and it has me quickly adding, "It's nothing bad."

"Okay."

I settle down in an armchair, relaxing back while Lara perches on the edge of hers, her hands wrapped tightly on her lap.

Shit, she has beautiful hands. Why didn't I notice that before?

Reaching across, I cover her hands with mine and give them a reassuring squeeze. "You're not in trouble. Relax, Lara."

I have to make an effort to set her at ease, or the stress will take her to an early grave.

She nods again, some of the tension leaving her shoulders. She's dressed in a pair of black leggings and a light blue t-shirt, her body slender beneath the clothes.

She still looks too fragile, making me feel protective of her.

It amazes me how she survived in Mazur's house for twenty-two years.

Needing to clear some things between us so Lara won't worry as much, I start by saying, "Don't apologize for every single thing. Okay?"

"*Evet*, Gabriel *Bey*," she answers with more obedience than usual. Hearing her try so hard to speak Turkish almost makes me smile.

"Stop worrying that I'll throw you out on the street or send you back to Mazur."

The corner of Lara's mouth threatens to lift into a smile as relief fills her eyes.

Those damn eyes.

"And I won't kill you, so stop worrying about that."

Her eyes are glued to mine, and I see the moment the fear leaves her. It's as if she exhales it from her body.

Fuck, I should've had this talk sooner.

Lastly, I say, "There are no more restrictions. You're allowed to move freely around the house. Murat will still be around but only as protection for when Emre and I are at work."

A look of wonder washes over her features. "I'm allowed in the east wing?"

"Yes." To make sure she understands, I add, "And you can walk around the house alone."

This time her mouth curves up into a breathtaking smile. "Thank you, Gabriel *Bey*."

"Just Gabriel," I murmur as I return her smile.

It feels like we've finally taken a step forward. "How do you feel today?"

"Much better." She scoots to the edge of the chair. "Can I leave my bedroom tomorrow?"

There's a twisting emotion in my heart. Having this woman constantly asking for my approval does something to me.

"Yes."

The intense grateful reactions she has to everything I give her, to everything I allow – it gives me more power than I should have.

I have absolute control over her.

The realization has me staring at Lara until she tilts her head and asks, "Is everything okay?"

"Yes." Out of pure curiosity, I ask, "If I gave you your freedom, what would you do?"

Instantly, her features tighten with concern and confusion. "I..." her tongue darts out to wet her lips, "I don't want to leave."

Trying again, I say, "If I gave you all the money you could ever need, and you could do anything you ever wanted to do, where would you go?"

Lara's breathing starts to grow shallow, panic darkening her eyes again, then she begs, "Please let me stay."

I reach over and place my hand on top of her clenched ones. "Relax. I'm not telling you to leave. I just want to know if you'd like to have your freedom."

She shakes her head, her eyes locked with mine and filled with so much emotion it hits me square in the chest. "There's nowhere I want to go. I want to stay here with Nisa *Hanim*, Murat *Bey*, Alya *Hanim*... and you." She turns her hands over, and her slender fingers wrap around mine. Then she leans forward and admits, "I'm safe here. It feels like I belong."

Lifting my other arm, I wrap my fingers around the back of her neck. We're so close, I can almost taste her desperation on my tongue. Leaning forward, I press my mouth to her forehead, then say, "This is now your home, Lara. You never have to leave."

Her eyes shimmer as she gives me a thankful look, her cheeks flushed pink. "Thank you, Gabriel *Bey*."

"Just Gabriel," I remind her. For some reason, it annoys me when she calls me mister or sir.

When she nods, I realize I'm still holding onto her neck. We're still only inches apart, and yet, she doesn't look uncomfortable.

And neither am I.

Three days of caring for this woman, and she's somehow changed how I saw her. I'm not sure what she is, but she's definitely not a burden.

175

She has the purest heart, and it shines through her blue eyes.

I move my hand to her forehead, and when she feels cool with no signs of fever, I smile but add, "Just because you can do whatever you want doesn't mean I'll allow you to work yourself to death again. Try to take things slower. Okay?"

"*Evet.*"

My smile grows, then I ask, "Is Nisa *Hanim* teaching you Turkish?"

She shakes her head. "I pick up on the words and try to remember them."

"You don't have to learn the language," I tell her, just in case she thought she had to. I settle back in the chair, then ask, "Can you speak Polish?"

"Very little."

"What was it like growing up in Mazur's house?"

Lara glances out the window, tension creeping into the lines around her mouth. "It was nothing like here."

"Did you get to go to school?"

She nods, her eyes still focused on the dark night outside. "Only until I was sixteen."

"So, you never graduated?"

Shaking her head, she answers, "No."

This is the longest conversation we've had, and I'm in no hurry for it to end. "Would you like to continue with your studies?"

Lara turns her attention to me, then tilts her head. "Go back to school? I'm too old."

"You can study online."

I watch as she thinks about it, then she starts to smile. "I'd really like that."

Again, I find myself smiling at her. "I'll have Murat get you a laptop so you can study."

"Thank you, Gabriel Be –" She stops the instant I shake my head, then she chuckles and says, "Just Gabriel."

"You'll get used to it." I glance at my wristwatch and notice it's almost two am. "Shit, you must be tired."

"No," Lara replies quickly. "I had to stay in bed the whole day. I'm not tired at all."

Before I can censor my words, I tease her, "Is that your way of asking me to keep you company?" The instant fear darkens her eyes, I quickly reach for her hand again. "I'm teasing, Lara."

I have my work cut out for me but come hell or high water, I'll somehow undo all the damage Mazur has inflicted on her.

My fingers wrap around hers, and I lean closer. With my eyes holding hers prisoner, I say, "You don't have to fear me. I want you to talk to me like you'd talk with Nisa."

Her eyebrows draw together, then she admits, "It's difficult."

"What's difficult?" I murmur, keeping my tone gentle.

"Not being afraid of you."

"Why?"

"You're a man. Nisa's like a mother to me."

Jesus, is she saying what I think she's saying?

Just to be sure, I ask, "Are you scared of Murat?"

"No, he's my guard."

It feels like I'm looking for a needle in a haystack as I ask, "How am I different from Murat?"

"You saved me," comes her simple answer that packs one hell of a punch.

"I didn't save you, Lara." I've always been direct and never one to lie. Not about to start, I admit, "I'm the one who shot you."

Chapter 21

Lara

Throughout our conversation tonight, I've started feeling more at ease with Gabriel, but I'm struggling to bring my point across, and it frustrates me.

"You saved me," I repeat, not knowing how else to explain to him what impact he's had on my life.

"Did you hear what I just said?" He tilts his head. "I'm the one who shot you. I almost killed you."

It still feels wrong arguing, but I can't keep the words back. "Because you shot me and brought me here, my whole life changed."

"Jesus, Lara." He stares at me as if I've lost my mind. "Just how fucking bad was it living at Mazur's that you see being shot and almost killed as a blessing?"

My eyes lower to where he's still holding my hand. I can't keep my voice from quivering as I admit, "You're the first man to hold my hand."

Instantly he pulls away, and I lift my eyes to meet his. "You're the first man who hasn't hurt me." Every good emotion I've felt since coming here bursts like fireworks in my chest. "You saved me."

Gabriel stares at me, and I watch as worry tightens his features. "When you say hurt, what does that entail?"

Traumatic flashes of beatings and whippings shudder through me.

Once I laid unconscious for a whole day after a beating. I couldn't use my right arm for two weeks, and my eyes were swollen shut.

Another time some skin came off with the shredded blouse after Tymon gave me fifty lashes for being five minutes late with his tea because the bus ran late after school. I couldn't sleep on my back for weeks and never returned to school.

I'm so lost in the hell I endured that I startle when Gabriel's palm cups my jaw. "Talk to me, Lara."

Not wanting to relive the hell I've been through, I shake my head and lie, "I guess I'm tired after all."

He tilts his head, his gaze searching mine before saying, "Then I'll let you rest."

We stand up at the same time, and I'm instantly overly aware of how close we're standing to each other. My head tilts back, and my stomach does the weird flip-flop when my eyes rest on his face.

"Maybe one day you'll feel comfortable enough to tell me what happened?" he asks.

It's on the tip of my tongue to apologize, but knowing he doesn't like it when I do that, I just nod.

Gabriel brushes past me, then I turn to watch him leave my bedroom, silently wishing he had stayed and slept on the armchair again.

For a moment, I just stand between the table and the bed, not knowing how to process everything that happened tonight.

Then the importance hits like a ten-pound hammer, the air whooshing from my lungs. I wrap an arm around my waist as I slump down on the side of the bed in total shock.

Gabriel has accepted me. More so, he was friendly, understanding, and even supportive. He went out of his way to set me at ease.

Lifting a trembling hand to my mouth, I shut my eyes, tears rolling down my cheeks.

He was willing to give me my freedom. Even though I'd never leave because I won't survive a day without his protection, just the thought that he was willing to give it to me means so much more than he'll ever know.

Gabriel has shown me a man can be gentle.

In his house, I've learned strangers can become family and enemies can become saviors. I've learned what it's like to be cared for, and I don't think I'll ever be able to live without it again.

The more affection I'm given, the more my soul craves it.

I never have to leave, and he won't kill me.

A peacefulness I haven't experienced before washes over me. I quickly wipe the tears from my cheeks, and standing up, I walk to the door. A smile wavers around my mouth as I pull it open and step out into the hallway.

Even though it's the middle of the night, I can't wait for the morning to come. I'm too excited.

I walk down the hallway and knowing it's allowed, I go to the kitchen. Just because I can.

I'm one of them now.

I take a seat at the table where Nisa and I have our meals and replay the conversation Gabriel and I had over and over in my head.

I'm no longer a prisoner but a part of the household.

The last of the tension leaves my body, and I almost laugh out loud. It's hard to contain all the happiness I feel.

This is my home now.

I enjoy my newfound freedom until the sun starts to rise. Getting up, I stretch my body before switching on the stove and setting a teapot on it so the water can boil while I get ready for the day.

With a smile spread over my face, I quickly go back to my room and change into a pair of jeans and a yellow blouse. The color fits my happy mood.

When I return to the kitchen, I start baking the recipes Nisa taught me so the pantry will be full. I ground pistachio nuts and place them between layers of phyllo pastry. While they're in the oven, I try making some Turkish delights which Nisa likes to have with her tea sometimes.

I wonder what Gabriel and Alya *Hanim* like to eat? I need to ask Nisa so I can make sure there are treats for them as well.

"*Allah Allah*, my heart," Nisa suddenly exclaims, making me jump with fright. "What are you doing up so early?"

A smile splits over my face. "I'm baking."

"I can see that." She walks closer and opens the oven. I notice the *baklava* is almost ready. Nisa looks at me again. "Why are you baking? You should be in bed."

I shake my head, my smile growing. "Gabriel said I can move around the house freely." Without thinking, I grab hold of Nisa and hug her. "I'm no longer a prisoner. I'm free."

She wraps her arms around me, then says, "You were never a prisoner, Lara. But I'm glad to hear you can move around freely. It's long overdue."

When we pull apart, she pours us some tea, then asks, "When did Gabriel *Bey* tell you this?"

"Last night. He said I don't have to be afraid of him and even said I can go back to school."

Nisa's eyebrows lift high on her forehead. "What else did he say?"

I glance down at the gooey mess I've made, then scrunch my nose. "How do you make Turkish delight?"

"That can wait," she scolds me. She takes hold of my arm and drags me to a chair. "Sit and tell me everything that happened last night."

"Gabriel just told me I can relax and that there are no longer any restrictions."

Nisa must not understand because she asks, "How did he say this? What were his facial expressions, his gestures."

Confused, I shake my head. "They were normal?"

"*Allah Allah.*" She glances up at the ceiling as if she's saying a prayer. "Did he smile or frown?"

"Oh." My lips instantly curve up. "He smiled a couple of times." Then I think to add, "He was really friendly and patient. It was nice."

Nisa slumps back in her chair, using a hand to fan her flushed face. "Getting information out of you is impossible," she mutters. "And here I thought I'd get a juicy story before breakfast." With a sigh, she stands up to look at the mess I've made, then she points at it. "This is not how you make Turkish delight."

Getting up, I take the *baklava* from the oven and set it down on a cooling rack. "Will you teach me?"

"Not today." She gestures at the mess again. "Clean this up so we can prepare breakfast."

Getting to work, my heart feels lighter than ever. My laughter comes easier. Everything tastes better. The sun shines brighter.

I'm happy.

Chapter 22

Gabriel

Hearing Lara laugh, I know I did the right thing by having the conversation with her last night.

I follow the sound until I find Lara outside in the garden where's she walking with my grandmother.

Babaanne points at a bush of flowers. "Those are my favorite. Peonies. They're easy to grow."

"They're pretty," Lara says, leaning closer to smell one. "They almost smell like Nisa *Hanim*."

"It's her favorite as well," my grandmother says before dragging Lara toward the rose garden.

I did the right thing.

Nisa and Lara joined us for breakfast. From today, they'll be having their meals with us in the dining room.

I kept finding my eyes wandering to Lara, and watching how much she enjoyed the food brought a smile to my face.

Nisa, on the other hand, was watching me as if she was trying to solve a riddle. Give the woman half a chance, and her mind will run away with her. I know what she's thinking. Why the sudden change of heart?

Heading back into the house so I can go to work, I'm cornered by Nisa, who's waiting at the front door. She lifts an eyebrow. "So, what made you change your mind?"

I let out a chuckle as I pull my jacket off the hook and shrug it on. "I had to ease up on Lara at some point or you and *Babaanne* would never let me hear the end of it."

"Oh." She deflates right before my eyes. "You better get to work."

I watch as she walks toward the kitchen, then I shake my head and leave the house.

While Mizar drives me toward Reckoning, which is situated near the Space Needle, I check my messages. There's one from a number I don't recognize, and opening it, it's to find a photo of Lara, Nisa, and Murat. It must've been taken when they went shopping a while back.

Frowning, I read the accompanying text.

Give her to me as a peace offering, and I'll forgive the attack.

I quickly dial Daniel's number.

"Boss?"

"Go to my house with two men and help Murat keep everyone safe."

"On my way."

I end the call and dial Emre's number.

"Are you on your way?" he asks the instant he answers.

"*Evet*. Twenty minutes. Mazur made contact. I've sent Daniel to the house to watch over everyone. You don't move around alone any longer. Have Kerem with you at all times."

"Okay. And you?"

"I have Mizar."

"What did Mazur say?" Emre asks.

"He knows Lara's alive. He somehow got a photo of her, Nisa, and Murat when they went shopping."

"How do you want to handle this?"

"We wait. Mazur wants Lara back, so he's bound to make a rash decision that can count in our favor."

"Let me know if anything else happens."

After we end the call, I get Elif on the line. I give her the number the message came from, ordering her to trace it when I make the call.

Knowing Elif's waiting, I press dial on the number. I'm actually surprised when it rings, thinking he would've gotten rid of it.

"Demir," a hoarse voice comes over the line.

Too many cigars, old man.

"Mazur."

"I see you got my message," he mutters arrogantly. When I remain silent, he demands, "Return the woman to me."

I let out a chuckle. "I've been wracking my mind trying to figure out why she's so important to you? Are you afraid she'll tell me something of importance?

"She's an imbecile," he scoffs.

Then maybe...

"Is she related to you?"

"She's nothing more than a dog I like to keep on a leash," he spits out.

"I've grown rather fond of her," I say to taunt Mazur. "She's so eager to please my every command." Wanting to piss him off, I add, "So submissive."

"I don't care what you do with her. Fuck her and send her back, and I'll forgive the attack. I won't make the same offer again."

"I don't want your fucking forgiveness, old man," I growl. "I want your blood dripping from my fingers."

"Why?" he demands.

"When we meet, face to face, I'll tell you why." Cutting the call, I take a deep calming breath before checking with Elif whether she was able to trace the call.

"It's pinging all over the world. I was able to narrow it down to Poland. He's definitely there. I'll check any CCTV footage for signs of him."

"Have you received proof from the contact you have in Poland?"

"Not yet. He's gone silent."

Fuck. He's probably been killed.

"Let me know the second you find something."

"*Kesin.*" (Definitely.)

By the time we reach the club, I'm so fucking tired of my phone I want to throw it out the window. Instead of doing that, I tuck it back into my pocket and climb out of the SUV. On guard, I glance around the area, my hand beneath my jacket and resting on my gun.

Now it's only a matter of time.

After talking with Mazur for the first time, it's hard to focus on my work. I'm walking toward the docking bays with Emre to check on shipments.

Why the hell does he want Lara?

No one fights for a person unless they're of value to them.

I stop in the middle of the hallway as the realization hits – I'm willing to fight for Lara.

Jesus.

When Emre notices I've stopped walking, he turns back and asks, "What's wrong?"

I shake my head. "Nothing.

I start walking again, my thoughts inundated with Lara.

I'm willing to fight so she can keep smiling. So she'll remain free.

Again I stop, and this time Emre frowns at me. "Is it the call with Mazur that's bothering you?"

"Why the hell does he want Lara?" I ask the question for what feels like the millionth time. "She has to be related to him, right?"

"But you said he denied it."

I level Emre with an impatient look. "Would you admit a person is family if your enemy had them?"

"Right." He shrugs. "How old is Mazur? Did he have children?"

I lock eyes with my cousin. "She could be his daughter."

He shrugs again. "But she was a maid."

"We know Mazur is fucked up, Emre. He's not the kind of man who cares about family." I think for a moment. "He just doesn't want her in his enemy's hands. It's a matter of wounded pride, not love."

"That makes sense," Emre agrees.

I shake my head again. "But he never told Lara he's her father? It still doesn't add up. He would've used it to keep her in line at the very least."

"Fuck if I know," Emre gives up, trying to solve the puzzle.

After getting the shipments on the road, we wait at the back of the club for a client to arrive. I keep going over everything I know about Mazur. I'm sure the man doesn't have children.

Lara said she came from Poland with her mother. What the hell did she say about her father?

I have to set my thoughts aside when a Mercedes pulls up. A woman in her early fifties gets out, looking like she just stepped out of a fashion magazine.

Carrying a briefcase with cash, Julia Liotta smiles at me as if I'm her next meal. The woman is ruthless. She deals in drug trafficking and sex slavery.

"Gabriel," she purrs. "It's been a while."

Not long enough.

"Julia," I nod. I gesture for Emre to take the briefcase.

Once he's checked the contents and indicates it's all there, Julia hands me a piece of paper with three number plates printed on it.

"I trust my trucks will have safe passage through Seattle?" she asks.

"They have one week," I warn her. "Only product is allowed to pass through my city."

The snake gives me a tempting smile before she turns around and casually walks back to her car, her guards flanking her.

When the Mercedes drives away, I mutter, "I hate doing business with that woman."

"She pays well," Emre reminds me. "At least we don't have to deal with her often."

"*Evet.*" Turning away from the loading docks, I head back inside so I can go home and ask Lara about her father.

Chapter 23

Lara

My cheeks hurt from all the smiling. Glancing over at Alya *Hanim*'s knitting needles, I watch as she makes a couple of stitches before I try again.

Mine aren't as neat as hers, but she told me to be patient. Practice makes perfect.

"*Selam*," Gabriel says *hi* as he walks into the sitting room. He presses a kiss to Alya *Hanim*'s temple, and it reminds me of when he did the same with me.

Instantly, my cheeks flush, and I quickly lower my eyes to the knitting needles in my hands.

Don't beat so fast, little heart.

Feeling rattled by the unexpected affection I feel toward Gabriel, I tuck the wool and needles back into the basket and get up.

Before I can dart out of the sitting room, Gabriel says, "I need to speak with you, Lara."

My feet come to a faltering stop, and just as I glance over my shoulder, he takes hold of my hand and pulls me out of the room.

Having his strong fingers wrapped around mine, attraction hits me hard. As my heart beats faster, I glance up at him.

He doesn't look angry.

We keep walking until we leave the house via a side door, and only once we're near the pool does he stop.

Turning toward me, his hand slowly releases mine as he asks, "What can you remember about your father?"

The question is so unexpected that I stare at him for a moment before shaking my head. "Nothing."

"Didn't your mother talk about him?"

I search my memory. "She said he died while she was pregnant with me." I shrug, not able to remember much more. "My mom didn't talk about him."

"And your mother worked for Mazur since you were born?"

"Yes. If I remember correctly, she started working for him long before I came along. Ten years, I think?"

Gabriel's eyes remain on me as he seems to think about something that's bothering him. "How did Mazur treat your mother?"

Like last night, I'm bombarded with traumatic memories of my mother covering me with her body while Tymon kicked her.

I glance at the swimming pool, the water a refreshing shade of blue. "The same way he treated me."

Gabriel's eyes soften a little, then he asks, "He never showed her any favor?"

I shake my head. "He treated us all the same."

But some he killed quicker than others.

My eyebrows draw together as I admit, "I always wondered why he never just killed me."

Whenever he picked up the bullet with my name on, I thought he would finally carry out his threat.

Gabriel lifts a hand to my shoulder, the touch a comforting gesture. He tilts his head, his eyes softening more with compassion. "I need to figure out why Mazur wants you back. Is there anything you know that will help?"

"No." The fear is instant and overwhelming, and I instinctively step closer to Gabriel.

Anxiety hits hard, and before I know what's happening, my breaths are coming too fast, and sweat breaks out over my entire body.

Gabriel's hands frame my face, and he steps into my personal space. Tilting his head, he keeps my eyes prisoner as he says, "Shh, you're not going back. You're staying right here. Breathe, Lara." His thumbs caress my cheeks, and I feel his breaths on my face.

My heart is pounding wildly in my chest, the turbulent emotions of fear and panic creating an ache behind my ribs.

"Breathe," Gabriel orders, and my lungs obey his command. A strangled sound escapes me, but I finally get some air in.

"You'll never go back," he assures me, the determined tone in his voice helping to set me at ease.

I nod to show I hear him and focus on bringing my breathing back to normal.

Once I've managed to calm down, Gabriel asks, "Better?"

I nod, becoming overly aware of his cool hands still framing my face.

Something weird crackles to life in the tiny space between us, and it's so alarming that I take a step back.

Gabriel also pulls back, then he inhales deeply before shaking his head.

Every ounce of my being feels the urge to apologize for what just happened, but knowing Gabriel doesn't like it, I bite my bottom lip to keep the words from escaping.

Shoving his hands in his pockets, his eyes narrow slightly as he stares at me. His voice is gentle as he asks, "Will you be able to handle more questions?"

Not wanting to disappoint him, I nod, even though I'm not sure what could be a trigger. I don't get anxiety attacks often, but lately, they've been happening more and more. I don't understand why, though. I'm finally safe and would think I'd stop having them.

Gabriel seems to hesitate, which is not something I've witnessed before. Usually, he asks whatever he wants.

"Did Mazur promise you to anyone?"

Huh?

I shake my head, not understanding the question.

Gabriel pulls a hand from his pocket and loosens the tie around his neck. I watch as he undoes the top button, and before he shoves the tie into his pocket, he mutters, "You have to be of some kind of value to Mazur." His eyes lock with mine again. "Mazur never said you were to marry someone or..." A look of disgust tightens his features for a moment, "had you sexually please any of his clients?"

My eyebrows pull together, and when I realize what Gabriel's asking, I start blinking, my face flaming up as if it's on fire. "No." I glance all over the garden, feeling stupidly self-conscious.

When Gabriel remains silent, I sneak a quick peek at him, only to find his eyes on me, surprise tightening his features as he realizes something. "You're a virgin. Fuck, that could be it."

I lower my gaze again, but then Gabriel asks, "Did Mazur deal in sex slavery?"

I quickly shake my head. "I don't know what kind of business he did. Sometimes I saw drugs and weapons."

"There were never girls coming and leaving the house?"

"None that I saw," I answer truthfully.

With one hand still in his pocket, Gabriel lifts his other hand to his face, his thumb wiping over his bottom lip.

Again I blink as my heart skips a beat, and there's a weird dipping sensation in my stomach.

His golden eyes drift slowly over me, then he murmurs, "You can go inside, Lara."

Nodding, I walk away and slip back into the house via the side door.

I feel frustrated that I couldn't be of more help, but Tymon had us all living in such fear that we never dared disobey him and kept our heads down.

It was the only way to survive.

Chapter 24

Gabriel

While I'm getting ready for the function I totally forgot about, I keep replaying the conversation with Lara in my head.

She's a virgin, but that can't be the reason why Mazur wants her back. The man told me to fuck her before sending her back, so it's definitely not to sell her virginity on the black market.

After I've put on a pair of diamond cufflinks and my Rolex, I let out a sigh. The last thing I'm in the mood for is socializing with people I don't give a shit about. I'm only going for my grandmother.

Dressed in a black tuxedo, I leave my bedroom and take the stairs to the lower floor. Emre's already waiting in the entrance hall, looking bored as fuck as he watches videos on his phone.

When he notices me, he says, "You have to watch this one."

"Emre, I'm in no mood to watch videos," I mutter as I let out another sigh. "Going to this fundraiser is torture enough."

"*Allah Allah*," my grandmother exclaims. "It's for the polar bears. You'll attend and donate enough to save the poor animals, and you'll do it with a smile on your face."

Putting a smile on my face, I take my grandmother's hand and help her down the last couple of steps. Dressed in a black gown, she looks like the monarch of the Turkish mafia that she is. "You look beautiful, *Babaanne*."

A happy smile graces her lips, then she wags her eyebrows. "I still have the touch."

"You certainly do," Emre compliments her as well. "Ready?"

"Let me just tell Nisa we're leaving," she says.

I follow her to the kitchen, where Nisa and Lara are cleaning up after dinner. Worried that my conversation with Lara might have set her back, I search her face for any signs of anxiety.

A smile spreads over her face, her eyes widening as she looks at my grandmother. "You look so beautiful, Alya *Hanim*," she breathes in total wonderment.

"Thank you, Lara. The child is so sweet." My grandmother turns her attention to Nisa. "We're leaving."

"You don't have to announce it," Nisa mutters. Over the years, Nisa and my grandmother have become good friends and more like sisters, so I know there's no malice in her words.

Lara glances at me, and I swear I see interest flashing in her eyes before she vigorously starts to wipe down the counters.

I stare at her until my grandmother pats my arm. "Stop daydreaming. We're going to be late."

Shaking my head, I hold my arm for my grandmother to take and lead her out of the house. The moment we're all seated in the limousine with Mirac at the steering wheel and Kerem in the front passenger's seat, my thoughts turn to Lara.

It feels like she's taking over my thoughts every chance she gets.

Staring out of the window, I wonder how such an innocent creature survived hell for so long. Lara's pure in every way.

So fucking beautiful on the inside, it shines from her.

My heart constricts, and I shift on the seat to rid myself of the weird sensation.

There was definitely interest in her eyes, and if I'm not mistaken, it's because she's attracted to me.

It could also be Stockholm syndrome, Gabriel. Don't read too much into it.

I exhale loudly, not happy about the thought. I fucking hope it's not Stockholm syndrome. The last thing I need is Lara becoming infatuated with me because she feels grateful and mistakes it for love.

Really? Would it bother you?

I shake my head, not liking the path my thoughts are taking. Lara probably doesn't know the first thing about relationships. She's already overwhelmed, just trying to navigate her way through a normal life and the good things we all take for granted.

But...

Why the hell am I even thinking about her? She's just another employee.

I shift in the seat again and glance down at my thighs as I dig deeper into my feelings.

She no longer annoys me, and if I'm honest with myself, I feel protective of her.

Only because she's so innocent.

The way she looks at me as if I've given her the world, her blue eyes sparkling like sapphires.

That's because you did give her the world. You've changed her entire life.

'You saved me.'

I close my eyes as her words drift through my mind, followed by her body dropping after I put two bullets in her.

Still, she believes I'm the hero in her story. So eager to please my every command.

I remember how good it felt taking care of her when she was sick and how she depended on me to make it easier for her to breathe. When she leaned on me because she had no strength.

When she was at my mercy.

The feel of her petite body in my arms. Her hands. Her eyes. Her fucking pure soul.

I fist my hand on my thigh when the sight of her kneeling at my feet flashes through my mind.

You fucking love it, you sick bastard.

There's a rush in my chest, need pours through my veins, and my muscles tighten as my predatory side flares to life.

I could take Lara, and she wouldn't fight me. She'd do everything I demanded in her desperation to please me.

Her innocence would be mine. I'd be the only man to touch her, and she'd worship me for it.

I've always been dominant, craving a submissive partner, but I never needed an emotional connection.

Until now.

She makes me fucking feel.

"Gabriel?" Emre's voice rips me away from my depraved thoughts.

I blink as I lift my head, the rush dying away and the need retreating to the darkness deep inside my soul.

"We're here," he informs me.

I nod and climb out of the limousine. Cameras start flashing as my eyes scour the crowds, and once I'm sure it's safe, I hold my hand out to my grandmother and help her out of the vehicle.

She has a graceful smile on her face as I lead her up the red carpet. Every muscle in my body is braced for an attack, and I don't let my guard down for a split second.

Once I'm inside the hall, I spend the next hour greeting people who are of no importance to me.

My gaze goes from one socialite to the next, all dressed in the latest fashion. Their heads are held high, the power of wealth wrapped around them like a cloak. Their laughter fake, and their smiles are perfected to lure in those wealthier than them.

They're all here to find a suitable husband in a crowd of old bastards who will be willing to leave their riches to a young bride.

Lara would never fit in here. She'd probably have an anxiety attack before the champagne is served.

I let out a bored sigh and check the time on my wristwatch.

Another two hours to go. God help me.

"Mr. Demir," a voice purrs behind me. Emre turns around, a smile instantly forming on his lips.

"I'm Madeleine Clark," I hear her introduce herself to Emre.

"Emre Demir," my cousin replies, the low sound of his voice telling me he doesn't intend on going home with us tonight.

The corner of my mouth lifts, and I shake my head lightly.

My grandmother tightens her hold on my arm and leans into me while gesturing at a couple in front of us.

"I hear the Thornes are having marital problems. They're only together because they don't want to split their wealth."

I couldn't give two shits.

"Hmm," I answer to show I'm listening.

A woman comes around the side of my grandmother, holding her hand out. "I'm Madeleine Clark."

Jesus.

"Mrs. Demir," *Babaanne* replies cooly.

Madeleine's eyes land on me. She doesn't even bother hiding the interest sparkling in her green eyes that are no match against Lara's striking blues.

When I don't bother returning her greeting, she brushes it off with a flip of her hair. "I hear you own most of the clubs in Seattle?" She steps closer to me and dares to place her hand on my other arm. Smiling up at me, she leans in, batting fake eyelashes at such a speed she might take flight at any moment.

She's blatantly flirting with total disregard for my grandmother.

Fucking ridiculous.

My gaze flicks to Emre, and I tip my head at the annoying woman. My cousin steps forward, and taking her by the arm, he leads her away from us.

Shock flashes over her features as she gapes at me. Then, her face tightens with indignation because I didn't bother acknowledging her existence.

Babaanne lets out a sigh, tugging on my arm. "Let's place our donation so we can leave before the rest of the vultures descend on you." As we walk toward a table, she mutters, "I can't take you anywhere."

Chapter 25

Lara

Just because I can, I go sit outside by the swimming pool when Nisa turns in for the night.

Pulling up my leggings to beneath my knees, I carefully dip my legs into the cool water and wiggle my toes.

This is nice.

I glance over at the flowers, illuminated by the garden lights, thinking how mystical everything looks at night.

Once again, my chest fills with gratitude, my lips curving up at how happy I feel.

I wish my mom could've experienced this before she died.

You were right, Mom. Fairytales do come true.

I glance up at the dark window of Gabriel's bedroom, thinking how handsome he looked in the tuxedo. He's pure power and testosterone.

My heart flutters, and I quickly dip my chin to hide the shy smile.

I don't know what to do with the emotions and attraction he makes me feel, and I can't talk to Nisa about it.

I love the way his face transforms whenever he smiles. It always makes my stomach flip-flop.

Mostly, I love how his eyes fill with satisfaction whenever I do something that pleases him.

God, I hope I never disappoint him.

"Want some company?" Gabriel suddenly asks.

My head snaps up, and I watch as he walks closer. He's still wearing his suit pants and dress shirt, but he's removed the jacket.

My lips instantly curve up, and I nod.

He rolls up his pants, and sitting down next to me, he dips his legs into the water. His arm presses against mine, then he glances down at me. "How was your evening?"

"I got to make a batch of Turkish delight," I tell him, glad to have finally gotten it right.

Looking into his gold eyes, my heart starts to beat faster.

"Do you like cooking and baking?" he asks, his gaze drifting over my face with a peaceful expression. It makes me feel safe.

"Very much." My smile grows. "I like everything Nisa *Hanim* and Elya *Hanim* teach me."

He stares at me for a moment, then murmurs, "It must be overwhelming for you."

Wiggling my toes in the water, I tilt my head. "What?"

"Experiencing everything all at once."

It is, but I'm slowly learning to deal with it. Glancing down at the water, I wiggle my toes again, loving the feel of the water.

"You should swim," Gabriel mentions.

"I can't." I shrug, then admit, "But one day, I'd like to learn."

"Do you have a bathing suit?"

I shake my head, then my eyes widen as Gabriel starts to unbutton his dress shirt. He pulls the fabric off his shoulders and sets it down on the paving.

Holy crap.

I stare at his muscled chest, my mouth going dry from the sight.

My lips part as he removes a gun from behind his back, dropping it next to his shirt. I watch as the muscles in his arms, shoulders, and back move when he slips into the water.

My abdomen tightens so much, I quickly press a hand to it. My heart keeps skipping beats.

"Get in," Gabriel orders.

"What?" I gasp, still in shock from seeing his bare chest.

"Get in the water, Lara." His tone leaves no room for argument, the command sending a wave of tingles through me.

Unable to deny him, I scoot a little closer. My hands grip the paving around the pool, and then a shriek leaves me as Gabriel grabs hold of my waist. I'm tugged forward and slam into his body, water splashing around us.

Gasping from the cold, my hands find his shoulders, and I hold on for dear life.

"It will get warmer," he says as he moves us away from the side.

Feeling awkward, I try not to hold onto him so tightly, but then he says, "Take a deep breath."

After I've inhaled deeply, he pulls me down beneath the water. It's only for a couple of seconds before our heads break through the surface again. Not thinking, I wrap my arms around his neck as I suck in a deep breath of air. The warmth from his body seeps into mine, making my stomach do a series of flip-flops.

When his hand brushes up and down my back, I realize I'm practically plastered against him. I quickly pull my arms back and let my hands drift through the warming water.

My eyes focus on his attractive face, the drops spiraling over his skin. With my heart scampering off at a crazy pace, I stare at Gabriel, who looks more handsome than ever.

He has one arm tightly wrapped around my lower back, and without much effort, he moves us through the water.

"How does it feel?" His voice is low and deep, the timbre vibrating through my body.

Incredible.

"Good." I try to focus on the water caressing my skin, then my lips curve up. "I feel weightless."

He brushes his hand through his hair, making him look hotter. I quickly glance away, staring at all the garden lights.

You need to calm down before he notices how attracted you are to him.

His voice is softer when he asks, "Do you trust me?"

Slowly, I bring my gaze back to his. I'm not holding onto him. He could let go of me any second, and I would drown. But I know he won't do that.

I still fear him because he has the power to end this beautiful life he's given me. But I also feel safe with him because he has never hurt me.

I know it's only been a month and a half since I came to live here, and a lot can change at any moment, but my survival instinct tells me Gabriel meant it when he said he wouldn't hurt me.

"Yes."

Emotion wells in my chest at the realization. I trust these people who've become like family to me.

I'm really safe with them.

Lowering my eyes, I'm met with the sight of Gabriel's broad shoulders and some of his muscled chest. There's a crazy fluttering in my heart, all my insides tightening as a wave of attraction hits again.

I've never experienced these emotions. They leave me feeling inexperienced and confused.

"What are you thinking?" he asks, the low tone of his voice making everything feel intimate, as if he's pulling me under a magical spell.

My voice is soft as I admit, "I feel stupid."

"Look at me," he demands, and my eyes dart up to meet his. There's a serious expression on his face. "Why do you feel stupid?"

Because I'm feeling all these things for you, and they're overwhelming. I don't want to do anything that will risk my staying here, and I don't know what to do.

Not willing to admit the truth, I answer, "Everything is new, and I don't know how to process it all."

Gabriel pulls me against his body, and his arms wrap me in a tight hug. His manly scent is in every breath I take, the heat from his body warming mine.

God, it feels magical to be in his arms.

"It will take some time, but you'll get used to everything." He clears his throat, then adds, "And you're not stupid, just innocent. There's a difference."

Unable to resist, I wrap my arms around his neck again. I close my eyes and relish in the feel of his embrace. It's soothing, secure, and... perfect.

"What's the difference?" I ask as I carefully splay my fingers over his warm skin. Tingles sap through my nerve endings, making goosebumps erupt over my body.

"Innocence is when you just haven't had the opportunity to experience things. It's actually rare." He pulls back until our eyes lock. "I like it."

When I see the truth in his eyes, a smile spreads over my face.

My hands have shifted to his shoulders, and before I know what I'm doing, they drift down to his biceps to take in the feel of his arms.

God, so much strength and golden skin.

The veins. Sigh. The veins.

Realizing what I'm doing, I yank them away from his skin, my cheeks flushing.

Gabriel tilts his head to catch my eyes, then asks, "Why are you blushing?"

I quickly shake my head, pressing my lips together so the secret won't escape them.

"Lara." There's a warning tone to his voice, then he demands, "Tell me." The order is filled with dominance.

Once again, I'm unable to disobey him. I squeeze my eyes shut. "Touching you feels intimate."

"Are you uncomfortable?"

I shake my head.

That's the last thing I feel.

"Do you feel it's wrong?"

I open my eyes, and frowning, I answer, "No, that's not what I meant."

Gabriel moves us back to the side of the pool, then he takes hold of my hips, and without any effort, he lifts me out of the water and sets me down on the paving.

With his hands still on my sides, he looks up at me. A predatory look shutters his eyes, then he mutters, "Put on my shirt."

As I reach for the dry fabric, I glance down. Seeing my own shirt is practically see-through, an intense wave of self-consciousness hits. I quickly shove my arms through the sleeves of his shirt and cover myself.

Instead of getting out, Gabriel pushes away from the side, his body gliding through the water. Only when he's on the other side of the pool does he turn to look at me. "Don't mistake gratitude for something it's not."

Huh?

Shaking my head, I admit, "I don't understand."

Gabriel lifts himself out of the pool and sits on the other side. With the light shining on him, I have a clear view of his muscled chest and abs, and Lord help me, his strong arms.

He's breathtaking.

I'm well aware of the weapon lying next to me and know it's a test. Gabriel is checking to see whether I'd shoot him if I got the chance.

That will never happen.

"I didn't save you, Lara. I shot you and stole you from Mazur, hoping you'd be able to give me information on him."

I still don't understand.

Letting out a sigh, Gabriel wipes the water from his face. "Don't make me out to be the hero, because that's the last thing I am. You're grateful and experiencing life for the first time. Don't confuse that emotion for more."

My eyebrows pinch together. "I'm even more confused now."

Gabriel gets up, and the wet fabric of his suit pants hangs so low on his hips, there's a V carved into his hips, pointing down. My mouth goes bone dry, and there's an intense tightening in my abdomen.

Wow.

I can't tear my eyes away from his beauty as he walks around the pool. Stopping in front of me, he holds out his hand, and once I've placed mine in his, he tugs me onto my feet.

He leans down, his eyes burning on mine. "You look at me as if I'm becoming your entire world, Lara. Don't mistake gratefulness for love."

Oh...

OHHHH.

Having been caught out with the silly infatuation I have for him, awkwardness and embarrassment wash over me. I pull my hand from his and nodding, I quickly turn around and walk toward the house.

Oh. My. God.

I'm going to die of embarrassment. I've been drooling over him, and he knows.

Kill me now.

My chest fills with a weird pressure, all the happiness being sucked into it until I feel empty.

"Lara!"

I stop on the spot, my body tensing.

Please, please, please, I just need to shove my head under a pillow until the mortification disappears.

I hear Gabriel behind me, and taking a deep breath for strength, I turn to face him.

There's a dark frown on his face, and it makes my heart sink. He stops in front of me, his eyes locking with mine.

"Don't walk away while I'm talking to you."

Lowering my head, I nod, almost saying, 'yes, sir.'

He lifts a hand to my chin, nudging my face up so I'll look at him. The touch is too much at the moment, making my bottom lip tremble.

I swallow hard on the embarrassment still whirling in my chest.

Gabriel shakes his head, his eyes softening on me. "Jesus, this is hard." Pulling his hand away from my face, he takes a step back before his gaze finds mine again. "I'm just saying to not mistake one emotion for the other."

He looks uncomfortable as well, and I start to worry, I've really gone and ruined things between us. I can't keep the words back and whisper, "I'm sorry."

He shakes his head, giving me an incredulous look. "What for?"

"For making you feel uncomfortable. I didn't mean to do that." My shoulders slump, and I wrap my arms around my middle, lowering my eyes to the cobblestones beneath my bare feet. "It wasn't my intention for you to find out."

No one was supposed to find out. I've barely had time to explore the things he makes me feel and none whatsoever to enjoy them.

Again he nudges my chin up. His eyes search mine, then he seems to realize something. "You really like me?"

I nod, my arms tightening around me. "I'm sorry. I'll stop it."

"Don't!" As I blink at his strong response, he adds, "There's nothing wrong with it, Lara. You're allowed to feel whatever you want. I just don't want you confusing your emotions for something they're not."

"It's really new," I admit.

His hand moves to my shoulder, and he pulls me against his bare chest. My eyes drift shut from how good it feels as he hugs me. His chin rests on the top of my head. "If you're ever unsure, you can talk to me about it."

I nod, my cheek brushing against his warm skin.

When Gabriel pulls back, I feel better and not as embarrassed.

"Thank you," I whisper. I gesture to the house. "Can I go inside?"

"Yes." Gabriel takes a step back, giving me a full view of his bare chest and the damp pants clinging to his strong legs.

Before he can see the strength of the attraction I feel for him, I quickly turn around and dart into the house. I don't stop until I reach the safety of my bedroom, and placing a hand over my heart, I try to calm the frantic organ down.

So, am I allowed to like him or not?

Chapter 26

Gabriel

Dressed in jeans and a charcoal sweater, I walk to the dining room for breakfast.

I think I made a mistake last night and only managed to confuse the fuck out of Lara.

"*Selam*," I mutter as I walk into the room where only Emre is seated. I take a seat at the head of the table and stare at the plate in front of me.

"You look like you had a shit night," Emre comments. "By the way, you owe me for taking one for the team."

My eyes snap to his. "You went home with the woman?"

"Nope. We went to a hotel. It's easier to leave in the morning."

I shake my head, and the conversation ends right there when our grandmother comes into the room.

"*Selam*," she says, a bright smile on her face.

"You look happy about something," Emre mentions.

She glances at me, a knowing look in her eyes. "I am. I saw something last night and hope it means wonderful news is coming soon."

Fuck. She saw Lara and me and is probably planning the damn wedding.

"What?" Emre asks, looking confused as hell.

"Just something." She waves a hand in the air. "What's taking Nisa so long to bring the food?"

"Nisa only has two hands," Nisa mutters as she carries a tray of dishes to the table. Lara follows behind her with another tray.

They set everything on the table, then Nisa says, "Eat before you all starve."

As Nisa and Lara take their seats, Murat comes in. He nods in my direction, and taking a seat next to Lara, he murmurs, "*Selam.*"

I pick listlessly at my breakfast as I keep stealing glances at Lara.

From the moment I set her down on the side of the pool and saw the wet material clinging to her breasts, everything went wrong.

Fuck, her breasts are exquisite.

I shake my head, shoving some eggs into my mouth.

Swimming with Lara was a new experience for me as well. I enjoyed her company. Holding her in my arms didn't feel weird, and it pleased me to learn she trusts me.

Then she fucking looked at me with interest, and I could see the appreciation in her eyes as she kept stealing glances at my body.

Holding her against me and having her hands on me was a rush I couldn't prepare myself for. I was hard as fuck and almost claimed her right there and then.

But everything else was a fucking shit show. After I told her to not confuse her emotions, the rejected expression on her face didn't sit well with me.

My eyes land on Lara, who's eating so fast she's bound to get indigestion.

"Slow down, Lara," I order, my tone harsh.

She swallows hard on the bite, and keeping her head lowered, she obediently murmurs, "Yes, sir."

Christ almighty.

Throwing the napkin down, I stand up and walk around the table. I take hold of Lara's hand, tug her up, and drag her after me.

"What did I miss?" Nisa asks as we leave the dining room.

"Hush and eat," *Babaanne*'s voice caries after us.

I pull Lara to the study and shut the door behind us before turning to face her. Her eyes are wide on me.

"Things went wrong last night," I say. "I didn't mean to make you feel rejected."

She nods, her full attention on me.

I exhale and let go of her hand. Locking eyes with her again, I continue, "You're free to feel whatever you want."

Her tongue darts out to wet her lips. "Just to make sure and I don't get in trouble, is it okay for me to like you?"

Her question takes a swing at my heart.

"Yes, Lara. You feel whatever you want. Just make sure it's not for the wrong reasons."

"Okay." The corner of her mouth lifts. "Thank you."

"Jesus, don't thank me," I mutter. I take hold of her shoulders and pull her against my chest. Wrapping my arms tightly around her, I press my mouth to her hair, and close my eyes.

She feels so fucking good.

I don't know how Lara did it, but she has me wrapped around her little finger.

I'm starting to feel things for her, I haven't felt in a long time. Protectiveness for someone that's not family.

Possessiveness that makes me want to selfishly claim her innocence.

I want this woman to obey only me. I want her to live to please my every wish. I want to dominate her.

It's fucked up.

My arms tighten around her as I take a deep breath of her fresh scent.

When I met Lara, she was definitely not the most beautiful woman. But, during the past month and a half, that all changed. The more I got to know her, her beauty surfaced.

She has zero experience. She's nothing like the socialites I've dated in the past. But she has a heart of gold and her inner beauty shines through. She's refreshing, and I can't stop the need to possess her from growing inside me.

Her innocence is fucking intoxicating, and it's starting to drive me insane.

Slow down. You need to think about this.

Letting go of her, I put some distance between us, then mutter, "Go finish your breakfast."

I wait for her to leave, then shut the door behind her.

Letting out a frustrated sigh, I walk to the window. I cross my arms over my chest, and not taking in any of the scenery of the backyard, I start to dissect my feelings.

What I thought was compassion has changed into something else.

It's that pure heart and fucking innocence of hers.

Christ, it makes me want to force every ounce of submission out of her so I can devour it. Lara makes my dominant side flare to life like nothing else has been able to do.

So what are you going to do it about? With a snap of your fingers, you can have her kneeling at your feet.

That's not what I want.

I don't want her pleasing me out of fear. That does nothing for me.

I want her eagerness.

I want her to melt beneath my touch and seek strength in my arms.

And all of that will take time.

First, she needs to be ready, and I have no idea how long that will take.

In the meantime, I'll have to be patient, and I'll encourage her whenever I get the chance, so it feels as natural as possible for her.

So you're really doing this? You're pursuing Lara?

I let out a humorless chuckle, thinking I don't have much choice in the matter.

The heart wants what the heart wants.

Chapter 27

Lara

After I was sick and the intense conversations with Gabriel, things seemed to have calmed down.

It's been a week since he gave me his permission to like him, but I haven't seen much of him.

Every day Nisa teaches me how to make something, and in the afternoons, I either sit and knit with Alya *Hanim* or we walk through the garden.

I no longer rush to clean the house as fast as possible but take my time with each room.

Standing in Gabriel's room, I dust all the surfaces. When I'm done, I pick up his laundry basket to take it downstairs. His woodsy aftershave wafts up from the basket. I take hold of the shirt at the top, and bringing it to my face, I take a deep breath.

He smells so good.

As if my imagination conjured him from thin air, he appears in the doorway, catching me red-handed sniffing his shirt.

Dear God, now you look like a stalker.

I shove the shirt back in the basket and walk to the door. Gabriel doesn't move out of the way, and my eyes dart to his face as I squeeze by him.

His fingers wrap around my arm, stopping me from making a quick escape.

"Wait here." He lets go of me and walks to his closet, pulling a dress shirt off a hanger. I watch as he squirts some of his aftershave onto the fabric, then he brings the shirt to me. There's a hot as hell smile tugging at the corner of his mouth. "At least this one is clean."

"Ah…" I take the shirt, bunching the fabric to my chest. "Thank you."

He leans his shoulder against the doorjamb and watches me as I walk down the hallway.

I'm not sure what to make of the interaction, but I feel it was a good thing. *Right?*

Stopping by my room, I place the shirt on my bed, then drop the basket in the laundry room so I can do the washing first thing tomorrow morning.

I keep seeing Gabriel's smile while I help Nisa prepare everything for dinner. As we carry the trays to the dining room, the thought hits – does Gabriel like me?

I'm stumped.

He hasn't said anything like that. He's always talking about my emotions.

Frowning, I unload the dishes onto the table.

"Why are you frowning?" Nisa asks.

I quickly shake my head. "No reason." We set the trays aside as Alya *Hanim* and Emre *Bey* come to take their seats.

"Come sit across from me, Lara," Alya *Hanim* says.

Not questioning her, I pull the chair out. It's only when Gabriel walks into the dining room and sits at the head of the table, that I realize I'm now seated next to him.

I give him a tentative smile, and wait for everyone to help themselves to food before I load some onto my plate.

"I found a new pattern we can knit," Alya *Hanim* says. "Baby socks. They're so adorable."

Gabriel almost chokes on the bite he just took, and I quickly push his glass of water closer.

Once he's taken a sip and clears his throat, I turn my attention to his grandmother, who has a wide smile on her face. "I can't wait to try knitting them."

She gives me a curious look. "Have you ever thought about getting married?"

Huh?

"*Babaanne*," Gabriel mutters, warning laced in the word.

Nisa sets her utensils down. "What's going on that I don't know about?"

Emre lets out a chuckle.

This is weird.

"Ah...no," I answer Alya *Hanim*'s question. My eyes dart around the table to try and figure out what's going on.

Nisa gives me a questioning look, and I shrug to show I have no idea.

For the rest of the meal, Alya *Hanim* talks about the changes she wants to make to the garden, and I forget about the fleeting weird tension.

After I help Nisa clean the kitchen, I finally get to retire to my room. I take a quick shower, and once I've dried off, I stand and stare at Gabriel's shirt.

He gave it to me so I can do with it what I want.

I pull the fabric on and button it, then smile at my reflection in the mirror. I look silly, almost drowning in the shirt, but I'm surrounded by his scent, so I don't care.

I roll up the sleeves as I walk back into the bedroom, and throwing the covers open, I crawl into bed. I let out a happy sigh because today was another good day.

With Gabriel's woodsy aftershave hanging all around me, my thoughts turn to him. I switch off the bedside lamp, and once darkness falls in the room, I allow my feelings for him to surface.

It's becoming a habit to think of him until I fall asleep, one I like very much.

I think back to the swimming pool and how good he looked without a shirt. I remember the feel of his muscled skin and the strength in his body as he kept me afloat.

And that V running down from his hips.

When there's a knock at my door, I'm ripped out of my thoughts. I sit up and switch the light on. "Yes?"

I'm surprised when Gabriel comes in and shuts the door behind him. When his eyes land on the shirt I'm wearing, a smile tugs at the corner of his mouth.

"I wondered whether you'd sleep in my shirt." He walks closer and sits down on the side of the bed. "I like it."

I pat a hand over the fabric, glad he's not upset that I chose to sleep in it.

For a moment, Gabriel stares at me, then he says, "I apologize for my grandmother. She saw us at the pool, and now her imagination is running away with her."

"She didn't do anything wrong."

He turns his body toward me and gestures for me to come closer. Obeying, I move out from under the covers and kneel a couple of inches away from him.

"Closer," he murmurs. I move until my knees press against the side of his thigh, then he smiles. "That's better." His eyes drift over my face. "I've been busy the past week, so I couldn't check in on you. How are you feeling?"

"About?"

"Everything."

I shrug, just happy that I can have a conversation with him. "I'm fine."

Gabriel tilts his head, his eyes sharpening on me. "Have you thought more about how you feel about me?"

I nod, then lower my eyes as I admit, "I still like you."

"How much?"

How do I explain that to him?

I take a deep breath as I try to gather my thoughts. "I think about you all the time." *Like ALL the time.*

A pleased smile forms on his face. "What kind of thoughts?"

My cheeks flush, and I glance down at my hands. Gabriel takes hold of one and brushes his thumb over the back of mine. "You can tell me anything."

I lift my head, meeting his gaze. "I think about what happened by the pool. You really look good without a shirt on."

A chuckle rumbles from his chest. "Glad to know you like what you see."

"Very much."

Our eyes lock again, then he asks, "Have you been kissed, Lara?"

I shake my head, nerves starting to spin in my stomach.

"Do you want me to kiss you?"

Without a doubt. "Yes."

He nods but doesn't make a move. Instead, he gets up and pulls me off the bed. When I'm standing in front of him, he lets go of my hand.

"Close your eyes."

I obey him and don't have time to wonder what he's doing because his hands frame my face right before I feel his breath on my lips.

My heart explodes in my chest, my stomach fluttering like crazy.

Gabriel brushes his lips over mine, once, twice, then he lifts his head. Stunned by how intense a three-second kiss felt, I watch as his eyes drift over my face.

Then he chuckles, "Breathe, Lara. I can't have you pass out before kissing you thoroughly."

I fill my lungs with air, the anticipation making me feel overwhelmed.

His thumb brushes over my cheek, the expression in his eyes both predatory and tender. Again, he closes the distance between us, and this time when his mouth meets mine, he doesn't just brush his lips over mine. His tongue licks at the seam of my mouth, then he demands, "Let me in."

I part my lips, and the moment his tongue strokes hard against mine, it feels like I'm leaving my body and floating on clouds.

Chapter 28

Gabriel

The purest sweetness bursts over my tongue, and I lose all rational thinking, devouring Lara until she's gasping for air.

My tongue flicks and strokes against hers, and I inhale her breaths. My teeth ravish her lips until they're swollen.

I'm on a fucking high because I have total control.

Catching myself before I move too fast and traumatize her more than she already is, I break the kiss and press my face against her neck. "Jesus," I mutter, my own breaths racing from me. "You're going to drive me insane."

Lara's chest rises and falls against mine, the swells of her breasts drawing my attention and making me harden even more.

Lifting my head, I look down at her flushed face, swollen lips, and eyes filled with wonder.

Like the fucking caveman I am, I ask, "How was your first kiss?"

"Perfect."

My chest swells with pride, and I brush a thumb over her pink cheek. "Everything you hoped for?"

"So much more." Lowering my arm, I take hold of her hand and press her palm over my chest. "You can touch me."

She nods, her eyes still shining like stars.

Tilting my head, I stare at her. "You've bewitched me with your innocence."

Her mouth curves up. "Can I ask you something?"

"You can ask me anything."

"Do you like me too?"

"I wouldn't have kissed you if it weren't the case."

Relief washes over her features. I hadn't realized it was something she worried about. I obviously haven't been clear about my own feelings. I've never been much of a talker and more of a watcher.

My eyes caress her face. "You've gotten under my skin, Lara Nowak. I don't know when or how it happened, but I'd like to see where this goes."

Confusion flutters over her face. "What do you mean?"

Lifting my hand, I tuck a couple of silky strands behind her ear. "There are no rules. Let's just enjoy whatever this is."

"Okay."

Needing to have this discussion with her, I ask, "Are you on the pill?"

She shakes her head.

"Do you want to start a form of contraceptive, or will I be using a condom?"

Her cheeks flame up, her eyes filling with shock because of the direct question she clearly wasn't expecting.

"If the relationship between us continues to develop, I'd like to know I'm not going to get you pregnant when we finally sleep together," I explain, my tone gentler.

"You choose," she murmurs.

Not wanting her to worry about swallowing a pill every day, I say, "I'll have the doctor come over so he can give you a contraceptive implant." I tuck a couple of strands behind her ear. "But we'll take the time to get to know each other better and enjoy each other before sleeping together."

"Okay," she agrees, relieved that I made the decision for her.

Wanting to see what kind of power I hold over her, I demand, "Kiss me."

Lara pushes up on her toes, and to keep her balance, she wraps her fingers around the back of my neck. To help her, I lower my head, and she doesn't hesitate to press her mouth to mine.

Intense satisfaction has my cock hardening to breaking point.

I break the kiss, and taking hold of her hips, I sit down and pull her onto my lap so she's straddling me.

"That's better," I murmur before hungrily claiming her mouth again. My tongue lashes against hers, and I love that I have total control over everything because she has no experience to challenge me with.

Lara wraps her arms around my neck, pressing her body against mine, and it situates her right on top of my cock. Her breathing hitches, and unable to resist, I thrust up against her heat.

Her breaths falter as she gasps.

Pulling my mouth away from hers, my eyes settle on her face before I thrust up again, watching her reaction closely.

Her eyes remain closed, and a look of pure ecstasy relaxes her features.

"Do you want me to make you come, Lara?"

My direct question has her eyes snapping open. I see embarrassment tightening her features, and I expect her to put a stop to this.

"Yes."

My eyebrow lifts in surprise while my dominant side orders, "Unbutton the shirt."

With trembling fingers, she pops one button open after the other. The moment she's done, I brush the fabric to the side so I can see her breasts.

Having her obey me makes satisfaction fill me. As a reward, I lower my head and flick my tongue over her already pebbled nipple. Her body jerks, and when I suck her into my mouth, she arches her back, eagerly offering herself to me.

Perfection.

Wanting to hear her moan, I slip my hand down her abdomen, and moving the fabric of her panties, my fingers brush over her soft curls. I find her slick heat and twirl my finger around her entrance.

Freeing her breast from my mouth, I look at Lara as I slowly push my middle finger inside her. Her lips part in a gasp, and her thighs squeeze against my sides.

"Good?" I ask to make sure I'm not hurting her.

She nods quickly.

"Touch me, Lara," I order.

"Where?"

"Wherever you want."

She lifts her hands to my shoulders as I slowly move my finger in and out of her tight opening.

There's no fucking way I'd fit inside her tonight. Not without hurting her badly.

Instead of my own burning need, I focus on Lara's. I massage her clit with my thumb until her breaths are nothing but short bursts over her lips.

When I see the pleasure filling her eyes, I pull my hand away and demand, "Rub yourself against me."

Her inexperience shows as she struggles to swivel her hips. I lie back on the bed, and pushing her panties out of the way, I help her move up and down the outline of my cock.

"That's it," I praise her. "Harder, baby."

She places her hands on my chest, her fingers digging into the fabric of my shirt, then she finally finds her rhythm. Pleasure builds in my balls, and my hands grip her hips tighter.

"Come for me, Lara. Let me have your first orgasm."

Her body starts to convulse, her eyes snapping shut as her features tighten, her mouth opening on a silent 'O.'

I drink in the sight of my shirt hanging loosely around her, her breasts on display. With her panties pushed aside, I can see her swollen clit as she rubs over my hard length.

The sight of her has me exploding in my sweatpants. Somehow, I manage to sit up. I shove my hand down between us, and thrusting my finger inside her clenching heat, I move fast to prolong her orgasm.

Lara buries her face in my neck as a whimper escapes her.

I wrap my other arm around her, my own pleasure forgotten as I focus all my attention on her.

Only when she stops clamping the fuck out of my finger, do I still, our rushing breaths the only sound in the room.

Intense satisfaction surges through me. I pull my hand free, and taking hold of her hair, I tug her away from my neck so I can see her face.

Tears shine in her eyes, her chin trembling. There is so much emotion on her face, she's never looked more alive than she does right now.

"Did I hurt you?"

She quickly shakes her head.

"Why does it look like you want to cry."

Unable to lower her head, she glances away from me, swallowing hard on whatever she's feeling.

"Lara." Her eyes swing back to mine. "Tell me what's wrong."

"Nothing." Her voice carries a world of vulnerability, then she gives in and admits, "There are too many emotions."

"Good ones?"

She nods, swallowing hard again.

She's just emotional.

"It's okay to cry," I encourage her, thinking it might help.

She shakes her head again, and I watch as she reins in everything she's feeling.

I don't like it one bit and hate that she's bottling it up. Frustration slithers into my chest, but not wanting to ruin this moment for her, I keep quiet.

When she reaches for the shirt to cover herself, I shake my head. "Don't you dare."

Her eyes lift to mine. "What happens now?"

"We talk." I let go of her hair and move my hand to her face. Cupping her cheek, I ask, "How was your first orgasm?"

She thinks for a moment, then replies, "I don't know how to describe it."

"Try."

I watch as she inhales, her breasts rising and falling. Lowering my hand, I brush my knuckles over her pebbled nipple.

"It felt like something exploded inside me."

The corner of my mouth lifts as I keep touching her, loving how goosebumps spread over her skin. "And?"

"It was intense."

I let out a chuckle. "Is it what you expected?"

My fingers brush over the scar left by one of the bullets, and regret trickles into my chest.

I almost fucking killed an angel.

"I didn't know what to expect."

My eyebrow lifts. "Haven't you made yourself orgasm?"

Looking a little self-conscious, she shakes her head.

My lips curve up in a satisfied smile. "All your firsts will belong to me." Lifting my hands to the sides of her neck, I pull her closer. My eyes keep hers prisoner as I demand, "Whenever you need to orgasm, come to me. Only I get to touch you. Understand?"

"Yes."

"Yes, who?"

With a world of happiness in her eyes, she murmurs, "Yes, Gabriel."

I stare at her, intense possessiveness filling every corner of my being.

Damn my soul, but I'm taking this angel for myself.

"You belong to me, Lara."

Chapter 29

Lara

Hearing Gabriel tell me I belong to him, something unfurls deep in my soul. It gives my emotions wings, making them soar impossibly high.

He's my boss and a dangerous man. Still, it doesn't stop me from wanting to belong to him.

Instead of hurting me like Tymon did, Gabriel has shown me pleasure. It's the sweetest torture I've ever experienced.

When he made me orgasm and my body was numb from all the pleasure, I wanted to cry. It was so intense I lost control of all my senses.

I could only see him. Feel him. Taste him. Smell him.

There was only Gabriel, and it felt like I was touching heaven.

It looks like awe fills his eyes as he stares at me. "I'm taking you as my reward."

"For?"

"Not claiming your virginity tonight."

Out of curiosity, I ask, "Why didn't you?"

A smirk tugs at the corner of his mouth. "You won't be able to take me. It would hurt too much."

I glance down at the wet stain on his sweatpants over his manhood. "Did you at least enjoy it?"

"Very much." There's a teasing tone to his voice, "You can see the proof."

My lips curve up. "That makes me happy."

"You love pleasing me," he states.

I lift my eyes to his. "Yes." *I live for it.*

His hands move down, over my collarbones, until he cups my breasts. "You're so fucking beautiful, *Ödülüm.*"

No one has ever said that to me, and hearing the words from Gabriel, makes me think it could actually be true.

Maybe I'm not as plain-looking as I thought.

Curiously, I ask, "What does the word mean?"

"My reward." His palms massage me until there's a tightening in my abdomen. With his eyes locked on mine, I feel him harden beneath me, then he warns me, "If I don't leave now, I'm going to lose control."

I lean into his touch, but he lowers his hands to my hips, picks me up, and sets me down next to him. Rising to his feet, he stands in front of me, buttoning my shirt.

When he's done, he nods toward the bed. "Get in."

I climb beneath the covers, my eyes never leaving him.

Gabriel braces a hand next to my head, and leaning down, he presses a tender kiss to my lips. I feel it all the way to my toes.

Straightening up, he mutters, "Sleep before I change my mind and fuck you."

I blink, intrigued because I find his dirty words hot.

I find everything about him hot.

I watch as he leaves my bedroom, pulling the door shut, and then I'm left with my thoughts and all the new emotions I've discovered.

Not once did I think something like this would happen between Gabriel and me. We're worlds apart. He's the head of the Turkish mafia, a powerful man, and I'm just a maid.

I sure didn't feel like a maid tonight.

My infatuation with him might be growing out of control, but I never thought he'd actually return my feelings. I don't know much about relationships, but I know it takes two people.

And tonight, Gabriel treated me like a woman he desired. He looked at me as if I was really beautiful to him. He kissed me as if he couldn't get enough of me.

He orgasmed.

God, it felt incredible to feel his hardness against me. I couldn't move fast enough, and there was an aching yearning to have him inside me.

I stare up at the ceiling, relishing in how amazing everything felt. When he kissed me, I became totally absorbed by him. When he touched me, my body melted.

Sharing such an intense connection with another person fills me with awe.

I belong to him.

With a wide smile on my face, I turn onto my side and switch off the light. I snuggle into my pillow, reliving every touch until I feel like laughing from all the happiness.

I belong to Gabriel Demir.

I watch as the list of guests for Alya *Hanim*'s birthday party grows until it fills an entire page.

That's a lot of people.

"I think that's everyone," she murmurs as she reads through the names. "Gabriel's family on his mother's side will arrive the day after tomorrow. We need to make sure the guestrooms are ready."

"Okay."

"How long will they stay?" Nisa asks, irritation lacing her words.

Alya *Hanim* lets out a sigh. "A week. Can you at least try to hide how much you despise them?"

"I can't promise anything. The second they start ordering me around as if they're royalty and I'm nothing but a peasant, I might forget I'm a lady and slap them."

Cautiously I say, "They don't sound like nice people."

"They're not," Nisa huffs. "You just stay with me while they're here."

"*Evet*," Alya *Hanim* agrees. "Let Nisa deal with them."

I nod, then ask, "Which guestrooms should we prepare?"

Before I can get my answer, Gabriel walks into the sitting room. "*Selam*," he murmurs.

My heart starts beating faster at the sight of him, and my cheeks flush when I remember what we did last night.

"I have to miss breakfast," he tells us. "Emre's already at work." After pressing a kiss to his grandmother's temple, he turns his attention to me. "Give me a moment, Lara."

I get up from the chair and place my hand over my stomach to contain the butterflies as I follow him to his study.

He shuts the door behind us and lets his eyes drift over my face. "How do you feel after last night?"

"Good." I give him a tentative smile. "Did you sleep well?"

He shakes his head as he takes a step closer to me. "Thoughts of you kept me awake."

My smile widens. "Me too."

Gabriel wraps an arm around my lower back and slowly lowers his head until his mouth brushes against mine. It's nothing like last night, but it still makes tingles spread through my body.

It makes me feel special.

When he lifts his head, his eyes caress my face. "The doctor is here to give you the implant. Are you ready?"

Even though I feel anxious, I nod.

"Wait here," Gabriel instructs. He leaves the office, and minutes later, returns with the older man. "You remember Dr. Bayram, right?"

I nod, too nervous to smile.

Gabriel gestures for the doctor to get to work. I glance toward the window, hearing as the doctor moves closer. Gabriel comes to stand on my right, and giving me an encouraging smile, he takes hold of my hand.

Suddenly I feel a prick as if I'm getting an injection, but the sensation passes. I glance at my left arm, then the doctor says, "All done."

"Thank you," Gabriel murmurs to the doctor. "You may leave."

Dr. Bayram lets himself out of the office as Gabriel pulls me into a hug. "Thank you for doing this for me."

A smile curves my lips. "You're welcome."

"I need to leave for work," he says as he pulls back.

"I hope you have a good day."

"I doubt I will," he mutters as he steps away from me and opens the door. "I'll be busy until the birthday party. I don't want you to worry if you don't see me."

"Okay." I love that he's reassuring me after the special night we shared, and it makes my heart expand with affection.

He gestures for me to walk, and we leave the office together. At the top of the staircase, his fingers brush against mine before he takes the stairs down to the front door.

I stand and stare after Gabriel, still finding it hard to believe how much things have changed between us.

I return to the sitting room, and when I take a seat, Nisa asks, "What did Gabriel want to see you about?"

Oh crap.

Thinking quick, I lie, "He had questions about my past."

Alya *Hanim* shakes her head. "I hate that Mazur got away."

"*Allah Allah.* There will be no talk of that man while we're planning your birthday party," Nisa exclaims.

Alya *Hanim* picks up the guest list again. "Right, where were we."

"Which rooms should we prepare for the family?" I remind her.

"The three on the first floor in the east wing. That way, they won't be near you and Nisa, and I can keep an eye on them."

Nodding, I say, "I'll get everything ready today."

With a lot of work to do, we go our separate ways. While I'm changing the sheets and airing out the rooms, Nisa is in the kitchen baking up a storm.

This will be the first birthday party I get to attend, and thinking I don't have a gift for Alya *Hanim*, my teeth worry on my bottom lip.

Gabriel said I'm allowed to come and go as I please, but I still feel like I should ask his permission.

Maybe he'll be home before I fall asleep, then I'll ask him.

Chapter 30

Gabriel

Emre and I have been busy checking all the shipments of weapons before dispatching them.

Usually, I'd have my men do it, but seeing as the shipments are for high-valued clients, I didn't want to risk something going wrong.

The moment I sit down to notify my buyers that their orders are on the way, my phone vibrates.

There's a message from an unknown number. Opening it, I read the text.

My patience is wearing thin.

"Fuck your patience," I mutter, instantly feeling aggressive.

When I don't respond, a call comes through from the same number. I answer but remain quiet.

"Bastard. Are you there?" Mazur barks.

"Watch your fucking tone," I warn him, promise of a cruel death lacing my words.

"What do you want for the girl?"

"Your bloody fucking heart in my fist," I growl, wishing the man was in front of me so I could strangle the life from him.

"What have I done to you? We've never crossed paths when it comes to business."

"We both have secrets, old man. You go first. Why do you want Lara?" I counter his question.

"It's none of your fucking business. You took what belongs to me, and I want her back."

Intense rage flares through me, and as I rise to my feet, my voice is filled with every bit of power I hold. "Lara isn't your property. I've claimed her. You fucking touch her, and I swear I will peel the skin from your body and fucking feed it to you."

"You have no right to claim her!" he shouts into my ear.

I inhale deeply, my voice deadly calm as I say, "She begged me on her knees. I spared her life, and that gave me every right. She's *mine*. Don't call again. I have nothing to say to you until we meet in person."

I end the call and throw the fucking phone across the room. Needing to release some of the rage coiling in my

257

chest, my fist slams into the desk, making everything on it rattle.

"Fucking bastard."

"Who?" Emre asks as he appears in the doorway.

"Mazur."

"You spoke to him again?" My cousin comes in and picks up my phone. "What did he say?"

"The same. The fucker wants Lara."

Emre takes a seat and places the device on the table. "She's the perfect bait to draw him out of his hiding place."

Unreasonable anger reignites in my veins, and before I can calm myself, I shout, "She's mine! I will kill anyone who tries to take her from me."

I'm so fucking upset, my body trembles.

It takes a moment to realize what I just admitted to my cousin. Shoving a frustrated hand through my hair, I turn my back to Emre and stare out the window.

I take deep breaths until the rage subsides to a simmer in my chest.

"She's yours?" Emre asks, his voice filled with caution. "When did this happen?"

Shaking my head, I mutter, "The past two weeks. I didn't even see it coming."

"Do you care about her?"

"I feel something," I admit.

"Well, it's definitely *something* from the strong reaction I just witnessed," he mutters.

I underestimated my feelings for Lara.

Fuck.

Up until now, it was all about possessing her, making her submit to my will.

"I'm done talking about Lara," I snap. Taking a seat behind my desk, I grab the phone and unlock the screen. At least the thing didn't break. "Don't breathe a word of this to anyone," I warn Emre.

"My lips are sealed."

"Take down this number and have Elif look into it," I order, turning the screen to Emre so he can see it.

When he's done, I dial the number for Petro Ramirez.

"*Hola*," the Mexican answers.

"It's Gabriel. Your shipment has been dispatched," I inform him.

"Good. I'll transfer the rest of the money as soon as it crosses the border."

"Emre will keep you updated."

We end the call, then I ask Emre, "Have you checked that the trackers were activated?"

"*Evet.*" He pulls out his phone to show me the map with all the dots moving slowly through the city, southbound.

I make the other calls and only then have time to check on the illegal gambling section of the club. By the time I'm done with work for the day, it's past two am.

Tired as fuck, I signal for Mirac that I'm ready to head home. During the drive, I rest my head against the seat, calculating that I'll have three hours of sleep before I have to wake up for work again.

Mirac brings the SUV to a stop in front of the house, and I release a sigh as I shove the door open. After stepping through the front door, I shrug out of my jacket.

Just as I reach the stairs, there's movement in the shadows to my left, then Lara comes into view.

"Why are you awake?" I ask, my voice still strung tight from all the shit I had to deal with.

"I need to ask you a question."

I exhale slowly and turn to face her. "What?"

"Can I go into town to buy a gift for Alya *Hanim*?"

"Yes, just take Murat with you."

Instead of cowering at my brisk tone, she steps closer, concern filling her features. "Are you okay?"

"I'm just tired. It's been a long day."

"I hope you sleep well."

Her soft voice makes some of the tension leave my body, and on the spur of the moment, I move closer to her and press a kiss on her forehead. "I'm sorry, *Ödülüm*. Once things calm down at work, I'll be in a better mood."

"I understand."

I gesture for her to head back to her bedroom. "Get some sleep."

I watch her until she disappears down the hallway, then head up to my bedroom to shower.

Only when I slide beneath the covers and rest my head on a pillow, do I worry about Lara leaving the house. I'll have extra men help Murat guard her to ensure nothing happens to her.

Chapter 31

Lara

Even though I only went to bed at three am., I wake up at six, knowing there's a lot to do today before the guests arrive.

I stretch out beneath the covers, and turning my head, it's to see Gabriel sitting in the armchair, already dressed for work.

He looks heartbreakingly attractive in a three-piece, midnight blue suit.

I quickly sit up. "Did you sleep at all?"

He stares at me until I feel self-conscious about my bed hair and morning breath. Finally, he shakes his head as he rises to his feet. "I'll arrange extra guards to accompany you today. Do everything they say and be on guard at all times. Try to make the shopping trip as quick as possible."

"Okay."

He comes to the side of the bed, and reaching a hand out to me, he cups my cheek. The touch is tender as his eyes rest on me with worry.

"I don't have to go," I murmur, not wanting to add to his stress.

His thumb brushes over my skin. "I don't want you living like a prisoner. You've had that for twenty-two years, and I won't add to it." When he leans over me, I quickly hold my breath. He presses a soft kiss to my lips, then pulls back and gives me a questioning look. "How did you do it, Lara?"

Lifting my hand, I place it over his. "Do what?"

"How did you bewitch me?"

I wish I knew because then I'd keep doing it.

A smile curves my lips as I admit, "I don't know, but I'm happy I did."

Some of the tension leaves his face, and he leans forward again to press a kiss on the top of my head. "Have a good day, *Ödülüm.*"

I love hearing him call me his reward. It makes my heart melt.

"You too."

I watch as Gabriel leaves the room before I climb out of bed and get ready for the day.

Wearing black jeans and a cream silk blouse, I've put on black ballet flats to match the outfit.

When I open my bedroom door, Murat's leaning against the wall, already waiting for me. He lifts an eyebrow at me. "I hear we're going shopping today?"

I nod, a smile tugging at my mouth. "It will be quick. I promise."

He walks with me to the kitchen, then asks, "What time do you want to leave?"

"After breakfast?"

"I'll get the men ready."

When Murat leaves, Nisa, who's been watching us, asks, "Where are you going?"

"Remember I told you I wanted to get Alya *Hanim* a gift? Gabriel gave his permission."

"When did he do this? The man hasn't been home."

I wonder what to say, and not wanting to keep lying, I murmur, "This morning."

Surprise flutters over her features. "He was home?"

"He didn't get any sleep, though," I voice my worry. "He's working really hard."

Unlike Tymon, who sat around all day barking orders while hurting and killing people.

I shove the memory away as quickly as it popped into my head and get to work. I've been making a conscious effort to not think about Tymon and what he's done to me.

I can't change my past, but it doesn't mean I have to think about it all the time and let it sour my future.

Once we're done having breakfast, Murat walks with me to the SUV we'll use. I'm surprised when I see nine other men waiting for us.

I expected one or two guards, not a whole crowd.

"So many guards?" I gasp.

"Gabriel *Bey* just wants to make sure you're safe. You won't even know they're there," Murat informs me.

Ten guards. You only have so many to protect something you think is really precious.

Swallowing hard on the emotion the realization stirs in my chest, I climb into the back of the SUV. We leave the property in an entourage of four vehicles, making me feel like I'm someone of importance.

Murat glances in the rearview mirror. "What do you want to buy for Alya *Hanim*?"

"A vase so she can have flowers in her sitting room?"

He nods. "Sounds good."

The other guard, Daniel, keeps quiet, but he's constantly searching our surroundings for a threat, and it's making me nervous.

Murat parks the car near the mall's entrance, and I'm ushered out of the vehicle and into the building so fast that I'm out of breath.

With Murat next to me, Daniel in front of me, and the other guards spread out around us, I walk to the nearest ATM so I can check my bank balance.

When I get the little slip with the information on it, my eyebrows draw together. "This can't be right."

"What?" Murat asks, leaning closer.

I show him the piece of paper. "There's too much money."

"Put your card in again."

I do as he says, and I watch as he presses another button making the machine produce another slip of paper. Looking at it, Murat shows me the transactions. "Look, there's the incoming transfer from Demir Group Int."

My eyes widen. "Gabriel gave me all this money?"

"Yes." Murat hands me the slip, then nudges my lower back. "Let's move. We can't stay in one place for too long."

Stunned out of my mind that Gabriel gave me twenty thousand dollars, I walk in a daze until Murat tugs me into a store.

"What about this vase?" he asks.

I focus my attention on the beautiful navy, turquoise, and red vase, the mosaic patterns forming a ten-pointed star.

"I think Alya *Hanim* will like it. Right?"

"Definitely. She loves blue," Murat agrees.

He calls a store assistant closer and asks for the vase to be packaged. When I'm standing at the counter to pay for my purchase, I glance around at all the pretty items, thinking I'd like to get Gabriel a gift to say thank you for everything he's done for me.

Glancing up at Murat, I ask, "What do you think Gabriel would like?"

He lets out a chuckle. "Nothing in here."

"A tie?"

He shakes his head. "He gets plenty of those from Nisa *Hanim* and Alya *Hanim*."

After I've paid for the vase, Murat carries the bag as we walk from store to store, looking for something Gabriel might like.

As we pass a boutique, a dress in the window display catches my eyes. I stop for a moment to admire the shimmering silver gown. With a low neckline, the material is folded softly around the front. The back is exposed, and it would stop right above my butt.

I wish I could wear something like this but won't dare with the scars on my back.

"Do you like it?" Murat asks.

I nod. "But I'll never wear something like this. It's beautiful, though."

Continuing my search, I finally find a store that looks like it caters to men. There are cigar boxes that I avoid.

I stop in front of a display case. There are beautiful pens encased in wooden boxes. One draws my attention, and I ask the man behind the counter, "Can I see the gold fountain pen?"

He places the rectangular box on top of the display case, and I stare at all the tiny watch mechanisms in the middle of the pen.

"He'd like that," Murat agrees.

I check the price tag and almost swallow my tongue.

Holy crap.

Murat's phone rings, and as he takes the call, I stare at the fountain pen.

It's five thousand, four hundred and ninety-nine dollars. That's a lot of money. My teeth worry on my bottom lip.

The money in my account came from Gabriel, so it wouldn't be a bad thing to spend it on him. Right?

I glance at Murat, who seems to be on a serious call, so I can't ask for his advice.

I look at the pen again, and really wanting to give Gabriel something back, I decide to get it. "I'll take it," I inform the man.

My stomach starts to spin like crazy as I watch the store assistant close the beautiful wooden box the pen comes in. When I have to pay, my hand trembles.

It's for Gabriel.

I swipe the card and enter my pin just as Murat joins me again. "Ready to head home?"

As I carefully take the package from the cashier, I press it to my chest, ready to guard it with my life.

I nod quickly. "Yes, let's hurry."

So I can hide the gift safely under my bed until I can give it to Gabriel.

Chapter 32

Gabriel

Worried about Lara, I can hardly focus on my work.

When Murat doesn't respond to my message, asking if they're okay, I press dial on his number.

He immediately answers after two rings, "*Evet?*"

"Is everything okay?"

"*Evet.* We should be heading back home in the next ten minutes."

"Did Lara find a gift for my grandmother?" I go stand in front of the window overlooking the street below.

"Yes, she found a vase." He pauses, then lets out a chuckle. "Lara was shocked when she saw her bank balance. She thinks it's a mistake."

"Tell her not to worry. Why are you still at the mall if she already found a gift?"

Murat pauses, then says, "Lara's... ah... she's looking at a dress."

"What kind of dress?"

"A shimmery one... Hell, I don't know. I know nothing about women's clothing. The kind they wear to events," he rambles, sounding uncomfortable.

"Does she like it?"

"*Evet.*"

"Get it for her," I order.

"What?" he balks.

"Get the fucking dress for Lara."

"But, Gabriel *Bey* ... she said she won't wear something like it."

Thinking he's afraid she'll argue with him, I say, "After you've dropped her off at home, you go back and buy the damn dress."

"I don't know her size."

"She's a four," I inform him. "Make sure she doesn't see it and put it in my room."

"*Tamam.*" He lets out a sigh. "I'll get the dress."

Ending the call, I check the time on my wristwatch. She should be home by ten. Taking a relieved breath, I leave the office to find Emre.

He's sitting behind the monitors, checking data with Elif.

"Any updates?" I ask.

Elif gives me an excited look. "He was spotted in New York." She brings up an image of Mazur and Dudek, his guard, leaving a hotel.

"Finally," I mutter as I lean closer. I stare at the old man, the need to take his last breath from him rearing up inside my chest. "Don't lose him."

"*Evet*," Elif says. "I'll get someone to follow him to make sure we don't lose him."

I have to wait until after my grandmother's birthday before I can attack and wipe him out once and for all.

"What do you want me to do?" Emre asks.

"Tell the men to be on standby. The day after the party, we're ending this."

With most of the work done at Vengeance, Emre and I head to Retribution, where they're busy renovating the club. I'm having an extra area built onto the main building where I can have another gambling section and offices.

I'm doing this with all the clubs, so I don't have to do all my business from Vengeance, and we can switch up our routines. Right now, we're making it too easy for the enemy to plan an attack against us. At least if we keep moving between the five clubs, they'll never be sure which one we'll be at.

Emre and I spend the day reviewing the floorplans and checking that everything we've ordered has arrived.

"You sure three docking bays will be enough?" Emre asks.

"Evet." My eyes scan over the plans again, then I explain, "Retribution is smaller than Vengeance. Having more docking bays will draw attention."

"Right."

It's after midnight by the time I mutter, "Let's get some sleep before Eymen arrives."

Emre lets out a groan as we head out of the building. "Eymen I love, but damn, Ayesenur *Hanim* and Eslem drive me insane."

"It's just for a week."

He gives me a tortured expression. "Please try to remember Eslem is not my cousin. The woman can't take no for an answer."

I let out a chuckle. "I'm glad I don't have to worry about you fucking her."

"Yuck." He pulls a disgusted face. "I wouldn't touch her with a ten-foot pole."

I'm not looking forward to their visit either and really wish my grandmother would reconsider this tradition of having a party just so they can visit. I know they're family, but I've never been close with them.

Even my relationship with Eymen is more business-related, with him controlling Turkey for me.

When we arrive home, and I walk into my bedroom, there's a big square box on my bed. I lift the lid, and seeing shimmering silver fabric, I pull the dress out and hold it up.

My woman has good taste. She'll look beautiful in this.

Carefully placing the dress back into the box, I take a piece of paper from my stationery drawer and write a short note. Folding the paper in half, I slip it beneath the silver bow on the lid and smile as I pick the box up.

Leaving my bedroom, I head to the lower level and carefully open Lara's door, so I don't wake her. I sneak into the room like a damn thief and place the box on the armchair I always sit in.

Moving to the side of the bed, I stare down at her sleeping face. Her arms are wrapped around a pillow, and I wish it was me instead.

Leaning down, I press a soft kiss to her temple.

Desperately needing some rest myself, I steal one more glance of the woman who's worming her way so deep into my heart that I'm starting to fear I'll never get her out.

Going back to my bedroom, I shower before climbing into bed. Letting out a sigh, I stare up at the ceiling, my thoughts turning to Lara and how quickly things are changing between us.

It's no longer just about dominating her.

I care about her.

Admitting my emotions to myself is no easy feat. I've never been an emotional person. Fuck, I've never been one to care about anything, really. It's all about facts and money for me.

I love my family, but I've never invested in a romantic relationship. It's not something I needed.

But I find myself in unfamiliar territory, needing Lara. It's definitely not about sex, seeing as I haven't fucked her.

Yet.

Our connection is on a much deeper level. My need to control versus her need to be controlled. My sinfulness versus her innocence.

She balances me.

I've never seen myself as the kind to settle down, even though my grandmother's been nagging me. At thirty-eight, there's just never been a woman I could see myself settling down with.

Could I see myself with Lara? Is it even something she's ready for?

"Jesus, Gabriel. Get some fucking sleep," I growl as I turn onto my side. I punch the pillow and let out a huff. "Just take it one day at a time. You don't have to plan your entire future right now."

Chapter 33

Lara

Standing in front of the box, I stare down at it.

A gift?

Maybe it's for Alya *Hanim*?

Carefully pulling the note from beneath the ribbon, I open it.

Ödülüm,

Wear this for me to the party.

Gabriel.

My eyes dart to the box, and my heart starts to beat faster.

A gift for me.

I sit down on the bed, taking in the beautiful box. It's black with a leaf pattern all over it. It takes me a moment to process the excitement of receiving my first gift.

I stand up again and kneel in front of the armchair. With trembling fingers, I take the lid off, and then my breath catches in my throat.

Oh my God. It's the dress from the window display.

I carefully lift the shimmering fabric from the box and hold the beautiful gown in front of me. My eyes start to mist up, and I blink fast.

Climbing to my feet, I quickly undress and step into the gown. I rush to the bathroom and lose my ability to breathe when I see my reflection in the mirror.

I look like Cinderella and not a maid.

But…

Emotions explode in my chest, and a sob bursts over my lips. Covering my face, I crouch down, my shoulders shuddering as sobs tear through me.

"*Allah Allah,*" Nisa exclaims. She pulls me up into her arms. "Lara, what's wrong?"

"The dress," I sob against her shoulder. "It's so beautiful."

"*Allah Allah,* that's not something to cry about."

Pulling away from her, I turn around. "I can't wear it," I cry, devasted that the one chance I get to wear something so beautiful to a party, the scars on my back ruin it for me.

"Oh." Nisa places a hand on my back and comes to stand next to me. Giving me a comforting look, she says, "You can borrow one of my shawls. I have a silver and black one that will match the gown."

My gaze snaps to her, hope unfurling in my chest. "Really?"

"Of course." Gently she wipes the tears from my cheeks. Her chin quivers. "Stop crying before I join you, and then we won't get any work done."

I swallow the tears and turn to look at my reflection in the mirror. The fabric falls softly around my body, and with every movement, it shimmers.

"Did you get the dress yesterday?" Nisa asks as she admires the gown as well.

I shake my head. "It's a gift." I swallow hard as my throat threatens to close from the pressure of not crying. "Gabriel gave it to me."

Nisa's eyes snap to mine, surprise and hope all over her face. "He did?"

I nod, and no longer able to hide things from her, I admit, "I really like him, Nisa *Hanim*." I brush a hand over the expensive fabric. "I think I'm falling in love for the first time."

Nisa's face crumbles, and I'm yanked into a tight hug. "Does he return your feelings?"

I nod against her shoulder. "I think so."

"*Allah Allah*, this is a great blessing." She pushes me back by my shoulders. "Tomorrow, I'll style your hair and help you with your makeup. You'll be the most beautiful woman at the party."

I nod, and laughter bubbles over my lips. "I can't wait."

She pushes me back into the bedroom. "Change so we can get to work. The family will arrive at ten am. We need to have everything ready."

I wait for Nisa to leave the room, then carefully step out of the gown. I let it hang against my closet door, so I can see it whenever I'm in the room.

I quickly dress in a pair of light blue jeans and a soft cream sweater, then slip on the black ballet flats again. I rush through my morning routine before hurrying to the kitchen.

I'm so busy, time flies. As I place a tray of *baklava* on a cooling rack, Nisa comes into the kitchen, grumbling, "They're already driving me insane."

"I'm sorry," I murmur, in no hurry to meet them.

"Nisa *Hanim*, this. Nisa *Hanim*, that," she keeps grumbling.

"Is there anything I can help with?"

She gives me a pleading look. "Will you take tea to them? They're in the sitting room with Alya *Hanim*."

"Of course." I quickly prepare the tray and give Nisa a cup so she can rest while I tend to the guests.

When I enter the east wing, I hear a burst of loud laughter. I don't understand what's being said as they're speaking Turkish.

The moment I walk into the sitting room, the conversation stops. I glance at the two women, noticing their features are much darker than Alya's. They have curly black hair, dark brown eyes, and it looks like they've been in the sun for days.

"*Bu kadın kim?*" The older woman asks.

"This is Lara," Alya *Hanim* answers. "Lara, this is Gabriel's aunt and cousin, Ayesenur *Hanim* and Eslem."

"No Turkish?" Ayesenur *Hanim* asks.

"No, Lara's Polish."

"*Allah Allah. Neden bir Polonyalı hizmetçi tuttun?*" Ayesenur *Hanim* exclaims, looking as if she's been insulted.

"English, Ayesenur. Lara doesn't understand Turkish," Alya *Hanim* chastises the older woman. "And I'll hire whom I please." She turns her attention to me. "Set the tray down, Lara."

Oh. Right.

The younger woman, who seems to be in her early thirties, looks me up and down as if I'm dirty, making me feel uncomfortable. Then she comments, "She's young for a maid."

"*Allah Allah*! Lara's not a maid. She's just helping Nisa until she starts her studies," Alya *Hanim* snaps.

I think I should leave. My presence seems to be upsetting everyone.

Giving Alya *Hanim* a tentative smile, I quickly exit the room and hurry to the kitchen.

"How did it go?" Nisa asks.

I widen my eyes. "I think my presence upset them."

She waves a hand. "Those two live for drama. Trust me, it's nothing you did."

Now that we have a moment to breathe, I ask, "Do you think I can phone Gabriel to thank him for the gown, or should I wait until he's home?"

She doesn't hesitate. "Wait until he's home. He's busy with work."

Pouring tea for us, I sit down at the table.

Nisa gives me an inquisitive look. "Did he say you must only call him by his first name?"

I nod, then take a sip of my tea.

She leans forward, her expression telling me she wants to know everything.

I hesitate, not sure what I'm allowed to share. I've learned Gabriel is very private, and I don't want to upset him.

"*Allah Allah*, tell me everything!" she exclaims impatiently.

I give her an apologetic look. "I'm not sure what I'm allowed to share."

Excitement widens her eyes. "Has he kissed you?"

A shy smile spreads over my face, making Nisa almost jump out of her chair with happiness.

"So this is what the help does during the day," Eslem suddenly says as she saunters into the kitchen. "I have to bring the tray back because you're too busy chatting."

I dart up and quickly take the tray from her. "I'm sorry."

"Don't apologize," Nisa snaps. "Eslem has two hands."

My eyes widen when Eslem levels Nisa with a glare. "How dare you? Alya *Hanim* clearly allows you to do whatever you want, but you won't talk to me like that. Know your place, *servant*."

It looks like Nisa's about to burst a vein as she rises to her feet. I quickly set the tray down and move in front of Nisa. Keeping my tone respectful, as if I'm dealing with

Tymon, I say, "We apologize, Eslem *Hanim*. Is there anything else you need?"

She looks at me as if I'm trash, then lifts her chin and leaves the kitchen.

I quickly turn around. Nisa's red in her face, her hands shaking. I take hold of them. "It's okay. Shh." Not knowing what else to do, I wrap my arms around her and hold her tight. "I'm sorry."

It's one thing having people talk to me as if I'm nothing, but it breaks my heart that Nisa had to experience it.

She sucks in deep breaths of air, and when I pull back, she shakes her head. "Gabriel *Bey* will hear of this," she says, her voice quivering.

Oh, dear.

"They're only here for a couple of days," I try to defuse the situation.

Nisa shakes her head again, then mutters, "Let's prepare lunch for the ungrateful snakes before one of them slithers into my kitchen again."

"I'll serve them," I say, not wanting them to upset Nisa again. I'm used to dealing with cruel people. When Nisa wants to argue, I shake my head. "No, Nisa *Hanim*. I'll serve them." There's a finality in my voice I've never heard before.

"Thank you." She gives me another hug before we start making food.

An hour later, when I carry the dishes to the dining room, I steel myself for whatever might come. Entering the room, only Ayesenur *Hanim* and Eslem are seated at the table.

I set the tray down and carefully unload the dishes.

Eslem looks at the food, then picks up the bowl of *Şakşuka*. It's an eggplant, zucchini, garlic, tomato, and chili recipe.

"This is the best you can do?" she asks, her tone filled with hatred.

I've learned people don't need a reason to hate, they just do.

Before I can ask whether I should take it back to the kitchen, Eslem slowly tips the bowl, pouring the dish over my shoes.

Instinctively, I lower my head as she stands up.

She pinches the fabric of my blouse between her fingers. "This is not what a maid wears. You're disrespecting my mother."

"I'm sorry," I murmur respectfully, so glad Nisa's not here.

Eslem picks up the bowl of *Kisir*, a Turkish salad, and pours the contents over my blouse.

That's going to leave a stain.

"What the fuck do you think you're doing?" Gabriel's voice cracks through the air like a whip.

I instantly drop to the carpet and start to gather the food into a bowl. Pins and needles spread over my body, my heart beating a mile a minute.

Suddenly my wrist is grabbed in a tight hold, and I'm pulled to my feet. Gabriel yanks my body behind his as he steps into his cousin's personal space. "I asked you a fucking question."

A man I've never seen before steps closer as well. "Eslem? What's the meaning of this?"

Ayesenur *Hanim*, who's been quiet up until now, stands up. "*Sakin olun,* Gabriel *Bay*."

His eyes snap to his aunt, his features tight with rage. I cower behind his back, not wanting any of his anger directed at me. His voice sounds deadly as he growls, "Don't tell me to calm down."

Suddenly I'm tugged to his side. "Lara is not a servant you can abuse and boss around to your liking."

"Then what is she?" Eslem asks with a raised eyebrow.

It looks like Gabriel is a second away from strangling her.

Eslem is either very brave or stupid.

"What's going on?" Alya *Hanim* asks as she enters the dining room.

Ayesenur *Hanim* lets out a string of Turkish words, and for a couple of minutes, I don't have a clue what they're saying, but it looks intense.

Everyone is upset, then Gabriel shouts, "Silence!"

Instantly the room grows quiet.

He pins Eslem with a dangerously dark look. "You will apologize to Lara."

"Gabriel *Bey*," Ayesenur Hanim gasps.

"I said to keep quiet. I've had enough of you," he warns his aunt. Turning his attention back to Eslem, he orders, "Apologize to the woman I'm dating, or so help me God, I will disown you."

What?

Gasping, my eyes dart to his face. He looks like he could murder someone with his bare hands.

Because of me.

Gabriel's defending me against his own family.

Eslem sucks in a deep breath, then locks eyes with me. "I apologize. I wasn't aware you were dating *my* cousin."

Gabriel lifts a hand, pinching the bridge of his nose. "Eslem."

"I'm sorry. Okay? Geez." She lets out a huff then injects sincerity into her voice. "I apologize for disrespecting you, Lara *Hanim*."

Leveling his aunt and cousin with a final look of warning, he says, "You will treat Nisa and Lara with the same respect you give me. They are not maids in this house. They're more my family than you'll ever be."

My heart fills with so much warmth it threatens to burst.

How can I not fall in love with this man when he's so amazing?

Still gripping my hand tightly, Gabriel pulls me out of the dining room as he orders, "Clean up the mess you made, Eslem!"

Chapter 34

Gabriel

The woman I'm dating?

I drag Lara to her bedroom and demand, "Change your clothes."

With uncontrollable rage simmering in my chest, I watch as she gets clean clothes and rushes to the bathroom. The moment the door shuts behind her, I suck in a deep breath of air in an attempt to calm down.

Christ, I almost slapped Eslem.

When I walked into the dining room and saw her treating Lara like she's a piece of shit, I lost it.

The woman I'm dating?

This time I can't ignore the bomb I dropped in the dining room. It seems my heart decided Lara's my girlfriend before my mind had time to catch up.

It is what it is. There's no denying it any longer.

Fuck being bewitched, I'm falling hard and fast for Lara.

Noticing the dress, some of my anger dissipates.

I wonder what her reaction was.

The bathroom door opens, and Lara comes back into the room. She gestures to the dress. "Thank you so much for the gift."

"You'll wear it for me." It's supposed to be a question but comes out as an order.

"Yes." Then she suddenly drops to her knees and pulls a slender box from beneath the bed. Standing up, a shy smile graces her lips. "I got you a gift, as well." She hands the wooden box to me. "It's to say thank you."

Staring at her, a smile forms on my face. I flip the box open and look down at the gold fountain pen. "I love it."

"You do?" She moves to my side and points at the toothed gears you'd find in a clock. "I really like that."

"Me too. It's unique." Taking hold of the back of her neck, I lean down and press a kiss to her mouth.

When I pull back, happiness shines in her mesmerizingly blue eyes. My woman was degraded by my aunt and cousin, and it doesn't look like it upset her.

"Are you okay?"

She nods. "Yes."

"You're not upset with the way Eslem treated you?"

Lara shrugs. "It was nothing, and she apologized."

"Nothing, my ass. I won't have people treating you like that," I snap. Taking a deep breath to calm down, I continue, "Don't ever let someone disrespect you again."

"What am I supposed to do?"

Setting the box down on the bed, I lift my hands to her face and frame her cheeks. With my eyes locked with hers, I say, "You stand up for yourself, Lara. You're mine, and I can't have someone treating you like shit. Not only does it reflect badly on me, but I won't stand for it."

A smile spreads over her face, her eyes softening with affection as she stares up at me. "I like that."

"Which part?"

"I'm yours."

My thumb brushes over her cheek. "You know what that means, right?"

She nods. "I belong to you."

I shake my head, and confusion washes over her face, which has me explaining, "It means this thing between us is serious. If you're not ready for a relationship, you need to tell me now. It's either everything or nothing." Leaning into her, I say, "I don't want your gratefulness, Lara. I want your heart, soul, and body."

Her tongue darts out to wet her lips.

"Take time to think about it," I add, not wanting to force her into anything. I want Lara to make the conscious decision to be with me. I want her to willingly submit to me.

"Okay," she murmurs.

Lowering my head, I claim her mouth in a searingly hot kiss. I pour all my emotions – the anger, the confusion of the past two weeks while I tried to figure out what the fuck I was feeling, and the fear of losing her – into her mouth.

I wrap an arm around her lower back and tug her right against my chest.

Lara's hands splay over my shoulders as our tongues massage, our teeth nip, and our breaths become one.

It feels like I'm losing my mind with need, my hands starting to eagerly move over her body. They explore the curve of her hips, her ribs, her breasts.

The kiss turns downright filthy as I pinch her nipples into hard buds. Lara lets out a needy moan, her hands finding the nape of my neck and tugging at my hair.

A knock at her door has me ripping my mouth away from hers and barking, "What?"

The door opens, and Nisa peeks inside, then her eyebrows fly into her hairline. "Nothing. Don't worry." She starts to pull the door shut. "Ah… continue."

Letting out a chuckle, I shake my head as the door shuts. When I look down at Lara, she's breathless, her lips beautifully swollen.

"As much as I'd like to continue this, I need to get back to work."

"Okay."

I lift my hand and brush the pad of my thumb over her bottom lip. "While I'm gone, there's something I want you to do."

"What?"

"Go to my bedroom tonight. You'll find a vibrator in the right bedside table drawer. I want you to climb between the sheets and make yourself come, but don't go too deep. Just use the tip, so your virginity remains intact."

Her eyes are wide on me, embarrassment darkening them and coloring her cheeks.

"Do you understand?"

"Yes."

Brushing my thumb over her lips again, I explain, "It's to help you stretch so you'll be able to take me."

"Okay."

"Only the tip of the vibrator. Don't you dare push it in deeper."

She nods.

I lean forward until my lips brush against her ear. "Also, rub it against your clit. It will make you come quicker."

"Okay," she breathes, desire filling the single word.

I straighten up and adjust my hard as fuck cock in my pants. "The things I do for money." I give her a quick kiss then walk to the door. "I better get back to work."

"I'll miss you."

Her words have me turning back to her, and grabbing hold of her, I kiss the ever-loving fuck out of her. "Imagine I'm fucking you when you make yourself come."

"Ah... okay."

Remembering to take the fountain pen Lara gave me, I leave the room before I give in to my hunger. I stalk to the east wing to find Eymen so we can get back to business.

When I walk into the dining room, it instantly goes quiet. I look at Eymen. "Are you done eating?"

"*Evet.*"

My grandmother gets up, and taking hold of my arm, she pulls me out of the room. There's a worried look on her face as she asks, "Is Lara okay?"

I nod. "For the love of all that's holy, let this be the last time they visit."

"*Evet,*" she agrees. "I won't force the issue again."

I press a kiss to her forehead as Eymen comes out. He gives me an apologetic look. "I'm sorry for their behavior. It won't happen again."

On my way out of the house, I run into Murat. "Go buy a phone for Lara. Set the thing up and make sure it's charged before leaving it on my bed."

"*Evet*, Gabriel *Bey*."

I might have to work, but I'll definitely make time to hear her come.

Chapter 35

Lara

I wait until the house is quiet before I sneak to Gabriel's room.

When I slip inside, I softly shut the door behind me. There's a light shining from the bed, and walking closer, I see it's a phone.

Gabriel's name flashes on the screen. I haven't handled a cellphone much, and after three swipes over the screen, I finally manage to answer the call. "Hello?"

"What took you so long?"

"I waited for everyone to go to bed."

"Open the drawer and take out the vibrator," he instructs.

I can't believe I'm doing this.

I pull the vibrator from the drawer and stare at the hot pink shaft.

"It's pink."

"Like your pussy, *Ödülüm*," Gabriel murmurs, his voice low.

Holy crap.

My face goes up in flames, but heat pours through my body from his filthy words.

"Strip naked and lie down on my bed," he orders, his desire tensing the words. Then he quickly adds, "Put the phone on speaker."

"How?"

"There's a little speaker icon. Press it."

I search for it on the screen and press my thumb to it. "How do I know if it worked?"

"You'll know," his voice fills the room.

"Won't the others hear you?"

"No. My bedroom is too far from theirs, so feel free to scream when you orgasm."

I place the phone on a pillow and quickly take off my clothes. When I crawl onto the mattress, I say, "I'm on the bed."

"Lie on your back and spread your legs wide."

I feel self-conscious as I carry out the order. With my heart pounding against my ribs, I reach for the vibrator. I've never used one, and pressing a button, I start laughing when it gives short bursts of vibrations in my hand.

"Press the button again until the vibrations are continuous."

I have to press it eight times, my eyes widening from the intense vibration.

"Are you ready, Lara?"

Nope. Not by a long shot. "Ah... I think so."

"Relax, *Ödülüm*. I promise it will feel good." He lets out a chuckle. "It's not my cock, but it will have to do."

Sweet Jesus. He can just keep talking, and I'll orgasm.

When he talks again, his voice is deep and seductive. "Slowly rub it over your clit."

I move the vibrator between my legs and jerk when it touches me. The pleasure is instant, ripping a gasp from me.

"That's it, baby, let me hear you. Slowly press against your entrance, then rub it over your clit again."

My abdomen tightens, the sensations so good, I start to move faster.

"How does it feel?"

"Really good."

"You'll only come when I give you permission. Use the head of the vibrator to stretch your opening."

I quickly pull the device away from my clit before I lose control and orgasm. My breaths explode over my lips,

298

then I slowly rub the head around my opening, I try to push it in a little, but it won't fit. "Ah... Gabriel?"

"Yes."

"I don't think it's going to fit."

"That's why we're doing this."

"Not you. The vibrator."

He lets out a chuckle. "I know, Lara. You'll need to keep stretching yourself until it does fit."

"Oh." I keep massaging around my opening, every couple of seconds trying to push it inside me. I start to feel feverish with need, and my butt lifts from the bed. The head pops in, scaring the living shit out of me.

"You gasped. It didn't sound like pleasure. What happened?"

"It went in." I quickly pull it out and sit up.

There's a dark tone to his voice as he asks, "Is there blood?"

I let out a breath of relief when I don't see any. "No. Thank God."

"You better thank the almighty. Do not take your own virginity."

"I won't." I bite my bottom lip, then admit, "I'd rather have you here. This is much harder than I thought."

"Lie back and relax, Lara. You will come tonight."

I lower myself to the bed, really wishing he was here.

"Close your eyes and just listen to my voice." I shut them, focusing on Gabriel. "Massage your clit, baby. Imagine I'm right next to you. Imagine it's my cock rubbing against you."

The device vibrates over the bundle of nerves.

So good.

"I love when your breathing hitches. It makes me so fucking hard." I hear him move, then he continues. "I have my cock in my fist, wondering how it would feel to have your fingers wrapped around it, stroking me." *Dear Lord.* "I want you on your knees, sucking my cock into the back of your throat while your innocent eyes stare up at me."

My body tightens, and my back arches as I whimper, "Gabriel."

"Come, baby. Let me hear your orgasm tear through you."

The world splinters into pure ecstasy, and I hear Gabriel groan as he seems to find his own release. "I need to fuck you so badly. I can't wait to come inside you."

My thighs squeeze together as the device vibrates against my clit, and I cry from how intense the pleasure is.

"Jesus, Lara," he breathes with awe in his voice. "Hearing you come is the most beautiful sound I've ever heard."

My body goes numb, and I gasp for air. "That... was... intense."

"You better scream like that when I pound into you," he growls.

"Pretty sure I will." I turn onto my side and snuggle into his pillow. "Are you coming home?"

"No. I'm in LA. I'll be back before the party."

"Can I sleep in your room?"

"Yes, *Ödülüm.*"

The words bring a smile to my face. "Gabriel?"

"Yes?"

"You're my reward as well."

Not long after the call ends, I drift into a peaceful sleep. I wake before the sun rises, and after getting dressed, I clean the vibrator and place it back in the drawer. I make sure the room is spotless before sneaking out and rushing back to my bedroom.

I take a quick shower, get dressed for the day, then head to the kitchen to make tea.

Today is Alya *Hanim*'s birthday, and I don't want anything to go wrong.

Nisa comes into the kitchen, followed by Murat. He places the phone on the table, then says, "It's your phone, Lara. Gabriel *Bey* said to keep it on you at all times."

"Oh." My cheeks flush bright red as I pick up the device.

"There are messages you need to respond to," Murat adds.

"How do I unlock the screen?"

Murat comes to stand next to me to help, and when the messages open, he moves away, muttering, "So not what I needed to see before having tea."

I read the two texts Gabriel sent.

I was so fucking hard hearing you come, baby.

I'm jealous of my bed.

I let out a chuckle, my cheeks flush bright red, and turning my back to Nisa and Murat, I type out a reply.

It was really comfortable.

I'm just about to put the device in my pocket when it beeps.

Can't wait to see you in the dress.

With a wide smile on my face, I get to work. I'm so excited about tonight. I feel like Cinderella going to the ball, and I have my own prince that will be there.

Chapter 36

Gabriel

When I get home, there is barely enough time to shower and dress in a clean suit before the party starts.

I hate that I couldn't get home earlier and missed most of my grandmother's birthday.

Hurrying to the entertainment hall, I hear the buzz of voices from the guests that have already arrived. When I walk into the room, there's an audible pause before the guests continue their conversations.

My gaze sweeps over all the people, and not seeing Lara, I walk to where my grandmother is standing next to Emre.

When I reach her, I pull her into a hug. "*Mutlu Yıllar, Babaanne,*" I wish her a happy birthday.

"I was worried you wouldn't make it," she chastises me.

"I hate all the guests but wouldn't miss it for the world." Turning around, I search through the crowd. "Where's Lara?"

"I'm not sure," my grandmother starts to say, but then exclaims, "There, by the door."

My eyes snap to where Lara is standing, and I lose the ability to breathe.

Holy fuck.

She's styled her hair in soft waves, and makeup highlights her cheekbones and lips. The fucking dress fits her like a second skin, showing every damn curve of her body. "Jesus," I mutter as I walk toward her, thankful for the shawl over her shoulders.

I clearly didn't think this through when I bought the dress for her.

Lara looks like a goddess and nothing like the maid I stole from Mazur.

I hate that other men will get to see her in the dress.

When I reach her, I take hold of her chin, tip her face up, and plant a possessive kiss on her lips so everyone will see she's mine.

Pulling back, I say, "You look breathtaking, *Ödülüm.*" Taking a step backward, my eyes drift over her body. "I hate that other men will see your beauty." Locking eyes with her again, I order, "Don't you dare leave my side tonight."

"Okay." She smiles, and I almost bark for her to stop because it makes her eyes sparkle like stars.

I'm probably going to kill the first fucker who looks at her.

Christ, help me.

Taking her hand, I link our fingers and pull her to my side. "I'd much rather take you to my bedroom and strip you out of that dress than attend this party," I mutter under my breath so the guests near us won't hear.

Glancing down at Lara, I see the excitement on her face as she looks at the décor, the food, and the guests.

It's her first party, asshole. Let her enjoy it.

I lead her to my grandmother.

"Lara, you look beautiful," my grandmother beams. Her eyes dart between us. "This is the best birthday gift ever. It's all I wanted."

"It's a lovely party," Lara says, the smile not leaving her face.

"Pfft." *Babaanne* gestures between Lara and me. "I'm talking about you and Gabriel. I'm happy you're a couple."

Happiness shines from Lara, making her sparkle like a diamond. "Me too."

"I'm going to make the toast." Giving Lara a pointed look, I say, "Stay with my grandmother." I glance at Emre. "No one comes near her."

"*Evet*," he mutters as he moves in behind Lara.

I walk to the small podium and tap on the microphone. Everyone goes quiet and turns to face me.

Christ, I hate this.

Clearing my throat, I say, "I want to thank you all for attending my grandmother's eighty-fourth birthday. She doesn't look a day over forty-eight, right?" There's a chorus of agreement.

A server brings me a flute of champagne, and I hold it up. "To the most amazing woman who raised Emre and me. Happy birthday, *Babaanne*."

Cheers erupt from the guests. I take a sip of the bubbly liquid, then make my way back to Lara.

"Short and sweet," Emre jokes.

I give my cousin a scowl. "The next time you give the toast."

"There's no next time, remember," he chuckles.

The music resumes, and setting down the glass on a nearby table, I hold my hand out to my grandmother. "May I have this dance?"

"Of course." She places her palm in mine, and I lead her to the middle of the room. Pulling her into my arms, I look into the eyes of the woman who dried my tears and guided me through this life. It's rare for me to say the words, but as I start to move with her over the floor, I murmur, "*Seni çok seviyorum.*" (I love you so much.)

She gives my hand a squeeze. "*Gözümün nuru.*"

Hearing her call me the light of her eye, a smile tugs at the corner of my mouth.

I glance to where I left Lara in Emre's care and frown when I see Arnold Forbes, a wealthy businessman, talking to them.

The moment the song ends, I take my grandmother back to Emre and pull Lara to my side.

"Gabriel, so nice to see you," Arnold says, holding his hand out to me.

I take it in a firm grip. "Likewise. I hope you enjoy the party."

Pulling Lara to the floor, I ask, "Can you dance?"

"No."

"Just follow my lead." I tug her to my chest, then smile down at the nervous expression on her face. "I won't let you trip."

"Okay."

Her eyes are locked on mine as I start to move, her body obeying mine.

Lara's smile is filled with wonder as I steer her across the dance floor, then she murmurs in absolute awe, "I'm dancing."

The music builds to a crescendo, and I spin her away from me. The shawl takes flight before floating to the floor. Suddenly Lara stumbles, and I dart forward to catch her by her shoulders, so she doesn't fall.

"I've got you," I chuckle.

Lara stands frozen, her lips parted, her face pale.

Tilting my head, I try to catch her eyes. "Lara?"

The next moment I hear gasps, my eyes snap up, and I notice the guests are staring at Lara with horrified expressions.

What the fuck?

I feel a tremor rock through her body, drawing my attention back to her. "Lara, are you okay?"

Slowly, she nods.

Nisa appears out of the crowd, her face tight with worry as she picks up the shawl. "Lara?"

What the hell is going on?

Noticing everyone is staring at Lara's back, I move around her, then shock shudders through me with the force of a tsunami.

Jesus fucking Christ.

Thick welts cover her skin in haphazard patterns.

Whip marks.

Having tortured people myself, I know exactly what kind of force it takes to make those kinds of marks. How the skin splits open as the metal spike tears through it.

A violent rage forms a red haze around my vision.

The excruciating pain she had to endure.

"You're okay," Lara whispers as if she's trying to reassure herself, her voice void of emotion. "You're okay. It doesn't matter. You're okay."

"Fuck," I snap, and quickly shrugging off my jacket, I wrap it around her shoulders.

"Leave," I shout, glaring at the murmuring guests.

The entertainment hall clears at the speed of light.

I wrap my arms around Lara, and lowering my head, I say, "Everyone's leaving."

She doesn't respond. When it's only my family and us, I pull back and frame her way too pale face. "Lara?"

There's a vacant look in her eyes as if all the life has been drained from them.

"You're okay," she keeps whispering. "You've survived worse. You're okay." The words are so soft I almost miss them.

My heart. She's shutting down.

"Don't you dare shut me out." Grabbing her by the shoulders, I shake her hard. "Look at me, Lara!"

"*Allah Allah,*" Nisa murmurs, distraught with worry.

My grandmother moves closer, a trembling hand covering her mouth.

Finally, Lara's eyes focus on mine, and I frame her face again, pleading, "Let me in. Don't hide this from me."

Her features contort with heartache. "I ruined the party."

"You did no such thing." I lean down, not wanting to lose her attention.

Her eyes start to shimmer with unshed tears, but she clenches her jaw to keep from crying.

"Jesus, Lara, you're killing me. Just let it out. Let me help you carry this."

She shakes her head and tries to pull away from me. "Don't you fucking dare!" I snap.

Instantly, she stops, then she gives me a pleading look, her chin quivering.

I'm fucking determined to get inside her head. Pressing my forehead to hers, I order with every ounce of dominance I have, "Let. Me. In."

There's so much pain on her face, it cracks my heart right down the middle. Suddenly a sob bursts from her, and she slams into my chest, burying her face against me.

My arms form steel bands around her as she finally gives in and breaks.

Looking at my family, I murmur, "Leave us."

One by one, they walk out of the room, giving us privacy.

I lower my head and say, "I've got you, baby. Let it all out."

Her sobs are pure fucking torture. I pull the jacket away from her, dropping it on the floor. Moving my hand to her back, I gently caress the marks left on her skin by that fucking mad man.

"Mazur did this to you?"

She nods, burrowing as close to me as possible.

With the height I have on Lara, I can see a part of her back and notice some welts are still healing.

"When was the last whipping?"

I think I already know the answer but can't brace myself in time as she says, "When... I was late... with the... food."

I close my eyes as a wave of suffocating regret hits.

She was beaten like an animal because of me.

My voice is hoarse as I whisper, "I'm so fucking sorry." I press a kiss to the side of her head, then pull back so I can see her face. Tears sparkle over her cheeks, each one cutting into my soul.

When her eyes meet mine, I repeat, "I'm sorry for the part I've played in all the pain you were forced to endure." Leaning down until there's only a breath between us, my voice is tight as I say, "I'm sorry for not finding you sooner."

Lara throws her arms around my neck, holding me as tight as she can. "You don't care... about the... marks?"

The way she hiccups through the sobs just shreds my heart.

"Of course, I fucking care but not for the reason you think." I brush a hand up and down her back, wanting her to know they don't change how I feel about her. "I hate that you suffered. I swear I'm going to fucking whip Mazur to death so he can feel what you felt."

She starts to calm down but doesn't let go of me. I hold her for as long as she needs and wait for her to pull back.

She gives me an apologetic look, then glances around the empty room. "I really ruined the party."

"You didn't. The people were aggravating the fuck out of me. You just gave me an excuse to get rid of them." I brush my thumbs over her cheeks. "Once you're ready, the party will continue."

"I need the shawl."

I crouch down, and picking up my jacket, I shrug it back on as I say, "You don't need it."

"But..."

I shake my head. "You have nothing to hide, Lara. You're fucking beautiful, so lift your chin high and wear your scars with pride." I frame her face again and look deep into her eyes. "You bled for them, and they show how amazingly strong you are. Never hide them."

"What about other people?"

"Fuck them all." I press a kiss to her lips. "Only I matter, and I love every inch of you."

Once the words are out, we both freeze. Lara's eyes widen on mine, her lips parting.

Your timing fucking sucks, Gabriel.

Letting out a chuckle, I pull back. "Well, that's out in the open."

With total disbelief, Lara asks, "You love me?"

Do I?

I search my heart and can only find one answer. "Yes."

For a man who doesn't like expressing his emotions, I've said those words twice in one night.

And I meant them both times.

Chapter 37

Lara

I'm starting to wonder if I died when I got shot, and this is heaven because it's all too good to be true.

Staring at Gabriel, his love declaration wraps around me like steel armor. It gives me a sense of confidence I've never had before.

It fills my heart like it's never been filled before.

The prince loves a maid.

Slowly my lips curve up. I lift my chin and pull my shoulders back, the love he is giving me flooding every inch of my being.

Ten years I went without hearing those words.

For ten years, I lived in absolute horror.

But that's my past, and before me stands my future.

"You love me," I breathe. The impact of this astonishing moment hits me so hard, tears instantly fill my eyes.

Gabriel presses a soft kiss to my trembling lips. "Yes, I love you."

He wraps me in his arms and holds me while I process the meaning of his words.

I am his, and he is mine.

Gabriel belongs to me.

Pulling back, he tilts his head, his eyes inspecting every inch of my face. "Feeling better?"

I nod, and not sure what I should say or do because I'm still too overwhelmed, I murmur, "I need to fix my makeup before the party can continue."

The corner of his mouth lifts. "Good girl. I'll gather the family while you freshen up."

I hesitate to turn my back on him, so I can walk to the door, and Gabriel immediately notices. "Go, Lara. Let me finally see that sexy ass of yours in the dress."

A smile trembles around my mouth as I slowly walk away from him.

"Jesus, what the fuck was I thinking buying you that dress?" he mutters incredulously. "You'll only wear it for me."

His words boost my confidence, and I lift my chin. I even dare to wiggle my butt.

"You're brave, *Ödülüm*. I have no problem fucking you right on this floor."

I let out a chuckle as I glance over my shoulder, and blowing Gabriel a kiss, I slip out the door.

I'm instantly met with Nisa and Alya *Hanim*'s worried faces.

Nisa darts forward, covering me with the shawl. "My Lara, are you okay?"

Alya *Hanim* hooks her arm through mine, patting my hand. "Don't worry about the party."

They keep fussing over me, and I don't get a word in. I'm ushered into my bedroom and only then manage to pull away.

"I'm okay." When the women I've grown to love just stare at me, I repeat, "I'm really okay. The party will continue. I just need to freshen up my makeup."

"*Allah Allah*, if Lara says the party continues, then it continues." Nisa shoves me down in a chair and starts to fix my makeup.

Alya *Hanim* sinks down in the other armchair, letting out a tired breath. "I'm getting too old for parties."

I reach across and take hold of her hand. "I haven't given you your gift yet."

She pats my hand. "I can't wait to see it."

"Sit still," Nisa chastises me. "I almost drew a line of mascara over your face."

When I don't look like a clown anymore, I finally get to stand up. I shrug the shawl off, saying, "Thank you for lending it to me, but I no longer need it."

A proud smile spreads over Nisa's face, then she nods and throws the fabric on my bed. "Let's dance." She does a little two-step as she walks to the door, making Alya *Hanim* and I laugh.

When we walk back into the entertainment hall, music is playing. Gabriel is standing with Emre, Murat, and the other guards. There's no sign of Gabriel's Aunt and cousins.

"I hope the three of you are ready to dance the night away," Emre teases.

Before Gabriel can take a step in my direction, Emre swoops me into his arms and spins me away from everyone.

"You want to die tonight," Gabriel calls after us.

Laughter breaks out around us, but I'm too focused on not tripping over my feet. It's not the same as dancing with Gabriel, and I keep looking down.

Emre steers us in a wide circle, and when we're about to pass the group, Gabriel's arm wraps around my waist, and I'm tugged away from Emre.

"Mine," he growls playfully before pressing a kiss beneath my ear.

Emre wags his eyebrows at Nisa. "Come on, gorgeous, let me take you for a spin."

She mutters a string of Turkish words but happily moves into Emre's arms.

I watch them with a huge smile, wrapping my arms over Gabriel's as I lean back against his solid chest.

Emre wasn't lying when he said we'd dance the night away. I take off my heels so my feet will stop aching because I'm having too much fun to stop now.

At some point, even I get a chance to dance with Nisa. We're all stumbling feet and chuckles, but I've never had so much fun.

When it gets late, everyone says goodnight. Gabriel takes a firm hold of my hand and leads me to his bedroom. Once he's shut the door behind us, he pulls me into his arms and starts to sway.

"Did you have fun?"

"Yes, it was amazing," I murmur as I rest my cheek against his chest.

"Are you tired?"

"A little," I admit.

Gabriel lets go, lowering his hands to my sides.

"There's something I want from you."

"What?"

"Your virginity."

Oh.

Instantly my stomach starts to spin with nerves.

"Unless you're not ready. I want you to give it to me out of your own free will. Don't feel forced."

"I'll give you anything you want," I admit.

His hands move up my body until he reaches my shoulders. "It's going to hurt, Lara, but I promise, this will be the only time I'll hurt you."

My heart beats faster, not because of the impending pain, but because of his words.

"I trust you." I take a step closer to him. "My body is yours, Gabriel."

"And your soul?"

I nod.

His voice lowers as he asks, "And your heart?"

I don't think there are words to explain how I feel. Gabriel is literally my life. When he shot me, he could've left me to die, but he didn't. He saved my life and gave me everything I could ever dream of having.

Slowly, I nod.

His body slams into mine, his mouth claiming me with a fierce kiss. He pulls the dress' straps down my shoulders and lets the fabric fall to pool around my feet.

Within seconds the man has me naked while he's still fully dressed.

I do my best to return the kiss while trying to loosen his tie. Suddenly I'm airborne and tossed onto the bed. I bounce once, then watch as Gabriel yanks the tie from his neck.

His features are tight with need, his eyes twin flames of unadulterated lust, making intense anticipation spin in my stomach.

My eyes are glued to his body as he undresses. I feast on the sight of his muscled chest, the lines carved into his abs, then he drops his pants.

Holy mother of God. That's going to hurt a lot.

For the first time, I stare at *that* part of a man, thinking it looks angry and beautiful.

Gabriel places his knee on the mattress, and taking hold of my legs, he pushes them open. "Grab hold of the covers, baby. You're going to need the support."

I fist the covers in my hands and don't know if I should feel self-conscious or turned on as he moves in between my legs and presses a kiss to the inside of my thigh.

He drags his nose through the strip of curls, then his tongue lashes at my clit.

I gasp, the pleasurable sensation of his tongue lapping at the sensitive bundle of nerves, unlike anything I've felt before.

My fingers tighten in the covers, and when his teeth scrape over me, my butt lifts off the bed, and I let out a moan.

Oh my God, that feels so good.

Gabriel starts to devour my clit, every couple of seconds, thrusting his tongue inside me. Within minutes my abdomen tightens, and my body begins to quiver.

"Gabriel," I whimper, desperately waiting for his command.

Moving up my body, he pushes a finger inside me, then growls, "Come, baby." He keeps fingering me, his palm massaging me.

Light splinters behind my eyes, my breathing stalls in my throat, and my body convulses as if I'm being electrocuted. The pleasure is intense, robbing me of all my senses.

Gabriel keeps moving in and out of me, his eyes burning on my face as he watches me orgasm.

Once I've come down, he doesn't stop fingering me. "Are you ready for me?"

I nod. No matter the pain, I won't deny him. It's the only thing I can give Gabriel that he can't buy with money. It's a piece of me. "I'm ready."

He positions his hard length between my legs and rubs it up and down my slickness before pressing against my entrance.

"Take a deep breath."

I inhale, my eyes locked on his. As I exhale, he rocks against me until he can finally force an inch inside me.

The pain is sharp, tensing my muscles. I grip the covers tighter. Instead of going deeper, he pulls out again and only thrusts the head of his cock into me until it starts to feel good and my body relaxes.

"Was that it?"

Chuckling, he shakes his head. "You'll know when I've taken your virginity and I'm fully inside you."

Okay. Deep breaths.

Just as I think about letting go of the covers so I can touch his chest, he pushes deeper into me.

This time it feels like I'm being torn in half, and a cry escapes me.

Gabriel presses a gentle kiss to my jaw. "Are you okay?"

I nod my head, the pain still too intense to talk.

"Deep breaths, baby."

I can't. My breaths remain shallow.

He pulls out a little, and I wince, then a scream is torn from me as he buries himself inside me.

"I'm so fucking sorry," he groans. Bringing his hands up, he frames my face and presses kisses to my mouth. "I wish it didn't have to hurt."

Letting go of the covers, I wrap my arms around his neck and cry.

Gabriel pushes his arms beneath me, holding me tightly to him as I work through the pain.

"Are you okay?" he asks, his voice tight with concern.

No. It' hurts so badly. "Uh-huh," I lie.

He presses a kiss to my mouth, and when I slowly start to adjust to his size, the ache lessens.

"Better?" he asks right by my ear.

"Yes. I think you can move."

He doesn't let go of me, but instead, his hold on me tightens as he slowly pulls out. The burn returns, and when he thrusts inside me for the second time, I smother a cry against his shoulder.

After being stolen by Gabriel, I've learned great pain is followed by pure happiness. I know this pain will be worth whatever follows.

He pulls his arms from beneath me, and bracing a hand next to my head, he looks down at me. "I can't hold out much longer. On a level of one to ten, how's the pain?"

"It's bearable. You don't have to worry."

He shakes his head. "Jesus, Lara, just tell me the level."

"Four?"

"I can live with that," he grumbles, then my nails dig into his shoulders as he moves at a much faster pace.

His body rocks against mine, and soon I don't mind the pain as I feel his hard length move inside me.

Now a piece of me will always belong to Gabriel.

Emotion wells in my chest as his features tighten and his thrusts become erratic. "Fuck, baby," he groans. My body jerks hard from his thrusts as he empties himself inside me. "*Mine.*" Thrust. "All." Thrust. "Fucking." Thrust. "Mine."

He slumps on top of me, his breaths racing over his lips. I love feeling all his weight pressing me into the bed.

Once he's managed to catch his breath, he lifts his head and looks at me. "You're so fucking tight. Christ, you're going to hurt for the next couple of days."

Gabriel pulls slowly out of me, and I clench my teeth, so I don't wince from the burn.

Warmth spills beneath my butt, and my eyes widen. I dart into a sitting position and look down at the mixture of blood and Gabriel's release.

"The blood is normal," He assures me. "After a warm bath, you'll feel better."

Emotions shoot through my chest, and I try to swallow them down.

Gabriel pulls me onto his lap and holds me tightly. "It's okay to feel emotional, *Ödülüm*."

I burrow against his chest, the warmth from his body seeping into mine while he gives me all the time I need to process the intimate moment we just shared.

Gabriel owns the most precious thing I could give a man. I'm so thankful it's him – the man I love.

Chapter 38

Gabriel

After forcing Lara to relax in a warm bath, I watch as she drinks the tea I made.

Now that I have time to look at her naked body, I'm noticing more scars. Some are faint, whereas others are clearly visible.

"How did you get the scar on your right arm?"

She glances down at the mark beneath her elbow. "I broke my arm."

"How?" I demand.

"Tymon stomped on it until it broke."

Intense rage flares in my chest. I close my eyes and count to ten, so I don't lose my shit.

That fucking bastard.

Once I have control over the merciless emotion, I look at her again. "And the scar on your hip?"

This time she shrugs. "I don't remember when I got it."

I look at the marks the bullets left, and getting up, I move closer and kneel before her. Lara sets the glass down on the table, watching me as I lean forward. I press a kiss to both of the scars.

"Those are the only ones I like," she murmurs. Lifting a hand, she brushes her fingers through my hair. She tilts her head, affection shining in her eyes. "They brought me to you."

My heart.

As I climb to my feet, I lean over her and press a kiss to her mouth. "Ready to learn something new?"

Her lips instantly curve up. "What?"

Wrapping my fingers around my hardening cock, I stroke myself. "I want to feel the heat of your mouth."

Lara's eyes lower to my manhood, then she fucking licks her lips as she moves off the chair and onto her knees. Tilting her head back, her mouth opens, and her eyes find mine.

Holy fuck. Perfection.

I stroke myself once more before stepping closer. Placing a hand behind her head, I nudge her to take me into her mouth. I watch as her lips stretch around my girth, unadulterated satisfaction coursing through my veins. "That's it, baby, take me as deep as you can."

Claiming her virginity, I had to be careful, but now I can fuck her mouth the way I wanted to fuck her pussy. My fingers tighten in her hair to keep her head in place as I start to thrust into her.

Jesus.

I move my other hand to her jaw, my thumb brushing against her bottom lip as I pull out.

Fuck, this is the most erotic thing I've ever seen.

"Bring your hands to my ass, and hold on tight," I order.

Lara's fingers dig into my asscheeks, and with my eyes locked on her, I thrust all the way in, the head of my cock hitting the back of her throat.

"Fuck," I groan with intense pleasure.

Losing control, I pump into her, the sounds of her gagging music to my fucking ears. I watch as tears spiral from her eyes and her saliva coats my cock.

My lips pull back from my teeth as I growl, the perfection at my feet sending me over the edge. I come so fucking hard, my legs go numb. Dropping to my knees, I wrap my fist around my cock, and jerk the last of the pleasure from my body.

I'm gasping for air as I lift my head, only to see my cum on Lara's lips. Her tongue darts out, and she licks it up as if I've just served her ice cream.

"So fucking hot." Grabbing her, I slam my mouth against hers, and when I'm able to taste myself on her tongue, I fucking devour her until we're both gasping for air.

Helping Lara to her feet, I mutter, "You better get in bed and sleep before I find another hole to fuck."

As if she's trying to tempt the hell out of me, she crawls onto the mattress, ass in the air. I grab hold of her hips, and bite her right asscheek, earning myself a shriek from her. I follow it up with a slap, which has her laughing.

"Under the sheets. Now."

She climbs beneath them and lies down, looking up at me with happiness.

Crawling in beside her, I pat my chest. "This will be your pillow."

Lara scoots closer and rests her head over my heart. "Good girl," I praise her. "You exceeded my expectations tonight."

"I aim to please," she teases me for the first time, making a smile stretch over my face. She's growing into her own person, and it's awe-inspiring to witness.

"It makes me want to dominate you," I admit.

She turns onto her stomach and rests her chin on her palm. "I want you to dominate me."

"Then we'll make a good couple."

"But..." her teeth tug at her bottom lip, "you told me to stand up for myself. What if you do something I don't like?"

"Then you tell me, so I don't do it again. Just because I want to dominate you doesn't mean you don't have any say in our relationship."

She nods, then says, "As you know, this is my first relationship." She nods toward the discarded covers with her blood on them. "Are there rules?"

"Yes." I fluff the pillows behind me and lean back against them. Lifting my hand, I brush my fingers through her silky hair. "I'm very jealous and possessive. You're not allowed to be alone with another man unless I've given my permission. It's not because I don't trust you, it's because I don't trust them."

"Okay. Who do you approve of?"

"Emre. Murat, Daniel, and Mirac. Those are the only four."

"What else?" Her full attention is on me, and I love every second of it.

"No revealing clothes. I don't want other men drooling over what's mine."

"You weren't joking when you said you're jealous," she chuckles.

"You'll learn that I'm an asshole," I'm not ashamed to admit.

"Can I make rules as well?"

"You don't want me alone with a man?" I tease her.

Smiling widely, she shakes her head. "You're not allowed to remove your shirt in front of other women."

It's something I'd never feel comfortable doing anyway, but still, I nod to please her.

She moves up, and resting her cheek on my chest again, she snuggles into my side. "What was your childhood like?"

"I was actually quite blessed. My grandmother raised Emre and me after my parents were killed. She worked so hard to provide for us, and I could only repay the favor when I was twenty-three."

Glancing up at me again, she asks, "How were your parents killed?"

Placing my hand on her back, I follow the marks with my fingers. "We moved to Seattle when I was a baby, and they opened a bakery. My earliest memories of them were always seeing them work." After clearing my throat, I take a deep breath.

"I started helping them at the age of six, mostly packing the shelves." A nostalgic smile tugs at my lips. "I loved watching my mom bake. The way her hands moved would mesmerize me for hours."

Lara's eyes are locked on my face.

"It was a hot day. I remember my shirt clung to my body from all the sweat. Mazur had been threatening my parents for weeks, and on that day, he sent men to shoot and kill them. First my father, then my mother. I watched them fall and their blood seeped onto the floor. I watched the life drain from my father's eyes, and I promised to make Mazur pay."

When I look down at Lara again, a tear spirals down her cheek. I catch the drop, and bringing it to my lips, I taste the saltiness of her compassion for me.

"I'm sorry," she whispers as she moves onto her knees and wraps her arms around my neck. "You've suffered much longer than me because of Mazur."

Holding her, I take a deep breath of her scent. "Even though I did my best to corrupt you, you still smell like innocence."

"Then you'll just have to corrupt me some more," she teases as she pulls back.

"I'll have to find creative ways seeing as you'll be sore for at least a day."

We spend the entire night talking and teasing, getting to know each other on a deeper level. It's only when the sun starts rising that we finally give in to sleep, and with Lara in my arms, it feels as if I've found the other half of me.

Chapter 39

Lara

After showering, I stand in my bathroom, looking at my reflection in the mirror.

I'm struggling to see the maid I used to be. My hair is healthier, and with the weight I've picked up, my curves have filled out, making me look like a woman and not a starving child.

Last night I had sex for the first time. Even though it was my choice to give myself to Gabriel, it amazes me that he chose me.

He could have anyone, but still, he was buried deep inside me.

He came inside me.

My skin heats as I remember the intimate moments we shared. How hot he looked when he orgasmed. How brutally attractive and powerful he looked while he came in my mouth.

My stomach explodes with butterflies at the memories.

I'm tender between my legs, and it makes my lips curve up because I can still feel him inside me.

Gabriel loves me.

My eyes drift over my face, and I wonder what he sees when he looks at me.

I know I'm not beautiful, but Gabriel's called me that several times.

I take in my nose, my cheekbones, and the curve of my lips.

"What are you doing?" Gabriel suddenly asks.

My eyes snap to him, my cheeks flushing because I was caught staring at myself. "Ah… nothing."

Dressed in a pair of black cargo pants and long sleeve shirt, he looks devastatingly handsome. Moving closer to me, his eyes slowly drift over my naked body.

"It didn't look like nothing." Locking eyes with me, he gives me a pointed look. "I hate it when you keep things from me."

My shoulders slump, and exhaling, I admit, "I wondered what you see when you look at me."

He lifts a hand to my face and brushes his finger over the bridge of my nose to the tip. "A cute nose." He continues to trail his finger over my jaw and bottom lip, then he cups my cheek and leans down, so we're eye to eye. "I see intoxicating innocence and mesmerizingly blue eyes that have imprisoned me."

My chest fills with confidence as his hand lowers to my breast, his palm following the swell before brushing over my ribs and waist. "Your body is perfect, Lara. Your breasts. Your curves." His hand slips between my legs, the pad of his middle finger gently stroking me.

A breath bursts over my lips, and my body instinctively leans closer to his. Lifting my arms, I place my hands on his shoulders, loving how broad they are.

He keeps massaging me, then takes a step closer, so his body presses against mine. His features tighten with a predatory look, his eyes starting to burn with desire.

"One touch is all it takes to turn me on. I want to fuck you, Lara. Until we pass out from pure exhaustion."

My breaths speed up as pleasure unfurls deep inside me.

"How sore are you?" he asks.

"Not much," I lie, knowing he'll stop if I tell him I feel tender down there.

Slowly he pushes a finger inside me. I lift onto my tiptoes and feel his breaths fan over my forehead. Tilting my head, I wrap my arm around the back of his neck and pull him closer until I can feel his breaths on my lips.

There's a weird mixture of pain and pleasure. It only makes me want Gabriel more. With a pleading expression, I whisper, "Please fuck me."

"Jesus, Lara." The words rumble from deep in his chest.

"Please," I beg. "Without holding back this time. I want to experience how you prefer to have sex."

With his eyes burning on mine, he tests me by thrusting his finger hard inside me before keeping still. The pinch is sharp, but all the beatings and whippings have taught me how to keep the pain from showing on my face.

"Please," I whisper again, this time brushing my mouth against his. My tongue darts out, touching his bottom lip, and when he opens, I slip inside. I mimic how Gabriel kissed me in the past, hoping I'm doing it right.

Lowering my right hand, I move my palm down his chest and abs until I reach the bulge in his pants. I start to rub his manhood, that's already hard. My body feels like it's going to combust, and I need him to continue fingering me.

My teeth tug at his bottom lip, and I squeeze his hard length, which seems to tip him over the edge.

Gabriel starts to unfasten his belt, and when he pulls his zipper down, goosebumps spread over my skin. He allows me to pull his cock out, and I start stroking him as my mouth searches for his.

He lifts a hand to the back of my head and takes over the kiss, pouring desire and dominance into my mouth.

My fingers tighten around his thick girth, my thumb brushing over the beading drop spilling from him.

With a growl, Gabriel grabs hold of my hips and lifts me against his body. He sets me down on the bathroom counter and steps between my legs. Raising a hand to my face, his thumb tugs at my bottom lip, his eyes filled with so much hunger it makes him look brutal.

And so, so sinful.

"Are you sure you can handle me?"

I don't care if it hurts the same as last night, I want to be connected to him. "Yes."

This kind of pain is good, and nothing like I've experienced in the past.

Gabriel's strong fingers wrap around his cock, and as he strokes himself, my mouth starts to water from the sight.

Dear God, I'm really going to go up in flames if he doesn't do something soon.

Pressing the head of his cock to my clit, he starts to rub me. Pleasure tightens my core, only creating a need for more.

He keeps teasing me until my abdomen is nothing more than a tight ball, and my hips are gyrating as I try to create more friction.

"Beg me to fuck you, *Ödülüm*," he demands, his voice strained as if it's taking all his self-control to not slam into me.

With my eyes locked on his, I submissively murmur, "Please fuck me, Gabriel."

He positions himself at my entrance, and with a powerful and painful thrust, he fills me. I grab hold of his shoulders and clench my teeth to keep the cry from escaping.

Like a beast, a satisfied groan rumbles from his chest. I watch as his features tighten with pleasure, and it fills me with pride.

Yanking at my hips until our pelvises are flush together, he forces his way even deeper inside me. The pain is sharp, the burning making me feel how he's stretching me. I've never felt so full before.

I look down and seeing where we're joined, heat flushes through my body from the erotic sight.

"Jesus, don't do that. You're tight as it is. If you clamp around me, I will come within seconds."

A smile curves my lips, pleased that I'm able to pleasure him. I use my inner muscles to squeeze around him again, and as reward, his mouth claims mine in a filthy kiss.

Gabriel begins to move, hard and fast. His pace is relentless.

"Lean back," he orders.

Bracing my hands behind me on the counter, I obey him, and it gives me a view of his body as he increases his pace until he's pounding into me.

The burning sensation starts to lessen, and slowly each stroke of his cock creates pleasure deep inside me. My senses are inundated by the forceful way Gabriel is fucking me.

The muscles in his neck strain, his lips pulling back to bare his teeth, and just like last night, he looks powerful.

The pleasure becomes so intense, cries and moans start to spill over my lips. When I see the satisfaction on Gabriel's face, I don't try to stop them.

"Louder, baby. I want to hear you scream," he encourages me.

My body begins to tremble out of control, and my hands search for something to grab hold of. Gabriel braces an arm against the mirror behind me. With him closer, I grab hold of his shirt, my fingers twisting in the fabric.

I'm repeatedly shoved back by Gabriel pounding into me, whimpers of intense pleasure escaping me. Something coils deep in my abdomen, my breaths rushing faster, my heart thundering.

"Oh, God," I whimper when it becomes too much.

Gabriel swivels his hips, slamming so hard into me that my butt shifts back. His fingers clamp around my hip to keep me in place, then he continues to hammer into me.

There's intense heat between us, making sweat bead on my skin.

When the pleasure builds to a breaking point, I close my eyes.

"Open your fucking eyes, Lara. You'll look at me when you come," he orders, his voice hoarse and so low it almost sends me over the edge.

"Please," I beg, my face contorting from the intense need to orgasm.

His cock fills every inch of me, stroking me hard, then he says, "Come, Ödülüm."

I can't tear my eyes away from his as I begin to convulse, overpowering ecstasy seizing every part of me.

I can't think. I can't move. I can't breathe.

I can only feel Gabriel as the orgasm rips through me.

"Jesus," he hisses through clenched teeth. His body begins to jerk, and he drives deeper inside me, sending more paralyzing waves of ecstasy through my body.

I feel his cock swell inside me, and it makes sobs of rapture fall over my lips.

Desperately I gasp to fill my lungs with air, tremors rippling through me from the intense orgasm.

Gabriel's hands frame my face as he thrusts once... twice..., then his body tightens as he empties himself inside me. His eyes never leave mine, his breaths rushing over his parted lips.

He's pure perfection as he finds his release.

Chapter 40

Gabriel

When I pull out of Lara and her blood coats my cock, my eyes snap back to hers.

"Did I hurt you?"

She quickly shakes her head. "I'm pretty sure everyone heard me orgasm."

True.

I glance down again, and this time the sight of her blood fills my chest with overwhelming possessiveness. "You keep bleeding on my cock, and I'm going to fuck you for breakfast, lunch, and supper."

"I like the sound of that."

My woman is growing braver.

Leaning into her, I brace my hands on the counter on either side of her ass. "It *sounded* like you enjoyed my cock."

Her cheeks flush a beautiful pink. "I did."

"How much?" the caveman in me asks.

"A lot. The orgasm felt much deeper this time. More intense."

My mouth nips at hers, murmuring, "That's because I was so fucking deep inside you."

Stepping away from Lara, I clean myself, pull up the zipper, and fasten my belt. "I need to get to work."

Lara remains seated on the counter, her legs pressed tightly together. Knowing what she's doing, a smile curves my mouth as I take hold of her thighs. I push her legs open and look down at my release, coating her skin. "So fucking hot."

Swiping the pad of my thumb through the cum, I bring my finger to her mouth. "Open."

Her lips part, and she obediently licks my finger clean. "Good girl," I praise her. Cupping her jaw, I lean in and press a tender kiss to her mouth. "Such a good fucking girl. You drive me wild, *Ödülüm.*"

Get your ass to work before you give in and fuck her again.

"I want you to move your clothes to my room," I tell her the reason I came to her bedroom in the first place before she distracted me.

Surprise flashes in her clear blue eyes. "Okay."

I give her a devious smile. "There, no one can hear you scream."

She lets out a chuckle and slowly slips off the counter. My eyes drift over her body. "You'll sleep naked from today. I don't want you wearing anything at night."

"Okay."

Grabbing hold of her ass, I yank her against my body and press a hard kiss to her lips. "Take a long, warm bath while I'm at work."

She nods. With all her attention on me, it's fucking hard to let go of her. I let out a sigh as I pull away and walk out of the bathroom before I give in to the insatiable hunger.

Just as I head for the front door, Nisa calls after me, "Don't you want to eat something before leaving for work?"

"No." Smiling at her scowling face, I add, "I'll grab something at work." I open the front door. "By the way, Lara's moving into my room."

Hearing Nisa gasp, I chuckle as I step out of the house.

"*Selam*," Mirac greets. He opens the back door for me. "Where to?"

"Vengeance," I answer as I climb into the SUV.

I hope Elif has been able to keep track of Mazur. Knowing he wants Lara makes me worry for her safety.

The only way to ensure she's never hurt again is by killing the fucker as quickly as possible.

While Mirac drives us to the club, I try to set my thoughts of Lara aside so I can focus on work, but I keep reliving the moment I took her virginity, how impossibly tight she was, and having her body trembling beneath mine. When she cried in my arms, it fed the darkness in me.

Jesus, it was an impossible task taking it slow, but this morning made up for it.

Stop!

I adjust the hard-on in my pants, so it's not as bothersome and shake my head. Glancing at my wristwatch, I notice it's actually afternoon and no longer morning.

She's even making me forget about time.

"We're here," Mirac announces, pulling me out of my thoughts.

"Right." Climbing out, I head into the club and make my way down to the offices.

"Finally," Emre mutters when he meets me in the hallway. "I'm not even going to ask why you're late."

"Good. I'm not sure you can handle the answer," I joke as I walk to Elif's office. "*Selam.* Give me some good news, Elif," I say as I stop next to her chair.

She glances up. "Mazur is still in New York, but…" she brings up CCTV footage of his house in Seattle, "there's activity at the mansion. Looks like his soldiers are starting to gather."

A pleased smile curves my lips. "Notify me the moment Mazur sets foot in Seattle."

"*Evet.*"

I glance at Emre. "Gather the men."

My cousin rushes out of the office as I glance at the footage again, then leaning forward, I say, "Rewind." When she gets to the part I want to see, I mutter, "Pause." I point at the man dressed in a suit. He looks nothing like a soldier. "Find out who that is."

"*Evet.*"

She scans his face into her facial recognition software, and we wait as it searches the database.

"This might take a while," Elif murmurs.

"Call me the second you know," I say before I walk out of the office.

My phone starts to ring, and pulling it from my pocket, I see it's my grandmother.

"*Selam, Babaanne.*"

"*Selam.* My wool is finished."

I let out a chuckle. "What do you want me to do about that?"

"Allow Lara to accompany me to the store. I want to get her, her own knitting needles and basket."

Fuck.

I want to encourage the bond between her and Lara, but now is not a good time.

"We'll be quick, and we'll take the whole army with us," she mutters. "We can't live like prisoners for the unforeseeable future. It might take thirty more years for you to kill Mazur, and I don't have that kind of time."

Jesus. I almost roll my eyes.

"Thanks for that vote of confidence," I mutter wryly.

"I promise it will be a quick shopping trip. Twenty minutes at most."

I let out a sigh. "Not a second longer than twenty minutes. I'll call Daniel."

"Thank you," she says sweetly.

Shaking my head, I end the call and quickly dial Daniel's number.

"Boss?"

"The women want to go shopping," I sigh into the line. "Twenty minutes is all they get. How many men do you have at the house?"

"Eleven."

"Take them all. Keep my women safe."

"Yes, boss."

Ending the call, I shove the device into my pocket and go look for Emre.

Chapter 41

Lara

I've just hung the last blouse in Gabriel's walk-in closet when Nisa comes into the bedroom, announcing, "We're going shopping."

My eyebrows draw together as I glance over my shoulder. "Does Gabriel know?"

"*Evet*. Alya *Hanim* phoned him. Come, he only gave us twenty minutes."

I quickly grab a pair of shoes and pull a brush through my hair. Picking up my handbag, I tuck my phone into it and follow Nisa out of the room.

"Where are we going?" I ask.

"Alya *Hanim* needs wool, so we'll only go to the craft store she likes to visit."

"Okay." When we meet Alya *Hanim* by the front door, I smile with excitement.

Leaving the house, we're met with twelve guards waiting for us.

Daniel steps forward. "You only have twenty minutes. Under no circumstances are you to leave our sight. Lara, you stay with Murat. Alya *Hanim*, you'll be by my side, and Nisa, you stay with Yusuf. If anything happens, just do as your guard instructs."

"So dramatic," Nisa mutters, then she bats her eyelashes at the guard I assume is Yusuf. "It's been a while, Yusuf *Bey*."

With a smile, Yusuf shakes his head as he opens the door for her. "Get in, Nisa *Hanim*."

"Ooh, I like it when you boss me around," she teases him.

This time I can't stop the laughter from bubbling over my lips.

"You're in this SUV, Lara," Murat says when I take a step toward Nisa.

"Oh." I quickly get in and watch as Alya *Hanim* climbs into the SUV behind ours. "Why are we taking separate vehicles?"

Murat waits for two guards to join us before he starts the engine. "It's for safety. If we're attacked, you're not all together."

I glance at the guard next to me and offer him a tentative smile before glancing out the window. The store isn't far from the house. When we reach it, we're bundled out of the SUVs and escorted to the doors. Only Murat, Daniel, and Yusuf follow us inside while the rest of the guards spread out.

My eyes dart over the shelves, drinking in all the arts and crafts. "Wow, there's so much to choose from."

"You take whatever you want, Lara," Alya *Hanim* says. "I'm paying, and there's no limit."

"Does the same count for me?" Nisa asks, already placing a wooden ring in her basket.

Alya *Hanim* chuckles. "Of course."

"What's that?" I ask Nisa, pointing into her basket.

"It's a hoop. You use it to keep the fabric in place for embroidery," she explains patiently. "Get the same one for yourself, then I'll teach you later."

I follow Nisa, loading the same supplies into my basket.

"Don't forget your knitting needles," Alya *Hanim* says as she comes to place a couple of sizes in my basket. Then she scowls at Nisa, "You can teach her embroidery once I'm done with the knitting lessons."

A burst of warmth fills my heart, but it chills when Daniel snaps, "Drop everything and run to the back. Murat, get them out of here!"

What?

Murat yanks the basket from my hands and throws it to the side. With his fingers clamped tightly around my wrist, he drags me to the back of the store.

Alya *Hanim* is right behind me, followed by Nisa and Yusuf. When I notice Daniel is staying behind, I reach for Alya *Hanim* and wrap my fingers tightly around hers. "Stay with me."

"I'm coming," she exhales breathlessly from having to move so fast.

"Wait, Murat!" I yank back against his hold. "Alya *Hanim* can't run."

He turns with a worried expression etched deep into his features. "Shit. Daniel!"

Daniel runs toward us. "Move!"

Suddenly there's a loud explosion, and my eyes widen as I watch one of the SUVs lift off the ground before crashing down in flames. The windows explode inward, ripping screams from Nisa and Alya *Hanim*.

Instead of panic, a strange calmness pours through my body, my mind becoming crystal clear.

"Move!" Daniel shouts again.

"Alya *Hanim* can't run," Murat says to Daniel. "You keep them back while I get them to safety."

"Just go." There's desperation in Daniel's voice.

Still holding Alya *Hanim*'s hand, I tug her further into the back. When I notice Nisa is still frozen with fear, I shout, "Nisa! Come."

She startles and quickly runs to join us.

Gunfire erupts outside the store. Searching the counter, I don't know what happened to the cashier. The lady must've made a run for it when the SUV was bombed.

Suddenly Murat shoves a gun into my hand. "If anything happens to me, you shoot whoever comes near you.

I only have time to nod.

As we make our way to the back exit, I check the gun to make sure the safety is off. I might never have fired a weapon, but I've seen Tymon handle one a million times.

The gunfire grows louder, and I hear Daniel and Yusuf firing their weapons.

Murat shoves a heavy door open and checks if it's safe before allowing us to rush out of the store and into an alley. Huge trash bins line the wall to our left.

"We'll hide," I say. "Between those." I point to the trash bins.

"Quick!"

I'm conscious of Alya *Hanim*, not wanting her to fall as I help her to our hiding spot. Reaching it, I press her against the filthy wall. "Get down if you can." I reach for Nisa and tug her to Alya *Hanim*'s side. "And don't make a sound."

I watch as they crouch down. This is clearly taking a toll on Alya *Hanim*, and I worry she won't be able to crouch like that for long.

Turning my back to them, I peek around the trash bin. Murat's by the door, where he can see what's happening, his weapon drawn and ready in his hands.

My fingers tighten around my gun, and I glance over my shoulder. Seeing pain on Alya *Hanim*'s face, I quickly look up and down the alley. Spotting a door, I whisper-shout, "Murat!"

He can't hear me with all the noise from the attack.

Gesturing with my hand to Nisa and Alya *Hanim*, I say, "Get up. There's a door a couple of feet away."

I hear them groan as they stand up. "Nisa, take Alya *Hanim* to that door. I'll cover you."

"*Allah Allah*," Nisa wails, but she does as I say. My eyes flick between Murat and the women. When Nisa pulls on the door's handle, it doesn't budge.

Crap. I quickly run closer, and training the barrel of the gun on the handle, I pull the trigger. I jolt from the force of the weapon but grin when the door shudders open. I check inside the dark space to ensure it's safe, then order, "Come! Quick!"

As I glance at Murat, I see him raising his weapon. The shots he fires echo down the alley. Not having time to tell him where we're hiding, I duck back inside and slam the door shut.

Breathless, I glance around for anything I can use to bar the door, and seeing a metal cabinet, I run to it. The thing is heavy, and I struggle to push it until Nisa comes to help me.

The metal grates over the concrete floor, but with Nisa's strength, we manage to push it in front of the door.

I check the dimly lit space that's filled with the sound of muted gunfire. Digging in my handbag, I pull my phone out and dial Gabriel's number.

"Lara!" His voice is filled with intense worry. "Are you safe?"

"Yes. For now." I glance around me again. "I think we're in an empty store close to the crafts store. Murat doesn't know. I didn't have time to tell him."

"Good. Fuck, I'm so proud of you. Daniel says you're armed."

"Yes."

"Do you know how to fire a gun?"

"Yes. Kind of."

He lets out a sigh of relief. "Shoot anyone you don't recognize."

"Okay."

"I'm on my way. Ten minutes. Just hold out for ten minutes."

"Okay."

There's a banging sound against the door, making me startle. "I have to go. They're trying to get in."

"No. Put the phone on speaker and give it to Nisa. I need to know what's happening."

I do as he says and hand the device to a trembling Nisa. "Just hold it."

As I turn around, I position myself in front of Nisa and Alya *Hanim*, raise my arms, and wrap both my hands around the handle. I suck in a deep breath, my eyes focused on the cabinet.

"Jesus, someone talk to me," Gabriel growls.

"*Allah Allah*," is all Nisa can get out.

"Lara's guarding us," Alya *Hanim*'s quivering voice sounds up behind me. "She's waiting. It's quiet."

There's another loud bang against the door, then a muted gunshot.

When my hands threaten to start trembling, I suck in a deep breath and let it out slowly.

You're okay.

You're all okay.

Just keep them alive until Gabriel gets here.

You can do this.

You've survived worse.

"It sounds like they're trying to get past the cabinet," Alya *Hanim* whispers.

"What cabinet?"

"The one Lara and Nisa pushed in front of the door. Lara had to shoot the door open so we couldn't lock it behind us."

"Good."

The worry in Gabriel's voice makes a tremble shudder through me. Once again, I focus on keeping my hands steady, pushing any fear trying to surface back down.

You can do this.

Stay calm.

Shoot anything that comes through that door.

Protect your loved ones.

I hear glass breaking somewhere behind me and swing around. The moment I see movement, I pull the trigger.

Nisa lets out a shriek that is drowned out by the sound of the shot.

"Almost there," Gabriel shouts. "I see the smoke."

Slowly I inch a couple of steps forward. A dark shadow moves, and I instantly fire a shot. Dust sprays into the air as the bullet hits a wall.

"We just want you, Lara. If you come willingly, we'll let the old women live," a man shouts.

"Don't you fucking dare, Lara!" Gabriel snaps. "I'm here."

"*Allah Allah*," Nisa wails softly. "Hurry, Gabriel *Bey*."

"Move in," I hear the man command. "Don't kill the target."

More glass shatters, and bodies pour into the store. I just open fire, trying to aim as best I can.

All hell breaks loose. Bodies drop to the floor. Nisa and Alya *Hanim* sob.

I hear the cabinet give way and fall over.

Then the gun clicks in my hand, all out of bullets.

God, help us.

I'm grabbed from behind. "I've got you," Daniel's voice sounds in my ear. He shoves me behind him, then his arm lifts, and he opens fire, not missing a target.

Flashes light up the dimly lit room, the smell of gunpowder filling the air.

Movement by the door draws my attention, and when I see Murat leaning against the doorjamb, blood staining his shirt, I break out into a run.

"I'm okay," he grinds out as I reach him.

Lifting his shirt, I find the bullet hole and press my palm to it as hard as possible. "Shit," he groans.

Silence descends around us, then I hear, "Where is she?"

My head swivels to the side, but I struggle to see anything through the cloud of smoke.

"Lara!"

"I'm here. By the door."

I hear his footsteps before he appears through the smoke.

"Murat's been shot. He's losing a lot of blood."

Mirac is right behind Gabriel, and he comes to help. Mirac pulls Murat's arm over his shoulders so he can lean on him.

"Where's Nisa and Alya *Hanim*?" I ask, moving back into the store to check on them.

"Emre and Daniel have them," Gabriel answers as he grabs hold of my bloody hand. "Let me just hold you!" He yanks me to this body and wraps his arms around me. "Jesus, woman."

I hear him suck in deep breaths of air, then the realization sinks in.

It's over.

We're safe.

"What the fuck are you made of?" Gabriel grumbles. He pulls back and frames my face, pressing a hard kiss to my mouth, then he grins at me. "My badass woman. I'm so fucking proud of you."

Chapter 42

Gabriel

I've just lost ten years of my life.

The moment we stop in front of the house, Lara darts out of the SUV and runs up the stairs. "Nisa! Alya *Hanim*!" she shouts as she runs inside.

I set after her, and I'm just in time to see her hug the older women. "Thank God," she breaths with intense relief. "I was so scared."

I stop and stare at the three women I love more than life itself, so fucking thankful Lara was able to ward off the attack.

Fuck, she's incredible.

I need to give her shooting lessons.

I glance at Emre, who's on a call. He's probably making arrangements for the injured men and those we lost.

Then Lara mutters, "I'm sorry you couldn't get your supplies."

I rub a hand over my face. My phone vibrating in my pocket has me pulling it out. Seeing an unknown number, I answer, "You don't train your men very well."

"That's just the start, Demir."

"We can meet right now and end this. I have some time available before dinner."

"Do you think this is a joke?" he snaps, clearly upset that he failed. "Just give me the girl, and no one has to die."

My eyes flick to Lara, who's staring at me.

"The only way you'll get Lara is by killing me, and that will never happen," I say with confidence lacing my words.

"Don't beg for mercy when I shove my gun down your throat," he tries to threaten me.

"I dare you to try."

"Let me speak to Lara," he demands, her name sounding bitter on his tongue.

"No."

"Let me speak to her!" he shouts.

Lara starts to walk toward me, and I shake my head. "Anything you want to say to her, you can say to me."

Mazur lets out a throaty chuckle. "Tell her Agnieska is alive. If Lara comes to me, I won't kill her."

Frowning, I bark, "Who the fuck is Agnieska?"

Lara's eyes widen with shock as Mazur mutters, "Her mother. Lara has twenty-four hours to return to my house in Seattle before I put her mother down like a dog."

I watch as Lara covers her mouth with her hands, her eyes glued to me.

I let out a humorless chuckle. "I know you're in New York."

"I'll be in Seattle tonight. We end this farce then."

"Oh, I'll end it." Then I think to say, "I want proof of life."

"I'll send it."

The moment I cut the call, Lara asks, "What did he say about my mother?"

I walk closer to her, not sure whether I should tell her. Mazur could be lying.

"Nothing."

"You're lying." Her chin starts to tremble. "Tell me."

"There's no proof."

"Of what?"

Just then, my phone vibrates in my hand. I open the message and press play on the video.

There's an older version of Lara sitting on a chair, the camera trained on her. Her face is covered in bruises.

Fuck.

'Lara…' She swallows hard as her face crumbles.

'Talk, woman!' a voice I don't recognize barks.

'Lara, nie przychodź tutaj. Biegać.'

"Bitch!'

The recording ends, and my eyes snap to Lara.

"Mama," she breathes, then she sinks to her knees and lets out a devastating cry. "Noooo!"

I quickly crouch and engulf her in my arms. "I'll get her back for you," I promise. "I'll go and fucking kill them all. I will bring your mother to you."

"She's alive," Lara sobs, then pulls back. "I need to see it again. I didn't understand what she said."

I hold the device between us and press play again.

'Lara, nie przychodź tutaj. Biegać.'

"Don't." Lara shakes her head, and I play it again. "Run? I don't understand!"

"I'll get it translated."

I forward the message to Elif with the instruction to translate it and see what else she can pick up in the background.

"We'll know soon," I promise Lara.

"Allah Allah," Nisa whimpers. "My heart can't handle this. Let's have tea."

Helping Lara to her feet, I wrap my arm around her shoulders. We all move to the kitchen, and as Nisa gets busy setting snacks out and making tea, my phone vibrates again.

Lara, don't come here. Run.

I show it to Lara, and as she reads it, her face crumbles with heartache.

I pull her against my chest, promising her again, "I'll find your mother and bring her to you."

"Please. I'll do anything to get her back," she begs.

Her words put the fear of God in my heart because I know without a doubt that Lara would sacrifice herself for her mother.

My eyes meet my grandmother. Today she looks eighty-four. The attack took a toll on her.

I can't let this go on for a second longer.

Pushing Lara back, I lean down to catch her eyes. "Don't leave the house. I'm trusting you to keep my grandmother and Nisa safe while I go get your mother."

She nods, her eyes swimming with emotion.

"Promise me you'll stay here," I demand.

"I promise."

I press a kiss to her mouth, taking a deep breath of her innocence. "*Seni çok seviyorum*," I murmur, then I let her go and walk out of the kitchen.

"What did he say?" I hear Lara ask.

"That he loves you very much," Nisa translates, tears in her voice.

Walking out of the house, I gesture to the guards that we're leaving. "Vengeance," I mutter to Mirac.

Emre jumps in next to me in a nick of time.

"Any news on the men?" I ask.

"Murat's okay. He's already on his way home." Emre glances at me. "Yusuf is still in surgery, and we lost four men. Doruk, Aslan, Dean, and Harry."

"Fuck." I glance out the window as sorrow for my men shudders through me. "Arrange their funerals and compensate their families."

"Already on it." I can feel Emre's eyes on me. "What's the plan?"

"We attack as soon as Elif can tell me what the fuck is going on in that house." Knowing she's not God, I let out a sigh as I pull my phone from my pocket.

I bring up Viktor Vetrov's number and stare at it.

He's a part of the Priesthood. You've been there for them whenever they needed you to help them.

Pressing dial, I bring the device to my ear.

"*Blyad*! This is a surprise. To what do I owe the honor," Viktor answers.

"I need your help."

"With?"

"I have an address. I need to know what's happening in that house, how many people there are, and if a certain target is present. I have to attack as soon as possible."

"Send me the details." I hear him move. "It will take me a couple of hours to get my ass to Seattle." Then I hear him shout, "Luca, Gabriel needs us."

Fuck.

I let out a sigh.

"We'll be there in three hours," Viktor says. "Where are we meeting?"

"My club. Vengeance."

The call ends, and I lower my hand to my thigh.

"You did the right thing," Emre mutters. "They owe you, and we can really use their help."

"I know."

I can't risk Mazur getting away this time. Or Lara's mother dying. There's too much at stake.

With Viktor's expertise in surveillance and being able to sniff out information, it will make things easier. The

369

man's part fucking bloodhound. Luca's powerful, he has the manpower to back mine.

Within the next twenty-four hours, Mazur will take his last breath, and Lara will be reunited with her mother.

Even if it costs my life.

Pressing dial on another number, I wait as it rings.

"Stathoulis," Nikolas answers.

"I need you in Seattle."

"Where?"

"Vengeance."

"I'm just kissing my wife hello and goodbye, then I'm on my way."

'Why are you kissing me hello and goodbye?' I hear Tessa, his wife, ask. *'Where are you going?'*

The call ends before I can hear his explanation.

Chapter 43

Lara

Nisa forced me to drink two cups of tea, and she hasn't left my side. Neither has Alya *Hanim*.

Now that there are no bullets flying around us, I sit and stare at the table, trying to process what happened.

Mom's alive.

Tymon lied to me. For years. *Why?*

Alya *Hanim* takes hold of my hand, giving it a squeeze.

My eyes lift to her face, and seeing how exhausted she looks, I murmur, "You should get some rest, Alya *Hanim*."

She shakes her head. "No more Alya *Hanim*. Call me *Babaanne* or Grandma, and I'm not leaving your side."

I turn my hand over and wrap my fingers around hers. "Thank you."

She looks visibly upset as her eyes meet mine. "That man must die. Gabriel will kill him."

"He will."

Nisa lets out a heavy sigh, and when Daniel walks into the kitchen, she asks, "Any news of Yusuf and Murat?"

"Murat should be here any moment now, and Yusuf's still in surgery."

"*Allah Allah*," she whispers, lowering her head.

I pat her shoulder, and getting up, I pour some tea for Daniel.

When he takes it from me, our eyes meet, and I say, "Thank you for protecting us."

"You're welcome." I watch as he leaves, then say a silent prayer for Yusuf and any other man that got hurt while keeping us safe.

I glance at Nisa and *Babaanne*, and needing some time alone, I leave to go to Gabriel's bedroom. Once I shut the door behind me, I walk to his closet and pull my box from the top shelf. Setting it down on the bed, I take off the lid and pull out the storybook. I open it and stare at the photo of Mom.

She wasn't much older than me when it was taken.

Remembering the video, I pull out my phone and figure out how to send a text to Gabriel. It takes me a couple of seconds, then I sit and wait. The device vibrates, and I quickly open the chat.

Why do you want the video?

I want to look at my mother. Please.

Suddenly the video pops up along with another message.

How are you coping with everything that's happened?

I type out a reply.

I just feel emotional. I'll be okay.

I love you, Lara. I don't think you fully understand how much.

I stare at the words that soothes the ache in my chest a little.

My fingers hover over the keypad, then I close the chat and press dial on Gabriel's number.

"Hi, baby." His tone is gentle.

"I love you," I say the words for the first time in ten years. "I love you, Gabriel."

"Love you too, *Ödülüm*."

My teeth worry on my bottom lip, then I ask, "Are you attacking tonight?"

"As soon as we're ready."

Worry for him strangles my heart. "Please don't get hurt."

"I'll do my best." I hear him take a deep breath. "If something goes wrong and I can't get back to you, I need you to call Liam Byrne. I'll send you his phone number. He's a friend who will be able to help you."

"I want you to come back to me," I argue, unwilling to settle for anything less.

"Just promise me you'll call Liam if you don't hear from me in twenty-four hours."

"Gabriel." My chin starts to tremble, and for the first time, I deny him something. "No. You will come back."

"Lara," his voice is filled with warning.

"No," I say with determination. "If I don't make this promise, it will guarantee your safety because there's no way you'll leave us here alone. As long as you know we're not safe, you'll keep fighting."

"Jesus," he mutters. "Only you can make me want to spank you and praise you at the same time."

"You can spank me all you want once you're home."

"Now that's what I call incentive," he chuckles, then he grows serious again. "Go to the closet and move my suits out of the way."

I do as Gabriel instructs and find myself staring at a floor-to-ceiling vault door. "What's the code?"

"Nine. Two. Nine. Eight."

I key it in, and when the door opens, I peek inside. There are piles of money and weapons.

"Take the guns out. They're all loaded. I've checked them myself. I want you to hide them all over the house where you can get to them should there be an attack. Keep one on you."

"Can I ask Daniel to help me?"

"Yes." He lets out a tired breath. "Stay safe, baby. I'll see you soon."

"Promise," I demand.

He lets out a sexy chuckle. "I promise."

When the call ends, I immediately go back to the chat and press play on the video. I turn down the volume so I can focus on my mother.

I stare at her blue eyes for the longest time, before taking in the fine lines and bruises on her face.

"Gabriel will save you," I whisper to her. "I can't wait to hug you." Slumping to my knees, I turn up the volume so I can hear her say my name.

'Lara...'

I press rewind and play again.

'Lara...'

"Lara?" I hear Murat call.

"In the closet," I call out as I scramble to my feet. I dart around the corner, and seeing Murat is alive and as well as can be expected, I throw my arms around him. "I'm so glad you're okay!"

"That makes two of us," he mutters.

Letting go of him, I point to the closet. "There are guns in there. Gabriel wants us to hide them all over the house in case of an attack."

He nods and walks to the vault. "God, I love my boss," he mutters with a grin as he takes a shotgun out. "Let's get to work."

For the next hour, Murat, Daniel, and I hide guns in potted plants, beneath chairs, in drawers, and just about anywhere we can find a spot.

When I pick a gun for myself, Daniel mutters, "A Heckler & Koch. Good choice."

A smile curves around my mouth as I tuck it behind me in the waistband of my jeans, covering the weapon with my shirt.

I shut the vault door and make sure it locks, then ask, "What now?"

"It would be easier for me if everyone was together and not spread throughout the house," Daniel says.

"The kitchen?"

He nods. "Thanks, Lara."

I leave the room with the men, and finding Nisa and *Babaanne* still sitting at the table, I say, "I'm preparing dinner. Any requests?"

"I can't eat," *Babaanne* murmurs.

"You need to keep up your strength," I argue as I start to take ingredients out for a Turkish pizza. "Nisa, can you please go get *Babaanne*'s knitting basket so she can knit a pair of baby booties?"

All eyes turn to me. "Oh no, I'm not pregnant. Not yet, anyway."

"*Allah Allah.*" Nisa throws her hands in the air. "Don't get our hopes up like that for nothing."

A smile starts to curve around *Babaanne*'s lips, then she asks, "Soon?"

Nodding, I promise, "As soon as Gabriel agrees."

She waves a hand, making a disgruntled sound in her throat. "Then I'll die long before I have great-grandchildren."

"I'll ask him nicely."

She chuckles, then Nisa says, "Just seduce him. The man will do anything for you."

The tension lessens, and some color returns to *Babaanne*'s face, making me feel better.

Chapter 44

Gabriel

After greeting the men, Viktor pulls his laptop from a bag and makes himself at home at my desk.

"Is Liam coming?" Luca asks.

I shake my head. "I need him as a backup plan should something go wrong. He's on standby to get my family out of Seattle if I die."

Luca locks eyes with me. "Do you have so little faith in us?"

"Clearly," Viktor mutters.

"I'm insulted," Nikolas adds.

"We're not just going up against Mazur. There's someone else involved, and I have no idea what kind of firepower he has."

"Jan Grabowksi," Viktor says. "He's Mazur's business partner."

"Since when did you have that information?" I ask.

"Two minutes."

"Jesus, Viktor," I mutter, moving to stand next to him so I can see the laptop's screen. There are so many programs open, I wouldn't know where to start. "Is there anything you don't know?"

He gives me a cocky grin. "Just one thing."

"What?"

"How to get rid of little Rose's thorns."

"You still have the girl?"

"Woman," he corrects me. "She's officially eighteen and of fuckable age."

I shake my head, wondering how he's getting away with this, seeing as his family is against any form of abuse against women. Curious, I ask, "How do Demitri and Alexei feel about this?"

Viktor shrugs. "They know I won't hurt her." Then he frowns at me. "I'm not a fucking rapist."

"Didn't say you were one."

"Guys," Luca mutters drily, "hate to break up the bromance, especially since Gabriel is actually in a talking mood for once, but we kinda have an attack to plan."

Suddenly, Emre rushes into the office. "We're under attack. They're coming in from the front and back."

"Fuck," I snap.

"Looks like the party came to us." Viktor shuts his laptop, puts it back in the bag, and pulls out two identical Glocks, then he grins. "Let's have some fun."

Luca arms himself with his Heckler and Koch, while Nikolas sighs as he gets up from the chair he was occupying.

Walking to the vault in my office, I key in the code. When the door opens, Viktor comes to stand next to me, letting out a low whistle. "This is why we're friends," he smiles as he helps himself to a couple of incendiary grenades.

"Try not to destroy my club," I mutter.

"You heard what I said, right?" Emre asks incredulously.

"Yes. Attack happening. We'll be there shortly," Nikolas answers.

Letting out a chuckle, I shake my head as I arm myself with an IMI Uzi submachine gun, my Glock safely tucked behind my back.

"Let me see what you have in there," Nikolas says. I step aside so he can take what he wants.

"Hey," Luca grins, "I sold you those grenades."

"*Allah Allah*," my cousin mutters as he stands by the door. "Have they breached?" he shouts at someone.

"Not yet," Elif shouts back.

"Okay, let's welcome them," I say as I walk to the door. I head to Elif's office, where we'll be able to see all the security cameras.

"It's an army," Elif says, concern etched over her face.

I check the monitors, and noticing there are easily thirty men in the docking bay, I wonder how many men are left at the mansion to guard Agnieska.

"Pull up footage of Mazur's house," I instruct Elif. Viktor comes to stand by us, then he leans over and shoves Elif's hands out of the way.

He brings up a completely different screen and seconds later says, "I'd guess a handful. Not much happening there."

Looking at Emre, I say, "Take men and go to Mazur's house. With the attack happening here, you might be able to get Lara's mother without any resistance."

"How do you propose I leave the club?" my cousin asks.

Viktor points to the ceiling. "The roof, unless you're afraid of heights."

Emre shakes his head, then glares at me. "You owe me for this."

I nod and watch as he leaves, then turn my attention back to the security monitors. "They're going to blow the back door. Let's move." I place a hand on Elif's shoulder. "Stay here until you have no other choice."

"*Evet.*"

We file out of the office, and I shut it behind us. "Docking bays are to the right. It will take them a while to breach from the upper floors."

"Docking bay it is," Luca says.

While they move down the hallway, taking cover in doorways, I instruct Mirac on what to do with the rest of my soldiers.

When everyone's in position, you can hear a pin drop on the thick carpet.

I hope to God Mazur is here and not hiding like a fucking coward.

Taking out my phone, I quickly send Emre a text.

If you find Mazur hiding there, bring him to the club. Have a man watch that damn tunnel so he doesn't escape again.

Seconds later, he replies.

I know what to do. You just focus on not dying.

Little shit.

I tuck the device away, then glance at the men who are willing to fight for me, while I impatiently wait for the action to start.

"Fuck this," Viktor grumbles. "I'm going to open the door for them."

The moment he moves, we all follow after him.

"That door can blow at any moment," Nikolas warns him.

"I doubt it. The fuckers have no idea what they're doing." Viktor pulls the heavy deadbolt securing the metal door, and yanking it open, he says, "Surprise motherfuckers."

I watch as he opens fire on the surprised men, spraying bullets everywhere.

"I could've stayed home and fucked my wife," Nikolas mutters as he leans against the wall, totally relaxed.

Suddenly, Viktor shouts, "Incoming! Run!"

We all fucking barrel down the hallway, then the building shudders as a grenade is launched against it. The explosion makes the ground vibrate beneath my feet and ducking into an office, I take cover from any flying debris.

Viktor lets out a bark of laughter, and I swear the man is just as insane as his uncle.

The enemy pours in over the debris of what used to be my backdoor, and all hell breaks loose. We open fire, my focus on Mazur's men as I take out one after the other.

We manage to push them back, and stepping over the rubble, the night air hits my face.

I move to the left, where I'll be able to take cover behind a concrete pillar. The floodlights come on, and I silently thank Elif, who must've turned them on so we can actually fucking see what we're shooting at.

When I take aim, a Bentley catches my eye where it's parked on the other side of the bay. "Anyone with a scope! Who's in that Bentley?"

"Mazur!" Bulut, one of my men, yells.

Not giving it a second thought, I run, jumping from the docking bay that's a good couple of feet high, my legs shudder with pain as I hit the ground in a crouching position. I'm up and dropping the Uzi, I fucking run as fast as I can.

The Bentley's lights turn on, and I hear the engine start. Pulling my Glock from behind my back, I fucking put every bit of strength I have into my legs.

Just as the car starts to drive through the exit, I launch myself into the air, plant a foot against the gate's pillar, and fucking fly onto the roof of the Bentley. I slide down the front and push myself to my knees, opening fire on the driver through the windscreen. The car serves, throwing me to the side, and I hit the ground fucking hard.

Pushing up, I watch as the car crashes into a telephone pole.

"Got you, fucker," I growl as I struggle to my feet, my entire left side banged up.

Luca comes running toward me. "Are you okay?"

"Yes." I walk to the car, yank open the back door and train my weapon on a semi-conscious Mazur. "Finally, we meet in person."

He lets out a groan, turning his head to look at me.

Switching my gun to my left hand, I reach into the car with my right, grab hold of the back of his coat, and drag his ass out onto the road.

"Need help?" Luca asks.

"No. I've got it," I mutter as I start to drag Mazur back toward the docking bays.

Luca lets out a sharp whistle. "Some help over here."

A couple of my men run toward us, and only when they're surrounding Mazur, do I let go so they can pick him up.

He groans something inelible, as they carry him toward the club.

Luca throws his arm around my shoulders. "That was some badass moves."

"Yeah, but I'm getting too old for this shit," I mutter. Glancing down at my ripped shirt, my left arm grazed and oozing blood, I let out a sigh.

"Age is just a number," Luca chuckles.

My phone starts vibrating, and I wince as I pull it from my pocket. Seeing Emre's name, relief floods my chest.

"Give me good news," I answer.

"I've got the woman. Sort of. She's like a damn wildcat.

"Call Lara so she can talk to her mother and calm her down," I order.

"I also have a man named Jan Grabowski who's willing to pay a shit ton, so I don't kill him."

"Bring him to the club."

"How are things there?"

"Hold on." I tuck the device in my pocket, and jumping, I grab hold of the ledge of a docking bay and pull myself up. Once I'm standing again, I take hold of the phone. "Everything's pretty much taken care of. Some damage to the back of the club. Bodies. Blood. The usual."

"And Mazur."

"On his way to the freezer."

I hear Emre suck in a deep breath. "Finally."

"Get your ass back here for the grand finale."

"On my way."

I end the call and follow my men as they carry Mazur to the freezer, where he will spend his last hours.

Chapter 45

Lara

When my phone rings and I see Emre's name, my heart shrivels into a black hole.

No.

God, please.

My hands start to tremble, and my thumb hovers over the little circle.

There's only one reason why Emre would call me. Something happened to Gabriel.

A sob builds in my chest.

"Your phone's ringing," Nisa says.

"I know." I take a trembling breath, swipe across the screen, and bring the phone to my ear. "Hello." My voice quivers.

"Hi, it's Emre."

"Uh-huh." I squeeze my eyes shut.

"I'm with your mother." My eyes snap wide open. "I need you to calm her down so she'll come with me."

"Yes!" I jump up from the chair and start stalking up and down, my heart instantly beating a mile a minute.

I hear movement, then Emre says, "Your daughter is on the line."

It takes a moment before I hear her sob, "Lara?"

"Mama." Tears begin to spill over my cheeks, and I don't care. Sobs strain my voice. "Emre is a friend. You can trust him. He'll bring you to me. Please go with him."

My mother lets out a heartbreaking wail, and it makes my own tears come faster, my chest shuddering. "Ma-ma," I hiccup. "Come to me."

"Okay," she squeezes the word out.

Seconds later, Emre's somber voice comes over the line. "We'll be there in thirty minutes."

"Thank… you."

When the call ends, I start to cry like I've never cried before. Nisa grabs me to her, holding me tight and making clucking sounds. "It's a happy day, Lara."

I nod, and when my phone rings again, I almost drop it. Through a blur, I can hardly make out Gabriel's name and swipe as fast as I can.

"Gabriel? Are you okay?"

"Yes. I've got Mazur. Did Emre call you?"

"Yes, a…" my throat strains from all the emotion, "a couple of seconds ago."

"I wish I could be there, but I have to deal with things at the club. I'll be home in an hour."

"Okay."

"Deep breaths, baby."

I nod, struggling to regain control over my breathing.

"That's better. You need to be strong tonight. Your mother is going to need your help. You can do that, right?"

"Yes." I fight harder for control, slowly starting to calm down.

"That's my girl."

"Are you really okay?" I ask just to be sure.

"Just a couple of scratches. I'll see you in an hour."

"Okay," I say before taking a deep breath.

"Give the phone to my grandmother."

Walking to *Babaanne*, I hand her the device. "It's Gabriel," I say unnecessarily.

"Gabriel?" she answers. Absolute relief washes over her features. "*Tanrıya şükür.*"

I glance at Nisa, who quickly translates, "Thank God."

Babaanne nods. "You make him suffer for what he did to my son, and then I'll bathe my black robes in his blood."

My eyebrows dart up at the hatred in her voice. Not that I can blame her. She lost a child because of Tymon.

"You did well. I'm proud of you, *gözümün nuru*."

I smile when I recognize the words. *The light of my eye.*

When she ends the call, she hands the device back to me, rises to her feet, and slowly walks out of the room.

I look at Nisa again, and it has her saying, "She needs to be alone. She can finally mourn Deniz."

"Deniz?"

"Gabriel's father," she answers. Groaning, she stands up. "Let's go wait in the entrance hall for your mother."

As we walk into the open space, the front door opens. For a moment, I freeze as Emre comes in, then my mother appears in the doorway, looking frightened as she glances around.

"Mama!" I cry, flying across the tiles.

"Lara," she sobs, stumbling forward.

We fall into each other's arms, then sink to the floor, our tears the only language we can speak after being apart for so long.

Thank you.

ThankyouThankyouThankyou.

Her scent has changed, but her arms still feel the same.

When I'm able to speak, I say, "I missed you so much."

Mom pulls back, her trembling hands fluttering over my face as her eyes drink in the sight of me. "I lived only for this day. My Lara."

Pulling back, my eyes greedily rove over her, then heartache fills every inch of me. She's skinny, the worn clothes hanging off her body, and there are bruises everywhere.

She's suffered.

"Come," I whisper, and climbing to my feet, I help her up before wrapping my arm around her lower back. "You're safe here," I say, knowing those would've been the first words I would've wanted to hear.

I take my mom to my old room, Nisa following right behind us. "What can I do?" she asks as I help my mom sit down on the bed.

"Can you go to Gabriel's room and bring me a pair of leggings and a sweater? Also, there's a pack of unopened underwear."

"*Evet.*"

When Nisa rushes away to get the clothes, I crouch in front of Mom and stare up at her, unable to believe she's really here.

Her eyes are locked on my face, then she whimpers, "You've grown so much."

"I'm twenty-two."

"I know." Her face crumbles. "I've missed everything. The photos they showed me weren't enough."

She slides off the bed and into my arms, her body trembling something fierce. Crying, she says, "I lived only for you."

"You're home," I murmur, swallowing hard on all the emotions creating a turbulent storm inside my chest. "You're home, and we'll never be apart again."

Nisa comes in with the clothes and sets them down on the bed. She takes one look at my mother, then leaves again, only to return with the first aid kit.

"Can you call Dr. Bayram?" I ask her, wanting to make sure my mother's not hurt badly.

"*Evet.*"

When she steps out of the room to make the call, I pull Mom to her feet. "Do you have the strength to change into the clothes?"

She nods but doesn't let go of me.

"I'll be right outside the door. Okay?"

I pull back, checking her face.

"Right outside the door?" she asks.

"Yes. Call for me when you're done."

She nods again and glances around the room as I step into the hallway, pulling the door shut. "I'm right here," I say to set her at ease. Thinking it will help, I continue to talk. "I still have the Cinderella book you gave me. And the photo." My mind races for things to say.

"Tell her we're good people," Nisa whispers.

"The people here are really good. They've become like family to me."

Nisa gestures for me to continue.

"Ah… are you okay in there?"

"Yes." Her voice sounds so vulnerable it's a blow to my heart.

"There won't be any more beatings," My voice breaks, and I take a calming breath. "No more pain."

"I'm done," she sobs.

I quickly go back inside, and we hug again.

I'll hold her until she feels safe.

"We'll get to know each other again," I assure her. "You can ask me anything."

"When did you escape?"

"It's been two months since Gabriel brought me here."

She closes her eyes, then asks, "He saved you?"

"Yes." A smile tugs at my mouth. "Emre is his brother."

Not wanting her to live in fear any longer, I say, "They're good men. I love Gabriel, and he loves me. We're safe here."

Her eyes search over my face again. "You look healthy."

My lips curve up. "I am. Nisa's cooking is delicious. You'll pick up weight in no time."

"Are you hungry?" Nisa asks, a hopeful expression on her face.

Mom hesitates before she nods, slightly cowering behind me.

"I'll prepare food." With relief, Nisa hurries away.

I pull Mom to me, keeping an arm around her. I have many questions, but I want her to settle in before asking them.

When our eyes meet, I give her a smile which she tentatively returns.

I have my mother back. I can't believe it.

Chapter 46

Gabriel

I kick Mazur's leg. "Wake up, fucker."

I have him tied to a chair and men guarding the freezers, while others clean up the mess outside.

Emre comes in. "Grabowski is in the other freezer. What do you want to do with him?"

"Is he conscious?" I ask.

"*Evet.*"

"Watch Mazur while I question the other fucker."

On my way to Grabowski, Luca stops me. "You need us for anything else?"

"Like helping with torture," Viktor offers, giving me a hopeful look.

"Sure, why not. Just don't kill the fucker until I have all my answers," I warn him.

As we walk to the freezer, I glance at Viktor. "Thanks for tonight."

"I always pay my debt."

"You didn't owe me shit," I mutter as we stop outside the door. "The fight against the Sicilians was for Nikolas."

Viktor shrugs. "I guess you owe me."

"Just give me six months before you collect," I joke.

He nods toward the door. "Let's do this."

We step inside, and I look at Grabowski with disgust. "I'm sure you know how this works. I ask a question. You answer. Don't, and my friend's going to make you suffer."

I pull a chair closer and take a seat, my body protesting against the movement.

Viktor goes to stand behind the man. "Please be stubborn and refuse to answer the questions. I have a lot of pent-up frustration to take out on you."

I chuckle, assuming he's referring to Rosalie, the granddaughter of the Sicilian we helped Nikolas kill a couple of months back.

Leveling Grabowski with a bored look, I ask, "What business ties do you have with Mazur?"

He lets out a heavy breath, the cold air making it visible. "Sex trafficking."

I raise an eyebrow, giving Viktor an apologetic look. "Seems he's a talker."

"A fucking pity," Viktor mutters as he crosses his arms.

I lean forward, resting my forearms on my thighs. "I'm guessing you had Agnieska?"

"The whore was a gift from Mazur," he spits out.

"Why separate mother and daughter?"

"Mazur used the daughter as a tool to keep the whore from trying to escape." He lets out a sigh. "I know you're going to kill me."

"Why answer my questions?"

"Promise me a quick death of my choosing."

"How would you like me to kill you?"

"A shot to the head."

I nod. "Tell me everything about the role you played in keeping Agnieska and Lara apart." I want every single fucking answer so I can give them to Lara.

"Like I said, the whore was a gift." He tries to shrug, but with his hands tied behind his back, he can't. "She served a purpose, and as long as I showed her photos of her daughter, she did anything I wanted." He lets out a humorless chuckle. "It's surprising what a woman will do for her child."

"You used Agnieska as a sex slave?"

He nods. "The best one I ever had."

It doesn't take much for me to figure out the rest. "But you wore her out, and Lara was going to replace her?"

"Yes."

"Why them?"

He gives me a wry smile. "I know they're not beauties, but they have an innocence that can't be ruined. It's exquisite. Like sampling a rare dish. It melts on your tongue."

My eyes flick up to Viktor, and I nod. Without any hesitation, he pulls his gun from behind his back, trains the barrel on Grabowski's head, and pulls the trigger.

He fires another shot. "I fucking despise sex traffickers."

"That makes two of us."

Standing up, I walk out of the freezer, telling the guards, "Clean up the mess."

Luca's leaning against the wall, but there's no sign of Nikolas. "Did Nikolas leave?"

He shakes his head. "He went to find a drink and call his wife."

I nod. "You don't have to stay. It's over."

"I know, but that would ruin the fun for Viktor, and I'd have to listen to him complain all the way home. Besides, I booked a room at a hotel."

I chuckle, admiring the brotherly bond the two men have.

I walk to Mazur's freezer, and seeing he's still out cold, I glance at Emre. "I'm going to head home and shower. I won't be long."

"Yes, you will," my cousin says as he shoves Mazur's head. "He better wake up."

"Call me the moment he does. Want me to bring you something from home?"

"Food."

I nod, then ask Luca, "Need a ride?"

"I thought you'd never offer," he chuckles. "No, I have a car waiting." He turns his attention to Viktor. "You coming or staying?"

"Staying. I want to be here when the fucker wakes up. Rough him up a little."

"The plane leaves at six am. With or without you," Luca warns.

I shake Luca's hand. "Thank you for tonight."

"No problem. That's what the Priesthood is for."

Our eyes lock for a moment. After tonight, I'll drop everything to help them.

When Luca heads down the hallway, I turn to Viktor. "Don't kill Mazur, and don't drive my cousin insane."

He glances into the freezer. "Emre loves me."

Shaking my head, I walk away. "You want me to bring you food, as well?"

"Yes. A lot. All the excitement is making me hungry."

I gesture that I heard him before stopping at Elif's office. "Mirac, we're heading home."

He kisses his wife, murmuring. "You go home. I'll be there..." He glances at me, and I hold up two fingers. "I'll be home in two hours."

As we leave the building and I climb into the back of the SUV, I worry about the difficult time lying ahead for Lara and her mother.

I'll have to get psychological help for Agnieska.

Fuck, I'm not sure whether sex slavery is something you can heal from.

Just give the woman a safe place and leave the rest to God.

Mirac brings the SUV to a stop in front of the house. Everything looks quiet, but I know it's not the case. Climbing out, I head inside. I walk to my bedroom, needing to shower and change my clothes because the women will worry if they see the state I'm in.

I open the door and switch on the light, then freeze. Lara's sitting on the bed, paging through a book. Her head snaps up, then she shoots off the bed.

401

"Oh my God! What happened?"

"Why aren't you with your mother?"

"You answer first," she demands as she slowly peels the fabric away from the dried blood on my arm.

"It's nothing. Just a couple of scrapes."

"Your arm is bleeding!" She scowls up at me. "Sit on the bed."

"Yes, Lara *Hanim*," I tease her. I take a seat, then repeat the question, "Why aren't you with your mother?"

"She's sleeping. After Nisa gave her enough food to feed a small army, she couldn't stay awake."

"How is she?"

Taking hold of the hem of my shirt, Lara pulls it over my head before carefully peeling the sleeve down my left arm.

Shaking her head, she answers, "I don't know. I told her she's safe here, but I don't think she believes me."

"It's been ten years, baby. She just needs time. Be patient with her."

"I know. I'm going to get the first aid kit."

She darts out of the bedroom, and I look down at the torn skin. It's really not that bad and should heal quickly.

When Lara returns, I let her fuss over me, thinking it will set her at ease. My eyes stay glued to her, searching for any signs that she's not coping after the day from hell.

"How are you?" I ask when she wraps a bandage around my arm.

"I'm okay."

"Lara." I wait for her to meet my eyes. "Don't lie to me."

She stares at me for a moment, then continues to fasten the bandage. Once she's satisfied, she starts to gather the used antiseptic wipes.

I take hold of her hand and pull her closer until she's standing between my legs.

"How are you, baby?"

I watch as she fights to keep control over her emotions.

"Come here," I murmur, pulling her onto my lap, so she's straddling me. Placing a hand behind her head, I press her face into the crook of my neck. "Talk to me."

Lara wraps her arms around me, burrowing as close to me as she can get, then she whispers, "I'm glad I have her back."

"But?"

"I'm worried about her."

"I'll get a psychiatrist to help her through this."

"What if she's never the same again?"

I press a kiss to her hair. "That's something you need to prepare yourself for. It's been years, Lara. You've changed, and so has she. You'll have to get to know each other again."

"I know." Her breaths fan against my neck. "At least I have her back." Lara lifts her head, and her eyes meet mine. "Did you find out why Mazur told me she was dead?"

I nod. "But I feel it's something your mother needs to tell you. When she's ready. Don't push her for answers on what happened to her over the past ten years."

Worry tightens her features. "Is it that bad?"

I nod again. "She's going to need a lot of care and time. That's all we can give her." A tear spirals down her cheek, and I reach up to brush it away. "Just be strong for your mother, and I'll be strong for you. Okay?"

"Okay." She hesitates, then asks, "Did you kill Tymon?"

"Not yet."

"Why?"

I shake my head. She doesn't need to hear what I have planned for him. "He'll die soon. Don't worry."

Lara lifts her hand to my face and frames my jaw. "Thank you for saving my mom."

404

"You're welcome, *Ödülüm.*"

Chapter 47

Gabriel

After I've given Emre and Viktor their food, and they're busy wolfing it down, I step into the freezer.

Mazur lifts his head, his left eye bloodshot from the knock he took during the accident.

"Finally. I thought you weren't going to wake up."

"Fuck you." He spits on the floor.

I shove the sleeves of my shirt up to my elbows, then take a seat across from Mazur. Locking eyes with the man, a smile lifts the corners of my mouth. "Tymon Mazur. Finally tied up like the pig he is. Ready for slaughter."

His features tighten, and I see a flash of panic. "Why did you interfere in my business? Why did you attack?"

I stare at him long and hard until he tries to shift in the chair. I take in his size, the fucking ridiculous mustache, the absolute cruel pull of his features.

Jesus, this is the man Lara had to serve all her life.

Inhaling deeply, I let the air out slowly, then say, "I honestly don't think you'll remember, but I'm a ghost from the past."

His eyes narrow on me. "I've never seen you before."

"You're right. You haven't."

He starts to look frustrated, and it makes my smile grow.

"First things first. You fucking tortured Lara." I lean forward, my eyes locked with his as rage simmers in my chest. "I'm going to do to you what you did to her."

"Answer me!" he shouts, his face almost turning purple. "What have I done to you?"

I stand up and take the time to move the chair out of the way. Turning back to Mazur, I say, "My mother was a baker. She loved it very much."

Confusion fills his face.

"My father opened a bakery for her. They made a modest living. I used to help after school, and one day while I was packing shelves, your men came in and killed them in cold blood. I watched my parents die, and I vowed to avenge their deaths."

Viktor and Emre come in, and Mazur's eyes flit Viktor. Instantly fear darkens his eyes.

"Looks like you know Viktor?" I ask.

"Everyone knows the head of the Bratva," Mazur mutters, his panic growing.

"Oh, we're going to get to know each other on a real personal level," Viktor chuckles.

"Mazur," I snap, getting his attention back on me. "Where was I?" I think for a moment. "Right. I probably would've taken over the store, but because of you, I worked my ass off to become the head of the Turkish mafia, all so I could get my revenge. This moment." I take a step closer. "It's all your own doing."

"You have the wrong man." He shakes his head. "What would I want with a bakery?"

"Once you got all the owners to sell their stores to you for next to nothing, you flattened it all. Then, you built a mall on that ground."

I watch as he starts to remember.

"Deniz and Sinem Demir. They were hardworking people, just trying to make a living, and you just had to fucking kill them." I gesture for Emre to untie Mazur, then say, "After tonight, my grandmother won't have to wear black anymore." Smirking, I add, "But first, you need to pay for the hell you've put Lara through."

Viktor steps closer, asking, "How can I help?"

"I need him lying on the floor."

Viktor places a hand on Mazur's chest, then grins at him. "Going down."

With a simple move, Viktor swipes Mazur's legs from under him. Mazur falls back, hitting the ground hard, letting out a grunt from the force, followed by a groan.

I move closer and step on his right arm. "Feel free to scream." Bringing my foot up, I stomp on his forearm until he's howling from the pain. Only when I'm sure it's broken, do I step back, asking, "Did Lara scream like that?"

Jesus, did she?

Intense rage clouds my vision, my insides starting to tremble as I imagine the woman I love lying on a cold floor while screaming with pain.

Swinging around, I kick Mazur right in the gut, earning an agonizing grunt from him. I watch as he struggles to breathe, and it gives me no satisfaction.

"Enough," he wails as he rolls onto his side, cradling his broken arm against his chest. "Enough."

"I'm only getting started," I grind the words out through clenched teeth.

I gesture for Emre and Viktor to help the man onto his knees. Walking to the table against the left wall, I pick up a cat-o-nine tail whip with metal spikes.

409

"I really don't have a taste for torturing people. Viktor, do you mind?"

"Thank God. I thought you were going to make me watch."

Letting out a humorless chuckle, I hand the whip to him. "Don't leave any skin on his back."

I check the time on my wristwatch as Viktor cracks the whip over Mazur's back. Mazur starts to crawl, trying to move away. Soon his sobs fill the air, and I watch as he begs for mercy, crawling on the floor like the fucking dog he is.

I wasn't lying when I said I have no taste for torture. I'd much rather shoot the man. But he needs to pay for what he did to Lara. For all the suffering he caused her.

I remember how she used to cower. How she used to flinch. The suffocating fear in her eyes.

Her on her knees, begging for her life.

How many times did she beg Mazur like that?

Viktor actually gets to work up a sweat. By the time Mazur passes out, his back is a bloody mess.

Viktor drops the whip to the floor. "Now I'm ready for bed."

"Thank you," I murmur, moving closer to shake his hand. "Don't hesitate to call me whenever you need something."

He lifts his chin before leaving the freezer. I turn to look at Emre, who seems to be half-asleep where he's leaning back against the wall, his arms crossed over his chest.

"You can go home," I say. "I'll finish up here."

"I'm staying," he mutters before yawning. "I'll get us some tea."

Just after Emre leaves, Mazur begins to stir. I'm surprised he's coming too so quickly.

Crouching next to him, I tilt my head. "Not feeling too great, are you?"

He groans pain etched with deep lines on his face.

"This is how Lara felt every time you whipped her."

Rising to my feet, I pull a bullet out of my pocket. I grab a knife from the table and start carving his name onto it. "I hear you like carving the names of your victims onto bullets." I crouch next to him again, smiling, "This bullet is for you."

Emre returns with the tea just as I carve the last letter, and I take a moment to drink some before loading the bullet into the revolver I took from the vault in my office.

Mazur somehow manages to move onto his knees, and tilting his head back, he looks at me. He seems to have realized he's shit out of luck, and his time is up. There's raw fear in his eyes, the kind you get when you're terrified because you have no fucking idea what comes after death.

I lock eyes with him. "While you rot in the ground, Lara will become a queen. I will take your business apart and wipe out every last man who worked for you. There will be nothing left of your life. But Lara? She will know only happiness, and after this day, you'll be forgotten."

Lifting my arm, I train the barrel on his head.

An intense tremor shudders through my body. I remember my parents laughing while they fixed the store, while they baked, while they danced at night right before we would go home.

Then I remember their blood and how my grandmother wept. The devastating loss that I never healed from.

"Babam, Annem, bu gece sizin intikamınizi alacağım. Bu geceden sonra benimle gurur duyacaksiniz.

I murmur, intense relief filling my chest as I pull the trigger. (Dad, Mom, I'm finally getting my revenge. Find peace and look at me with pride.)

My arm lowers as I stare at Mazur's half-open eyes, where he's lying on the floor, blood pooling around his head.

"It's done," Emre whispers.

As I lift my eyes to my cousin, he comes to embrace me. I wrap my arms around him, and we take a moment to savor our victory.

Thirty years of planning, working, and fucking living for this moment, and now that it's over, I can focus on my own life.

"Let's go home," I say as I pull back from him. "You're driving."

Emre lets out a chuckle, and as we leave the freezer, he instructs men to dispose of the body.

On the way home, exhaustion sets into my bones. I want to sleep for a fucking week.

When Emre stops the car, I climb out and wait for him. Together we head inside and walk to our grandmother's bedroom.

I knock on the door.

"Come in," she calls out.

I knew there was no way she'd sleep before hearing Mazur is dead.

When I step inside with Emre, emotions wash over her features. She keeps the tears in, lifting her chin high.

My own eyes start to burn as I drop down to one knee in front of her. Taking her hand, I kiss her knuckles, then draw her hand to my forehead. "I've avenged our family."

"*Tanrıya şükür*," she thanks God.

I pull back and climb to my feet, then help my grandmother to stand up. She opens her arms and hugs both Emre and me. "My boys. You've given me peace."

Intense relief fills my chest, knowing I've given my grandmother her only wish. I was worried that I would run out of time.

Chapter 48

Lara

When I wake up, I find myself in Gabriel's arms. I snuggle closer, taking a deep breath of his scent.

Then my eyes pop open.

I have my mom back.

Emotions wash the last of my sleep away.

"Morning, *Ödülüm,*" Gabriel murmurs, his voice hoarse. The sound makes goosebumps spread over my skin.

"Morning," I whisper, ducking my head because I'm conscious of my morning breath.

"Did you sleep well?" he asks, his arms tightening around me.

"Surprisingly, yes. And you?"

I really like this. Us starting the day together.

"Hmm," the sound rumbles from his throat.

My stomach flutters, my heartbeat speeding up. Pulling free, I climb out of bed.

"Where are you going?" he asks, opening his eyes to look at me.

"Bathroom." I dart inside, and shutting the door, I quickly relieve myself before brushing my teeth and hair.

When I step back into the room, Gabriel gets up to use the restroom. I walk to the closet and grab underwear, jeans, and a blouse.

"What do you think you're doing?" Gabriel asks as he comes to stand behind me, brushing his fingers over my back.

"Getting dressed," I answer. "There's a lot to do today."

His arm wraps around my front, and I'm tugged back against his chest. I feel his hardness pressing just above my butt.

"Not before you've satisfied me."

Thank God I brushed my teeth.

Like a caveman, Gabriel lifts my feet from the ground, walks to the bed, and throws me on it. I land on my side, and before I can move, he takes hold of my hips and forces me onto my stomach.

Heat spreads through my body, then he yanks my butt into the air and shoves a pillow beneath me.

My eyebrow lifts as I glance at him from over my shoulder. I watch as he wraps his fingers around his hard length, and when he strokes himself, there's an intense tightening in my core, warmth flooding between my legs.

It's so freaking hot when he does that.

"Like what you see, baby?"

"Yes," I admit shamelessly. "It's a turn-on watching you stroke yourself."

His thumb brushes over the beading pearl at the tip, only making me rub my thighs together for friction.

"Do you need my cock, *Ödülüm?*"

"Yes." I'm already breathless. "Please."

Gabriel keeps stroking himself slowly. "Open your legs wide."

Bracing my arms on the mattress, I move my knees apart. Suddenly I feel his fingers as he brushes them over my clit. My body jerks, and I instinctively push myself back against him.

He starts to massage the sensitive bundle of nerves, then I feel the head of his cock pressing against my entrance. Slowly, he pushes an inch inside me, and with rocking movements, he only fucks me with the head of his cock.

My insides are trembling for all of him to be buried deep inside me. I bite my bottom lip as I moan, trying to push back against him. "Gabriel," I complain.

"Do you need more?"

"Yes."

"Beg me."

"Dear God, please fuck me," I beg, rotating my hips. "Please, I need to feel you deep inside me."

Gabriel takes hold of my hips, and with a single hard thrust, he buries himself to the hilt. My lips part on a silent cry, my eyes falling shut from how he stretches me as he fills me.

Moving his hands to my buttcheeks, he starts to massage them. "Grab hold of the covers for support," he orders as he pulls all the way out.

I fist my hands in the covers, and my muscles tighten as I brace myself.

Still, nothing could prepare me as Gabriel slams back into me. Air bursts over my lips, and I don't get a chance to take a full breath as he starts to pound into me as if he'll die if he doesn't.

I can't stop the cries and sobs of pleasure as intense waves crash through my body. It's continuous, gripping me tightly in an earthshattering hold.

"Fuck," Gabriel growls as he keeps hammering into me, the sounds of our skin meeting filling the air. "You take me so well."

My abdomen clenches hard from his praise, making me sob as the orgasm keeps building, remaining just out of my reach.

"Gabriel," I plead, the intense friction as his hard length fills me relentlessly, becoming too much.

Even though he knows the answer, he asks, "What do you need, baby?"

"To come," I whimper breathlessly, sweat beading over my body.

"How badly do you need to come?"

"Desperately." My fingers grip the covers so tightly, I fear I might tear them. Knowing it will make Gabriel lose his mind, I say, "And I hope I bleed on your cock again."

"Jesus," he growls, fucking me so hard that I lose touch with reality. "Come, baby."

The world explodes within me, my arms give way, and burying my face in the covers, I scream from the unrelenting pleasure paralyzing my body.

This is the most erotic moment of my life. Gabriel slams into me three more times, then buries himself deep, his pelvis flush with my butt as he finds his release.

I glance over my shoulder, and seeing his body wound tight, every muscle bulging, more pleasure rockets through me.

I struggle to catch my breath as he pulls out of me. With a left hand firmly gripping my hip, he keeps me in place while he rests a right palm on my back. I hear him suck in deep breaths of air, then his fingers brush over the marks covering my skin.

He bends over me and presses a kiss to my back. "I love every inch of you."

My mouth curves up, my heart expanding to the size of the universe.

He flips me onto my back, then braces himself over me, his golden eyes burning into mine. I lift a hand and caress my finger over the stubble on his jaw.

"Did I hurt you?"

I shake my head. "I don't care if it's sore because then I'll still feel you inside me."

Pure satisfaction washes over his handsome face. "You're fucking perfect."

"*Aşkım,*" I say the word Nisa taught me. It means *my love.*

A smile spreads over Gabriel's face, then he demands, "You better call me that whenever you speak to me."

"*Evet, Aşkım.*"

With a chuckle, he leans down and presses a tender kiss to my mouth, then murmurs against my lips, "I love you so fucking much, *Ödülüm.*"

I wrap my arms around his neck, pulling him down until all his weight pushes me into the mattress.

It doesn't take long before I feel him harden, and as he starts to devour my mouth, he fills me again, slowly making love to me.

Chapter 49

Lara

After we've gotten dressed, and I notice Gabriel's wearing jeans and a charcoal sweater, I ask, "Are you staying home today?"

He nods, and pulling me against his chest, he says, "I need the day off."

"I agree." I tilt my head back and stare into his eyes.

Lifting a hand, he brushes some hair from my face. "Mazur is dead."

He watches me closely for my reaction, and it makes me search my emotions. I don't feel anything but relief, knowing that monster won't be able to hurt or kill anyone else.

My lips curve up. "Thank you, *Aşkım.*"

I absolutely adore calling him my love, and I'm happy he likes it.

"Are you ready for today?" he asks, worry creeping into his eye.

"No, but I'm going to do my best." I have no idea how I will cross the bridge of ten years between my mother and me.

"I'm here for you," he says.

I nod, and wrapping my arms around his waist, I rest my cheek against his chest. "You make me feel so strong."

"You were strong long before I came along. I just helped you to see it."

A soft smile curves my lips. "My mom used to tell me the story of Cinderella." I tilt my head back again so I can look up at Gabriel. "She said fairytales exist and that one day I'd find my prince."

He smiles at me with affection softening his eyes.

"You're my prince," I murmur lovingly.

Lowering his head, he presses a tender kiss to my mouth. "I killed the dragon and stole the princess who I claimed as my reward." He lets out an amused chuckle. "If you want me to be your prince, I'll be your fucking prince, baby."

When I pull away, Gabriel smacks my butt. "Go make us some tea while I check on everyone."

With happiness bubbling in my chest, I leave the room. Gabriel heads toward *Babaanne*'s sitting room while I take the stairs down to the kitchen.

When I enter, my lips part with surprise. Nisa's standing at the stove with Mom, teaching her how to make the tea.

The memory flashes through my mind as I remember her doing the same with me.

Dear Nisa. I love her so much.

Nisa notices me, then exclaims, "*Allah Allah*, look who finally woke up."

"Gabriel's home," I mutter in my defense, which makes Nisa chuckle.

Walking to Mom, I wrap an arm around her waist and give her a sideways hug. "How did you sleep?"

She nods, her eyes drifting over my face as if she can't believe I'm really here. "Okay."

It's on the tip of my tongue to ask her how she's feeling, but I swallow the words down. I can see how she's feeling, and it's not good.

Lifting a hand, I tuck some of her hair behind her ear. "When I first arrived, Nisa took me shopping, and I got a haircut. Would you like to do that?"

"Ah… okay?"

I give her a comforting smile. "I'd like to get you your own clothes so you'll have something that belongs to you."

Emotion wells in her eyes, and she quickly looks down as she fights the tears. Pulling her into a hug, I whisper by her ear, "It's okay to cry. It will help you feel better."

I hear movement behind me, and freeing Mom from the hug, I glance over my shoulder. The moment Mom lays eyes on Gabriel, she ducks behind me. She takes hold of my blouse in a tight grip.

"It's okay," I say, keeping my voice gentle. "This is Gabriel."

Mom peeks around my shoulder at Gabriel. He keeps perfectly still, his expression neutral.

"Welcome, Agnieska. I hope you find peace in my home," he murmurs.

As if I couldn't love him more, my heart just keeps expanding for him.

Pulling out a chair, Gabriel takes a seat.

"Tea, Gabriel *Bey*?" Nisa asks.

"Please."

I feel Mom's grip on my shirt lessen. Reaching behind me, I take hold of her hand, giving it a squeeze as I pull her to stand next to me.

There's a serious expression on Gabriel's face, as he looks at Mom. She quickly lowers her eyes to the tiles.

"Agnieska, look at me," he demands, his voice firm.

425

She quickly obeys, and I can feel the fear coming off her in waves.

I used to fear him like that. God, so much has changed.

It hurts to see her like this, but I know with time, she will get better.

"You are free," he says. "You are now in control of your life. There will be no beatings, no whippings, no threats of death." His eyes fill with compassion. "And you will not be expected to do anything you don't want to. Your body is your own."

Mom nods, her throat straining from keeping the tears back.

"I will arrange a doctor to help you work through the trauma you've suffered. If at any point you feel afraid or uncomfortable, tell Lara or me, and we'll deal with the problem." He tilts his head. "Do you understand?"

"Yes, sir," she murmurs obediently.

"You will not call me that. Just Gabriel." He stands up and takes a step closer. "Lift your chin." Mom quickly does as he says. "Straighten your shoulders." Again she obeys. "You are no one's slave, Agnieska. You are free. No one here is going to order you around. We're a family, and we take care of our own."

Mom nods, her chin quivering so bad. I place a hand on her back and softly brush it up and down to comfort her.

Nisa sets the tray of tea on the table, her eyes flitting between Gabriel and Mom.

Gabriel gives her a compassionate look. "Just focus on healing so you can enjoy the rest of your life. Don't let those bastards take your future from you. I've killed Grabowski and Mazur, so you are safe from their cruelty."

Mom takes a staggering step back. Her eyes widen with disbelief as she lifts her trembling hands to cover her mouth. Then she asks, "They're dead?"

"Yes." Gabriel keeps his eyes locked on hers.

Mom takes a step forward, falls to her knees at his feet, and sobs, "Thank you."

Just as I move to pull her up, Gabriel crouches in front of her. "Get up, Agnieska. You will never kneel again."

She quickly scrambles to her feet, and taking a step away from him, her hand searches for mine.

"I think that covers everything," Gabriel says. He turns his attention to me. "I'll be with my grandmother if you need me, baby."

"Okay." Pulling my hand free from Mom's, I walk to Gabriel and wrap my arms around his waist. "Thank you. It means so much to me."

"I know," he murmurs. When I tilt my head back, he presses a soft kiss to my mouth. "I'll see you at breakfast."

He turns his attention to Nisa. "Yusuf's surgery went well. He can receive visitors."

Intense relief washes over her face. "Thank you, Gabriel *Bey*."

When he leaves, I turn to look at Mom, who seems much calmer.

She clears her throat, then asks, "Is everything he said true?"

I quickly nod. "Yes. I promise. I wouldn't lie to you."

"This is a good house," Nisa adds. "No evil lives here."

Some relief flutters over Mom's features, then she nods and asks, "Is there work I can do?"

Knowing she needs to keep busy until she's grown used to the Demir household, I say, "I can show you how to make Turkish bread."

"Okay."

We get to work, and Nisa keeps correcting me whenever I get the ingredients wrong. At one point, she even manages to make Mom smile.

Just like me, she will get better and learn all the wonderful things I've learned. She'll experience good emotions and happiness.

Chapter 50

Gabriel

After I took a short break of one day, Emre and I have been working our asses off to get the repairs done to Vengeance from the attack.

All the renovations have been completed for Retribution. I also released the staff who used to work for Mazur, giving them each enough money to start a new life. Lara was happy to hear this.

With everything back to normal, the women have been shopping like crazy. My grandmother redid her entire wardrobe, filling it with colors, and they've bought enough clothes for Agnieska to last her two lifetimes.

Walking into the house, I hear Nisa say, "Slower, Agnieska *Hanim*! You don't have to clean everything in an hour."

"Don't snap at her," Murat mutters, and in a gentler tone, he continues, "Agnieska, I think it's time for a break. Take a walk in the garden with me."

"I wasn't snapping," Nisa huffs.

My eyebrow pops up, and I head toward them. Just as I come down the hallway, Agnieska and Murat exit one of the sitting rooms, his hand on her lower back.

"What's happening here?" I ask, my eyes searching Agnieska's face for any sign of fear or panic. Not seeing any, I relax.

"Nothing," Murat answers.

"The question was directed at Agnieska," I mutter. Locking eyes with her, I ask, "Are you comfortable with Murat?"

She nods quickly. "Yes, Gabriel."

I turn my attention to Murat. "Don't push her into doing anything she doesn't want."

"I'll never do that."

When I nod, they continue to walk toward the side doors as I stare after them. It's clear as fucking day that Murat is interested in Agnieska even though he's ten years younger than her.

I let out a chuckle, shaking my head, then the realization hits that Agnieska is only four years my senior.

Holy fuck.

It makes me realize how much younger than me, Lara is. Sixteen years. It's never even crossed my mind until now.

Doesn't change a fucking thing.

Like Luca said the other day, 'Age is just a number.'

Taking the stairs up, I hear laughter coming from the east wing. When I walk into my grandmother's private sitting room, I find her and Lara knitting.

"He used to run around without pants, his adorable bottom on display for the world to see."

"*Babaanne*," I mutter, realizing she's telling Lara about my childhood.

"Oh, you're home early," Lara comments, a wide smile on her face and laughter dancing in her eyes.

"Work isn't so busy anymore." I press a kiss to my grandmother's forehead, then walk to Lara, placing my hand on her shoulder. "Finish what you're doing."

"I'm done," she says quickly, shoving the needles and wool into a basket.

I notice what they're knitting, and my eyebrow lifts. "Are you seriously knitting baby shoes?"

"Yes," *Babaanne* answers, then she gives me a triumphant smile. "Lara said it's only a matter of time before I'll get to hold my great-grandchild."

"Is that so?" I shrug. "If Lara says so, who am I to argue."

My words make my grandmother's smile grow.

Lara gets up, and I take her hand. I pull her to our bedroom, and when I shut the door, I pin her with a questioning look. "Babies?"

She nervously tucks hair behind her ear, then explains, "Your grandmother wants a great-grandchild, and I couldn't bear to tell her no. I said you have to agree as well, but that I'm okay with it." She gives me a pleading look. "The news made her so happy, *Aşkım*."

Tugging her against my chest, I stare at her until her teeth worry on her bottom lip. "You want to give me children?"

Lara doesn't hesitate to nod.

A smile curves my lips, and I place my hand over her abdomen. "I'd like to see you pregnant with my child."

The nervous tension leaves her, relief filling her eyes. "I'd like that too."

"But first, there's your twenty-third birthday next month. I have a surprise planned for you. After that, we can talk about having the implant removed."

"Okay."

Wrapping my arms around her, I press a kiss to her mouth. Her lips eagerly part, and time slips away as I show her how much I love her until her lips are swollen and we're both breathless.

She rests her cheek against my chest, and I just hold her, so thankful I didn't accidentally kill the women I want to spend the rest of my life with.

"I need to help Nisa prepare dinner," she murmurs.

"Okay." I free her from my arms, and I walk with her to the kitchen.

Emre's sitting at the kitchen table, shoving *Baklava* into his mouth.

"When will you find a nice woman to settle down with?" Nisa asks.

"Never," he mutters around a mouthful. "I plan on becoming the most eligible bachelor in Seattle now that Gabriel's off the market."

"*Allah Allah*," Nisa exclaims, throwing her hands in the air.

It's good to see my cousin at home, getting some well-deserved rest.

I grab a slice of *Baklava*, and popping it into my mouth, I leave Lara with Nisa and go look for Murat and Agnieska to make sure she's okay.

I find them by *Babaanne*'s rose garden just as Murat picks one to give to Agnieska. She takes it with a blushing face.

Hating to disrupt their moment, I say, "Murat, give me a moment alone with her."

He gives her arm a squeeze, then moves out of hearing distance, still keeping an eye on her. I scowl at the man who's quickly becoming possessive of Agnieska, before turning my attention to her.

"How are you holding up?" I ask.

"Much better." She still struggles to meet my eyes, but she doesn't look as terrified anymore.

"Are the therapy sessions helping?"

"Yes." She nods quickly, glances at me, then looks at the rose.

"Are you really comfortable with Murat?"

"Yes." This time she holds my eyes for a couple of seconds longer. "He's... gentle and makes me feel safe."

"Good. I'm happy to hear that."

A nervous smile tugs at her mouth.

"I have something I'd like to ask you." Again she glances up at me, giving me a nod to continue. I clear my throat. "Will you give me your blessing to marry your daughter?"

Her eyes widen, then emotions crash through them, and she sucks in a quivering breath. "You want to marry Lara?"

My heart starts to beat faster, and I feel a trickle of nervousness that she might not give me her blessing.

Clearing my throat again, I answer, "Yes. I love her with all my heart. I'll keep her safe and put her happiness first."

Agnieska looks down again, then a tear spirals over her cheek. "You have my blessing."

Slowly, I lift my arm, and placing my hand on her shoulder, I give it a squeeze. "Thank you. It means a lot to me."

She shakes her head, swallowing hard. "Thank you."

"For?"

"Saving us."

The corner of my mouth lifts. "You're welcome." I glance at Murat, gesturing that he can come back.

When he jogs toward us, I let out a chuckle.

Yep, the man has it bad.

The moment he sees how emotional Agnieska is, he wraps an arm around her. "Are you okay?"

She nods quickly, then explains, "The happiness is overwhelming."

Leaving them to continue their walk, I head back to the kitchen. I feel better now that I know Murat's there to take care of Agnieska.

I sneak up behind Lara as she sets a tray down on the counter and wrap my arms around her. She startles and lets out a chuckle before leaning back against me.

I press a kiss to the side of her neck, then spin her around. Lifting her off her feet, I hoist her over my shoulder.

"*Allah Allah*! We're busy with food," Nisa chastises me.

Hungry for something else, I mutter, "I'm kidnapping Lara."

"She's already yours," Nisa calls after us as I carry a laughing Lara out of the kitchen. "Don't be late for dinner!"

I take my woman to our bedroom and feast on her body until the early morning hours.

Chapter 51

Lara

The excitement is killing me as I open the door to the bedroom and step inside.

The women kept me busy, taking me to a spa for my birthday. We also had our hair and makeup done by professionals.

Mom looks so pretty, and she seemed to really enjoy today. I'm so thankful for everyone going out of their way to make her feel like she's part of the family.

My feet come to a sudden stop when I see a breathtaking ballgown hanging in the walk-in closet.

Oh. My. God.

It's made of satin, the color a dusky rose.

Slowly, I step closer, and lifting a hand, I caress the luxurious fabric.

Wow.

Gabriel said my gift would be waiting in the room, but I never thought it would be such a beautiful dress. Slipping it from the hanger, I carry it to the bed, and lay it over the covers.

I hurry to strip out of my clothes, and remembering Gabriel's order to not wear any underwear tonight, I carefully step into the satin fabric. It falls softly around my body. I adjust the straps over my shoulders and the plunging, sweetheart neckline.

Moving to the mirror in the closet, I stare at my reflection. There's no sign of the plain girl I used to be, and as I step into my high heels, I feel like the most beautiful woman in the world.

I turn and look at the scars, visible because the fabric falls softly to my lower back.

Gabriel chose this dress, and I'll wear it with pride.

I choose a silver clutch from the collection I started a couple of weeks ago, and placing my phone and some tissues in it, I leave the bedroom.

The house is quiet as I take the stairs down to the entrance hall, then Gabriel steps into my line of sight. My breath catches from how devastatingly handsome he looks in the black tuxedo.

With awe on his face, he steps forward, holding his hand out to me. "Your carriage awaits, princess."

A smile spreads over my face, a burst of happiness quickening my heartbeat.

When I place my palm in his, he murmurs, "You look absolutely breathtaking, *Ödülüm*."

"Thank you," I say before joking, "You look too handsome to leave this house."

Gabriel's eyes are filled with love, making me feel like the luckiest woman in the world.

"Are you ready for your birthday party?"

I nod, excitement bursting in my chest. "Yes."

"Let's go." He leads me out of the house, where a limousine waits for us. He opens the door and helps me climb into the backseat, where two flutes of champagne are on a small counter.

My God, this is so romantic. I feel like Cinderella going to the ball.

Enjoying the bubbly liquid while Mirac drives us to our destination, Gabriel asks, "No underwear, right?"

I nod.

He moves off the seat and kneels in front of me. "Don't make a sound."

What?

Then Gabriel pushes the fabric up and pulls my legs open. He lifts one over his shoulder, and some champagne splashes from the glass and onto the seat when he plants his face between my legs, sucking and licking the ever-loving hell out of me.

I clamp a hand over my mouth and set the flute down before I drop it. With the hand I have free, I grab hold of his hair, my head falling back from the intense pleasure.

It takes only minutes for me to shatter, and I struggle to muffle the moans as the orgasm paralyzes my body, and I grind against his face.

Gabriel pulls himself up, shoves my hand out of the way, and claims my mouth. I taste my release on his tongue, my body spasming with residual pleasure.

Just as he ends the kiss, the limousine comes to a stop.

Gabriel murmurs, "Happy birthday, *Ödülüm.*" Then he quickly adjusts my dress, so I'm covered.

Opening the door, he helps me out of the vehicle, my legs still trembling from the orgasm.

He takes hold of my hand, and linking our fingers, he leads me into a building with a sign that reads, '*Vengeance.*'

It's dark, and fairy lights decorate the walls, showing the path we need to follow. "It's so pretty," I whisper, then my lips part, and emotions wash through me.

The hallway opens up to a floor where our family waits, all dressed in formal clothes. Mom looks so pretty in a gold-colored gown. Murat has a possessive arm wrapped around her.

"Happy Birthday!" they all shout.

There's a table overloaded with gifts. An enormous birthday cake stands near it, seven layers high. Lights sparkle everywhere, pink and silver balloons floating against the ceiling.

"Wow," I breathe, tears filling my eyes.

Turning, I plow into Gabriel's chest, wrapping my arms tightly around him. He engulfs me against him, pressing kisses to my hair.

"Thank you," I squeeze the words out through a tight throat, fighting hard not to cry so I won't ruin my makeup.

"You're welcome, baby." He rubs his hand over my back. "But you need to let go so I can give you your gift."

"You already did," I say as I reluctantly pull back.

Gabriel tugs me to the middle of the floor, where a soft spotlight shines. I glance around me, a smile quivering on my lips, then my eyes widen as Gabriel kneels before me for a second time tonight.

He wouldn't... would he?

Just before I can have a heart attack, he takes a small black box from his jacket and opens it.

Holy shit!

I burst out in tears, covering my face.

"Look at me," he orders.

I shake my head.

"Baby, look at me."

I lower my hands and meet his eyes.

"Marry me," he demands.

"You have to ask her!" Nisa cries. "*Allah Allah,* have I taught you nothing?"

Laughter bursts through my tears, and I nod as quick as I can. "Yes. YesYesYes!"

Rising to his full height, he pushes a stunning diamond onto my ring finger, then kisses me hard, applause and cheers filling the air.

Cinderella was right...

Being kind, having courage, and believing in a little magic brought me to Gabriel and a family filled with good and caring people.

Epilogue

Lara

Seven years later…

"Come out, come out, wherever you are," I call playfully.

I hear Deniz's chuckle, and knowing he's behind the armchair his grandmother is sitting in, I pretend to search everywhere for him.

"It's time for your bath," I say, smiling at my mother as she reaches behind the chair to tickle him. Laughter bubbles from him. "Oh, I can hear you. Are you behind the curtain?" I yank the fabric back.

"No," he shouts.

"Are you hiding…" I make a show of looking in the vases, "between the flowers?"

"Nooo," he laughs.

Gabriel leans against the doorjamb, and crossing his arms over his chest, he watches as we play hiding-go-seek.

"Have you looked beneath the table?" Gabriel asks.

"I'm not there," Deniz calls out, then suddenly he jumps up with what he thinks is a scary face. "Wha!"

He runs toward me, and I hold open my arms, sweeping him to my chest. "Ready for your bath?"

He nods. "Can I have hotcho…golate?"

"Just a little. It's almost time for bed."

Carrying our five-year-old while pregnant is no easy task. Gabriel takes him from me, saying, "You're getting too big, little man."

"Like you." Deniz wraps his arms around Gabriel's neck.

When we walk past a framed portrait of *Babaanne*, my heart squeezes with sorrow. She got to see her great-grandchild and spent three wonderful years with him before passing away in her sleep.

I smile at my husband and our son, Deniz, the spitting image of his father.

Entering Deniz's bedroom, I head to the bathroom, opening the faucet so the water can run while I get his pajamas.

Gabriel and Deniz are wrestling on his bed as I pull the clothes out of the chest of drawers.

Giving them a playful scowl, I say, "Time to bathe."

"You heard your mother." Gabriel nudges Deniz toward me, making himself comfortable on the bed.

I take Deniz into the bathroom and help him out of his clothes. Checking the water, I close the faucets, then lift him into the tub.

As I begin to wash his body, he asks, "Tell me the 'tory."

"Once upon a time, there was a girl named Lara. She lived in a mansion ruled by an evil dragon. He breathed flames and devoured anyone who came near him."

"Like cookies?"

"Yes." I nod, a soft smile around my lips as I scrub his feet. "Lara –"

"Like you?"

I nod again. "Yes, like Mama. She scrubbed the floors and washed the windows, staring at the world outside and wondering what it was like."

Deniz splashes the water, wetting the front of my shirt. "Then *Baba* came!"

"Yes, I rode in on my black horse, slew the dragon, and stole the princess," Gabriel suddenly says behind me.

I pull Deniz out of the tub and dry his body. Once I have him dressed in his favorite PJs, covered with tiny planes, Gabriel tucks him into bed.

"My hottochogolate," Deniz demands.

Just like his father.

"I'll get it," Gabriel says, rubbing a hand over my pregnant belly before leaving the room.

I sit down on the side of the bed, caressing my fingers through our son's silky black hair.

"Is it true?" Deniz asks.

"The story?" When he nods, I smile. "Yes. Your daddy's my prince."

"Am I one too?"

I nod, leaning forward to press a kiss on his cheek. "Yes, and one day you'll also save a princess."

"No, I'll steal her," he argues. "Just like *Baba*."

I let out a chuckle. "Yes, you probably will, and then you'll live happily ever after."

———————————

Gabriel

Fifteen years later...

"Why are you so nervous?" Lara asks as she adjusts my tie.

"It's her first date."

She raises an eyebrow at me. "And?"

After twenty-one years of marriage, my love for the mother of my children still keeps growing.

"I'm just nervous," I growl, unable to explain why. "I don't want to fuck up tonight."

"You won't, *Aşkım*," Lara assures me. She stands on her tiptoes and presses a kiss to my mouth. "I'm going to check on Alya. She's probably still soaking in the tub."

I nod, moving to stand in front of the mirror so I can make sure everything's perfect.

When Lara leaves the room, I open the vault and take a box from it. I flip the lid open and stare at the platinum chain with a heart pendant made from sapphires, the color of her eyes. It lies on a bed of red velvet.

I hope she'll like it.

I suck in a breath of air as emotion washes over me.

It's my baby girl's fourteenth birthday, and I'm taking her on her first date, so she'll know how future dates should treat her.

If they get past me.

Closing the box, I leave the room to wait in the entrance hall.

"You look so handsome, Gabriel *Bey*," Nisa says as she comes from the kitchen.

"Thank you." I adjust the tie, then ask, "Is Deniz back yet?"

"No. I'm sure he'll be home soon."

"That boy's testing my patience," I mutter. "Since I bought him the R8, he's never home."

"He's nineteen. Let him have some fun," Nisa chastises me.

Movement catches my eye, and I turn to glance up as Alya stops at the top of the stairs. She's wearing the pale blue gown I got her, stealing the breath from my lungs.

"Jesus," I mutter, once again swallowing hard on the emotions in my chest. "You look beautiful, *gözümün nuru*."

I now call her what my grandmother used to call me. The light of my eye. That's what my daughter is to me.

When she reaches me, I stare down at my little girl, who's growing up way too fast. I lift the box between us and open it, presenting my gift to her. "Happy birthday, Alya."

"Oh, *Baba*!" Her face lights up as she carefully lifts the necklace from the velvet. "Will you help me put it on?"

"Of course."

She turns so I can attach the clasp behind her neck, then beams a smile at me. I have to take a deep breath as I hold my arm for her, then I lead her out of the house and into the limousine.

My daughter shines like a star as I take hold of her hand, giving it a squeeze.

I clear my throat, then say, "If a boy doesn't treat you like the princess you are, he's not worthy of you. Tonight I'm going to show you what to expect on a date, and you won't settle for anything less. Understand?"

"*Evet, Baba.*"

"This doesn't mean I'm allowing you to date," I warn her.

Her shoulders slump. "But when, then?"

"Once I've taught you how to defend yourself, so you can kick a boy's ass if he tries to get fresh with you."

Alya stops right before she's about to roll her eyes, knowing not to even try that shit with me.

"It's for your own good," I mutter. "You need to be able to protect yourself."

"When will you teach me?"

"Soon."

Not for at least another two years. There's no way I'm letting my little girl date before she's sixteen.

The limousine comes to a stop in front of the five-star restaurant I booked for the evening. I help Alya out of the car, then lead her inside, where a single table waits, a candle flickering on the white table cloth.

I pull out her chair, and when she's seated, I help her scoot forward. "The boy will always pull out your chair for you."

"Okay."

I take a seat across from her. "And he'll open doors for you, stepping inside first so he can take the bullet instead of you. Never walk first. This is why your mother always stays slightly behind me. It's for protection."

"Okay, *Baba*."

A waiter brings us a bottle of sparkling water and welcomes us.

When he leaves to get our food, I continue, "You will tolerate no disrespect. You're a Demir, Alya. We come from a proud family."

She nods.

"And if he touches you without your permission or makes you uncomfortable..." I shake my head hard, murder already coursing through my veins.

"You'll kill him. I know that part already."

"Don't forget it."

Our meals are brought to the table. I ordered Alya's favorite, cheeseburgers and fries.

"Mama will be angry if she finds out you had a burger," my daughter teases me.

"You won't tell her."

"Then let me go to a party on Saturday," the little shit starts to negotiate.

"No."

"Please, *Baba*. Everyone will be there!"

Letting out a sigh, I stare at her pleading face until my fucking heart melts.

God help me.

"Only if Deniz goes with you," I relent.

"Yes! Thank you!" She darts up to give me a hug, making me smile from ear to fucking ear.

She's just like her mother. Has me wrapped around her little finger.

Alya starts to talk about the upcoming party, and I don't follow a word of what she's saying. But I listen, nodding every couple of seconds.

When we're done eating, her fingers brush over the sapphires.

"There's a tracking device in it," I say. Her eyebrows draw together as she glances down at it. "See the little button at the back?"

"*Evet.*"

"Whenever you're in danger, or even just a little scared, press it, and I'll come."

And fucking kill whoever dares to threaten you.

"I'll always come." My voice cracks over the words.

"*Seni çok seviyorum, Baba,*" she whispers, her bottom lip trembling.

"I love you more, *gözümün nuru.*"

Jesus, I'm about to cry like a baby.

Clearing my throat, I stand up and hold my hand out to her. "May I have this dance?"

She wipes a tear from her cheek and lays her small palm in mine. I pull her into my arms, the safest place on earth for her, and steer her slowly across the floor.

Leaning down, I press a kiss on her hair. "You'll always be my little girl."

She nods, resting her cheek against my chest, just like her mother's done a million times.

"Do you believe in true love?" she whispers.

"*Evet.*"

"Do you think I'll find it?"

"Definitely." I press another kiss to her hair, then promise, "Just like your mother and I, you'll find your happily-ever-after."

The End.

Published Books

The Sinners Series
Mafia / Organized Crime / Suspense Romance
(Can be read in this order or as standalones)

Taken By A Sinner
Nikolas Stathoulis

Owned By A Sinner
Liam Byrne

Stolen By A Sinner
Gabriel Demir

Chosen By A Sinner
Luca Cotroni
COMING AUGUST

Captured By A Sinner
Viktor Vetrov
COMING SEPTEMBER

The Saints Series
Mafia / Organized Crime / Suspense Romance
(Can be read in this order or as standalones)

Merciless Saints
Damien Vetrov

Cruel Saints
Lucian Cotroni

Ruthless Saints
Carson Koslov

Tears of Betrayal
Demitri Vetrov

Tears of Salvation
Alexei Koslov

Beautifully Broken Series

Organized Crime / Suspense Romance
(Can be read in this order or as standalones)

Beautifully Broken
Alex & Nina

Beautifully Hurt
Eli & Quinn

Beautifully Destroyed
Ethan & Finlay

Enemies To Lovers

College Romance / New Adult / Billionaire Romance

Heartless
Reckless
Careless
Ruthless
Shameless

Trinity Academy

College Romance / New Adult / Billionaire Romance

Falcon
Mason
Lake
Julian
The Epilogue

The Heirs

College Romance / New Adult / Billionaire Romance

Coldhearted Heir
Arrogant Heir
Defiant Heir
Loyal Heir
Callous Heir
Sinful Heir
Tempted Heir
Forbidden Heir

Stand Alone Spin-off
Not My Hero
Young Adult / High School Romance

The Southern Heroes Series

Suspense Romance / Contemporary Romance / Police Officers & Detectives

The Ocean Between Us
The Girl In The Closet
The Lies We Tell Ourselves
All The Wasted Time
We Were Lost

Connect with me

NEWSLETTER

FACEBOOK

AMAZON

GOODREADS

BOOKBUB

INSTAGRAM

Acknowledgments

The love I received for The Saints series inspired The Sinners series. I never thought my niche would be Mafia Romance, but I'll write what my readers want. Thank you so much for all your support.

To my alpha and beta readers – Leeann, Sheena, Brittney, Sherrie, Kelly, Sarah, and Allyson thank you for being the godparents of my paper-baby.

Candi Kane PR - Thank you for being patient with me and my bad habit of missing deadlines.

Yoly, Cormar Covers – Thank you for giving my paper-babies the perfect look.

My street team, thank you for promoting my books. It means the world to me!

A special thank you to every blogger and reader who took the time to participate in the cover reveal and release day.

Love ya all tons ;)

Made in the USA
Middletown, DE
08 September 2024

60545144R00255